Dare to Tell

by

Stacey Wilk

Big Sky Country

Dare to Tell

Cover Art by *Lisa Dawn MacDonald*

The Wild Rose Press, Inc.
PO Box 708
Adams Basin, NY 14410-0708
Visit us at www.thewildrosepress.com

Publishing History
First Edition, 2026
Trade Paperback ISBN 978-1-5092-6298-4
Digital ISBN 978-1-5092-6299-1

Big Sky Country
Published in the United States of America

Dedication

To my amazing editor, Roseann Armstrong.
Thank you for making me a better writer.

Chapter One

Careers went to Backwater, Montana, to die. Maeve Barnes knew that firsthand. She had returned to her hometown to bury her life's work—and her father.

The afternoon had the nerve to be sunny and mild. A perfect May day. A total contrast to the storm raging inside Maeve. She would have preferred dark storm clouds, inches of rain, and coverage under large black umbrellas.

Mourners shifted from one leg to the other while the pastor finished his sermon. Everyone from town was in attendance, all lined up in rows with heads bent, hands clasped, and sad eyes covered by dark glasses.

Maeve missed her father. Her mind fought the image of his body lying in the mahogany casket covered in a spray of white roses. Deny it all she wanted, but nothing would change the truth. Her father was gone—and her career was over all in the same month.

The expensive high heels she had purchased as a reward for landing a lead role in a major motion picture sank into the grass while she battled the grief of losing her father and the guilt for thinking about her job.

She should be grateful no paparazzi invaded their privacy and tried to capture her in another meltdown, but the lack of photographers only sealed the deal for her. She was a pariah. Her lost career was all her fault, and yet it wasn't.

Her brother nudged her side with his elbow. "Maeve, put the flower on."

Maeve glanced at the casket. Life changed in ways that twisted the soul until it cried out. Why hadn't she come home sooner? She had a million reasons.

One reason stood tall and rugged to the side of the crowd, wearing a well-fitted dark suit. His three brothers flanked him. Lock Ryker had given her a million reasons to stay away all by himself.

The rose's stem was cool in her hand. A tear leaked and slipped down her face. She placed the flower on top of the cascading arrangement of roses and moved away from the shiny box holding the man who had been the one stable thing in her life. Dad had been as strong as any oak and as constant as the changing seasons. She had not come to his side in his last weeks. Shame had paralyzed her, closed her throat against the words he would have listened to with a quick nod and a pat on her shoulder. But the love would have been in his eyes and in the lines around his mouth. She should have counted on that, but she had stayed away.

She hadn't the heart to tell her father her life had fallen apart. She couldn't tell the man who had rarely screwed up that she had on every level.

Exquisitely screwed up. If she were going to make a mess of her life, at least she had done it in a big way.

The crowd thinned out. Friends and neighbors drifted to waiting cars and pickup trucks. A breeze swelled and offered its own goodbye.

Everyone would return to their lives, and she and Zeke would have to pick up the pieces of their father's. After that, she would once again leave Backwater because its tight borders and small ideas no longer fit.

Where she would go was another issue and not one she wanted to decide on as she stepped away from her father for what would most likely be the last time.

The Rykers were ahead of her. She slowed her pace, having nothing to say to them except thanks for coming. Gage, the oldest, put an arm around Lockwood's shoulders for a brief moment and pulled away. The two men shared a glance.

Lock stopped walking and looked over his shoulder as if he could feel her stare burning on his back. She couldn't make out his gaze through the dark glasses, but the set of his chiseled jaw said it all. Under those glasses, his gaze would say "Stay away." She tilted up her chin and took the hill down to the parking lot without looking back. He was still angry. The man held a grudge better than most.

Maeve pushed out a long breath. Lock had been Zeke's best friend since elementary school. She had grown up with him and never given him a second thought until one day he was all she could think about.

They had been good together once, but she wasn't one who got everything she wanted. A sacrifice always waited to claim its prize. She had a father, but her mother had died when she was young. When her dream finally came true, her relationship with Lock, the one other men struggled to measure up against, had come to an end.

Maeve shoved away any more thoughts of her life with Lock, but without much luck. She hadn't missed his broad shoulders in that dark suit. Or the way the sun reflected off his black hair. He and his brothers seemed stamped from the same mold, but Lock's face was more defined than the others. He was the tallest—not by much, an inch or two. His eyes had often held a playfulness that

3

accompanied his nature. On lonely nights, she longed for the closeness of his easy spirit.

Someone gripped her elbow and effectively extinguished visions of Lock. She turned to discover Mrs. Thatcher, who had lived next door to their farm for decades. She had been the one to find her father.

"Maeve, dear, I just wanted to tell you how very sorry I am for your loss." Her white hair was styled in a bob that curled near her chin. She wore a smart lavender scarf around her neck that added a hint of color to her otherwise plain gray dress.

"Thank you." She didn't want to hear condolences. She didn't deserve them. She wanted to tell Mrs. Thatcher to go talk to Zeke.

"Ray was such a good neighbor and a friend to my Marvin when Marvin couldn't get around as well." Mrs. Thatcher pressed a crumpled tissue to her lips and shook her head. "I promised myself I wouldn't fall to pieces. If there's anything I can do for you or Zeke, please come calling."

"We will. Thank you." She would leave that to Zeke, who probably would not ask for any help. It wasn't in his DNA.

Mrs. Thatcher squeezed her hand and walked away. When Maeve turned around, the Rykers were gone.

Just as well. She and Lock had said all they were going to say six years ago. His roots went deep in this town. She resembled a white pine whose short roots could fall over in a good storm.

How she was standing now was beyond her. The worst storm of her life had blown in, knocking her off balance. All the wrongs in her life could not be set right. She wouldn't know where to begin.

The limousine that had brought her and Zeke to the cemetery gleamed under the bright sun. She leaned against the trunk and pinched her nose. A headache pulsed behind her eyes.

"Maeve?" Another female voice floated over to her.

She opened her eyes and met Karen Ryker's gaze behind her black-framed glasses. Karen was a petite woman with blonde hair and bangs. She pressed her lips into a thin line.

"I'm so sorry about your father." Karen gripped her arm but pulled away quickly. "If there's anything I can do for you, please let me know."

Maeve stood up straight and forced her camera-ready smile onto her lips. The one she used for junket interviews and red carpets. The one that never met her eyes. Or at least that was what she had been told in reviews.

"Thank you, Karen. Your kindness means a lot to Zeke and me, but we're fine. Really. It was nice to see you." She hoped Karen would get the hint. Maeve couldn't bear the kindness from Lock's mother. Karen had been like a second mother to her, and when she had broken Lock's heart, she had lost Karen in the process too.

Karen had never sent her away, though. Instead, Karen had found her before she left for Los Angeles and told her how much she cared for her. Maeve had allowed the guilt to eat away at her insides like a corrosive oil. How could Karen continue to care for her when she had hurt Karen's son?

"The offer stands, if you change your mind." Karen waited a beat, but when Maeve only stood there unable to say another word, Karen turned and walked to a pickup truck with the Ryker Ranch logo on the side.

Maeve watched as the truck pulled away and weaved along the cemetery road.

She couldn't stay in town even if she had nowhere to go. Someone back in Los Angeles would let her stay with them. But she would have to tell her secrets, and she couldn't face those either.

She had no one and nothing.

And no one else to blame but herself.

Chapter Two

"Lock, sweetheart, do me a favor and take this over to the Barneses' place. Would you?" His mother handed him an aluminum tray covered in foil and still warm to the touch.

Lock had a thousand things to do today. Jett had been up his backside about fixing the roof on two guest cottages. His Backwater Pathfinders had a meeting tomorrow, and he needed to prepare for five fifth graders and all their questions about the three badges they needed to earn to advance to the next level—Flickers. He didn't have time to run an errand that would take him clear across town.

He glanced around the kitchen in hopes a ranch guest or someone—anyone—would come in and interrupt her. A fire always needed to be extinguished on their ranch. She would understand he couldn't run the errand. Not that he didn't want to help out the Barneses in their time of need. It wasn't that at all. He did not want to see Maeve or stand close enough to her that he would accidentally get a whiff of her perfume.

"I can't, Mom. I have to get back to work. The funeral took up half the day." He handed the pan back.

She adjusted her black glasses on her nose. "I was afraid you'd say that. You're going to have to put the past aside for ten minutes. I know you can do it."

"It has nothing to do with the past. Can you ask Gage

or Kace?" He turned his gaze toward the window that looked out onto the field. She would be able to see right through him if he looked at her.

His mother had occupied a front-row seat to everything that went down between him and Maeve, and she knew her children as well as they knew themselves. Sometimes better.

"I've already asked your brothers. I'd do it myself, but I have a doctor's appointment in a half hour. I really wanted Zeke and Maeve to have a warm meal tonight. I'm sure after the funeral everyone left them on their own. It's how it goes. People get busy."

"Mom, I'm sure someone in this town has brought over a casserole." If he had to guess, a meal train was probably going around on a Facebook group. Besides, Maeve was incredibly independent. Lock was certain she could defrost a baked ziti.

"You're right." She waved the air as if she could clear her idea out like an unwanted smell. "It's not as if the Ryker Ranch is a fixture in this town or that people would expect us to set an example."

She was going to guilt him into this. "Since when do you care what the people of this town think?" His mother had made many choices in her life that others found questionable. Not once had she worried about the opinions of others.

"I don't care about what other people think, but I do care about you. You should go over there and see Maeve."

"No, thank you." He and Maeve had said their piece. She'd told him she was leaving for her career and didn't want to be tied down to a long-term relationship, and he had said goodbye. What else was there to talk about six years later?

"The ranch has a reputation to uphold. And it isn't as if Zeke is your best friend or anything. He couldn't possibly need his friend now. And then there's the fact that Gage is the sheriff. No one would look badly on Sheriff Ryker if he didn't bring by a tray of food to the grieving family," she said.

"Have Gage do it. He can make his own tray of food, can't he? Does he need his mother to do it for him?"

Karen arched a brow over the top of her glasses. He'd pushed too far. His mother continued to watch out for this family even when they claimed they didn't want her to, and he loved her for that.

"Go visit your friend, Lockwood. He needs you now, not later." Mom handed him back the tray. "I know you don't want to talk about the tough stuff with Zeke. Men like the two of you don't have emotions. You don't have to say a word. I know he could use a friend. Go."

"I have emotions." Hell, he had laughed his ass off only two days ago.

She pressed her lips into a thin line. "Yes, I'm aware. I wasn't sure you were."

"Mom, what is this all about?" He hoped she wasn't trying to matchmake him and Maeve.

She kept her gaze from him and folded a dish towel. "Nothing. I worry about my boys, is all."

"You don't have to worry about me." He had a full life, owning this ranch with Jett. He had friends, his volunteer work, and the occasional no-strings-attached relationship.

"Don't I? Are you truly happy?"

"I can't have this conversation right now. I have to drop off this tray and get back to work before Jett kills me for skipping out."

"Oh, pooh. Jett will do no such thing. I'll tell him I sent you out. Just tell me. Are you really happy?" She smoothed out her folded dish towel.

"I can't think of anything to make me happier." He kissed the top of her head. His mom barely cleared his chest. She was so small and not getting any younger. Maybe her four boys should be watching out for *her*.

"It's okay to want more." She gripped his arm.

"I don't want anything, except to drop off this food and get back. I'll see you later." He hurried from the kitchen before she came up with another great idea.

He navigated the country streets and his winding thoughts. Was he happy? He never gave it much thought. He loved his job. Working the ranch with Jett was all he'd ever wanted. He wished his other two brothers had been a part of the family business. But they had different careers. He missed his little brother, Ajay, every day. Ajay would have worked the ranch with them.

He took a turn down Main Street and waved to most of the people on the sidewalk. Howard Hornsby washed down the space outside his hardware store with a garden hose. Barry Pearce, the deputy sheriff, juggled a tray of coffee cups, almost dropping it as he waved back.

The shops faded into his rearview, and the rolling landscape of farmland and greenery spread out before him. He took a deep breath and opened the window, allowing the smell of fresh grass to flood the cab of his truck.

Being a part of this land made him happy. Montana soil was in his blood. Sure, sometimes he wished he had a serious relationship, like his brothers, but he also enjoyed the easy arrangement he kept with most women.

He was always up-front about what he looked for from a partner: no commitment, nothing serious, a good time. He didn't want to hurt anyone, especially himself.

He turned onto the long drive for the Barneses' farm. The front field was empty. Mr. Barnes used to rent the field to a cattle farmer, but that arrangement had ended a year ago. Zeke didn't want to rent out the field. Zeke didn't want to be a farmer. Sometimes the children found themselves in the roles laid out for them whether they had asked for that role or not. Maybe *he* wasn't happy running the ranch. Lock pushed that crazy thought aside. He loved the ranch.

Lock parked in front of the old farmhouse badly in need of a paint job. The white wooden slats had aged into a dingy gray. The porch steps creaked under his feet, and the railings showed signs of rot. He hadn't been here in a while. He and Zeke often met in town to hang out. Kennedy's bar was a favorite spot.

He rang the bell, unsure if he should just walk in. Zeke's truck was parked over by the shed. Another car was in the driveway too. A plain four-door sedan with out-of-state plates. It had to be Maeve's rental.

Zeke pushed open the screen door, banging it against the house. Dark half circles hung under his bloodshot eyes. He had lost weight since his father became sick. Zeke had been burning the candle at both ends for a long time now.

"Hey, man. Sorry about the door. It gets away from me. Need to fix those hinges. Come on in."

"If now's a bad time, I don't have to. I... This is from the family." He handed over the tray of food.

"From your mom? Cool. I'm starving." Zeke stepped aside to let Lock in.

He hesitated. What would he say to Maeve when he came face-to-face with her? "I figured the whole town would've dropped off food by now."

"They have. Mrs. Thatcher has been cooking for two straight days. Come in." Zeke turned, leaving Lock little choice.

The front living room was as worn as the outside. A round braided rug took up most of the hardwood floor, but the rug had faded from years of sun streaming in the window and miles of footsteps across it. A tan recliner sat alone in the corner, facing a flat-screen TV. The material on the sofa had thinned on the arms and sagged in the middle. The house smelled as musty and moldy as old animals.

"Maeve put everything in the freezer this morning. Had to keep busy, I guess." Zeke edged past a ladder propped in the hallway on his way to the kitchen at the back of the house.

The upper and lower cabinets were mostly removed from the walls, revealing old pink wallpaper. A layer of dust coated the counters of those still left behind. Dishes were piled into the sink because a hole existed where the dishwasher had once been. The linoleum floor had worn down in spots to the subfloor beneath it.

"Looks like you started the work." He pointed to the obvious demo of the kitchen. He found an empty spot and placed his keys on the counter.

"Yeah. I didn't want to wait any longer. I've been itching to update this place, but Dad always fought me on it." Zeke grabbed two forks from a drawer and held out one.

Lock shook his head. "You still thinking about selling?"

"I don't know. Maybe." Zeke pulled back the foil to reveal Mom's homemade eggplant parmigiana.

That dish was one of Lock's favorites.

Zeke shoved the fork into the pan and shoveled in a mouthful. "Farm life gets harder and harder every year. It's mainly me now. I'd have to hire some people. I doubt my sister would stick around and help. Not the famous actress." He had lowered his voice and pointed to the ceiling with his fork.

Maeve had wanted to be an actress since they were kids. She was in every play in high school and college. When she couldn't get a part on television or in a movie, she settled for the community theater in town. When she was on stage, she transformed into each character as if she had stepped into their skin, and he never tired of watching her.

But she couldn't break in, not even when she left Backwater and tried to make a go of it in LA. She came home discouraged, and for reasons he could never quite understand, she started laughing at the jokes he used to cheer her up. She'd spent more and more time with him until, without realizing it, he was in love with her.

"She's got a pretty busy life of her own." He shouldn't defend her to Zeke. Maeve had gotten that big break after all and left town, kicking up dirt in her wake without a look back.

"Do you know sometimes she's only on location for a few weeks? She could live anywhere besides LA. Other actors do it all the time. Who's that guy…" Zeke snapped his fingers. "The one who did all those chick flicks, then switched to that series on that major streaming channel. You know the station, the one with all the letters that spell a name."

"No clue."

"Yeah, you know. He plays the bongos."

"Bro, truly not a clue. I don't watch movies." He wasn't telling the complete truth. He used to avoid movies because he didn't want to accidentally see Maeve on the screen. But after a few years of being apart, he wanted to see her in her element. He would go to the movies alone when one of hers was in theaters.

"Well, whatever his name is, he lives in Texas or something with his wife. She's hot." Zeke shoved another forkful of food into his mouth. "All I'm saying is why not live here and help me out a little? It wouldn't kill her."

Lock thought living in Backwater actually might kill her. She wasn't cut out for this town. She had dreams too big for their small-town living. "You'll have to talk to her about that. Do you need any help with the renovations?"

"I'm fine for now. I'll let you know if I do, though," Zeke said around another bite.

Lock shoved off the counter. "You might want to slow down before you choke on that food."

"Sure." Zeke didn't lift his gaze from the tray.

"And maybe don't refer to other men's wives as hot." Sometimes Zeke had the manners of a bull. "I have to get back to work. Just wanted to drop off the food. If you need anything, let me know, okay?"

"Sure. But I'm fine. Thanks."

"If you say so." He wasn't sure if Zeke was telling the whole truth about being okay. He had lost his dad, and they'd been close. Ray had been a great guy. The kind of guy anyone would want as a father.

Lock didn't remember much about his own dad. His

father had passed away when Lock was only six. He wondered what kind of a relationship he would have had with his dad had he lived. Would they be close? He liked to think so. At least he had three older brothers. Most times that was enough. He sure as hell never wanted to think about losing one of them. That would kill him.

Zeke followed him to the door. He turned to his friend, ready to say something, but his gaze drifted up the steps to the second floor, and all he could think about was Maeve. She was probably upstairs, avoiding him.

"I feel like I'm forgetting something," Lock said. He couldn't think of what it was, except maybe a way to stall in case Maeve was about to come downstairs.

"Whatever it is, you'll figure it out. Thanks for stopping by." Zeke held out his hand.

Lock glanced at it and, for a split second, wondered if a hug would be better. He opted to shake. He and Zeke didn't hug.

"I'll see you around." He trotted down the porch steps to his truck. With his hand on the driver's door, he remembered what he had forgotten.

****

She had to pee. Again. Maeve grabbed her makeup bag from her suitcase and went into the upstairs hall bathroom across from her childhood bedroom. She locked the door and leaned against it.

Every step she took in this house seemed to take all her effort. Her father was in all the nooks and crannies. Even in the bathroom, his toothbrush sat waiting in the glass beside her brother's.

Her father's house was a mess, and that made her insides ache for the days when life was simpler and the future was in front of them all. Zeke had basically torn apart the kitchen already, sending plaster dust in thin sheets across every surface, including halfway up the steps. Anyone with a breathing issue would be hard-pressed to stay here.

The little half bath downstairs under the steps was being used as storage now. The bathroom off her father's room was also half demolished, but Zeke swore the shower still worked. The upturned master bath explained why Dad's toothbrush was in the hall bath.

She moved away from the door. If she had to guess, the worn burgundy terry bathrobe hanging on said door was also her dad's. She had bought it for him for Christmas almost a decade ago. She grabbed the fabric and pressed it to her nose, inhaling the clean scent of his laundry detergent. Her insides ached more.

The half-finished projects were as if Zeke had attempted one, become distracted by a shiny object, and begun another before finishing the first. Had he developed ADD in the last year? She had no idea how long this erratic demolition had been going on, but she hated to think of her father living in this squalor. She should have come home sooner. That thought would haunt her.

Now she was forced to share the small hallway bath with her brother for the duration of her stay. Just like when they were kids. Sharing wasn't all bad. Or at least, that was what she would tell herself each time she started to feel queasy.

She had been feeling off the past few mornings—maybe the last week or so. She had lost track but wanted to chalk it up to nerves about coming home and seeing old friends. But the upset stomach had started before she got the call from Zeke.

Her list of friends in Backwater was sparse, so seeing them shouldn't have ignited nerves. A few old friends from high school had come to the funeral, wished her well, and gone back to their regular lives without missing a beat.

She did have some secrets she didn't want to share with anyone. She didn't have a long list of friends who knew her well enough to figure out she was hiding something, like her relationship with Michael had ended a month ago. She had discovered he had spent all her savings, had lied about having a job for months, and wasn't who he said he was. She had been duped by a con artist because she had been desperate to be loved.

She had ignored her turbulent stomach long enough. Nature really did call. She unzipped her makeup bag.

Voices drifted up the steps and huddled outside the bathroom door in an undefinable mutter. Whoever had stopped by was at the front door talking with Zeke. Privacy was a commodity in the house with walls thin enough for a whisper to seep through.

Probably another well-meaning female neighbor with a tray of food had come to pay her respects. Many of the single ladies had vied for a date with the eligible Ray Barnes over the years. Or Mrs. Thatcher had returned for the third time.

All those women, and he had barely turned his head. Maeve wished her father had spent his final days with a companion. Someone to have held his hand and told him that it was okay if he was ready to go, that he didn't have to suffer any longer.

Well, whoever was at the door, Maeve hoped their food wouldn't smell like something that made her want to puke. "What am I going to do?" she said to herself.

She was a smart woman. She didn't need a test to tell her what she suspected but didn't want to admit. No matter what her brain knew, her skin broke out in a sweat. Her hands shook with terror. Her heart wanted to run and hide from the truth.

Should she wait until the visitor was gone? What if they were there for her? Maybe she should put off the inevitable.

But she had come in here with a purpose. Running from her fears never helped. Whoever had stopped by was not likely to barge into the bathroom and would certainly wait for her.

She had put it off long enough and set to the task of peeing on a stick. All she had to do was wait one minute for the results. One minute wasn't long, and she could keep telling herself that as the seconds turned at a snail's pace.

She finished up and washed her hands, counting to sixty in her head. Losing track somewhere around forty, she started over, but those fears would have the final say, and she dared a glance at the test.

Two lines. Two lines confirmed the biggest problem to come along and cut her off at the knees, leaving her ill-prepared to bounce back from this.

The room spun. She reached for the side of the sink to keep from falling over, but her hand missed, and she swiped at the glass with the toothbrushes, the soap tray, and Zeke's shaving kit. Everything landed with a crash.

Her legs buckled, and she followed.

Chapter Three

Lock pushed open the screen door. "Zeke, I left my keys on the counter."

Zeke popped his head out around the kitchen doorframe. A fork was midway to his mouth. His eyebrows stood at attention as if he was surprised by anyone being at the door.

"Huh?" was all Zeke said with a mouthful of food. "Oh. Sorry. I'll grab them for you."

Something loud crashed on the floor above. A woman yelled. Maeve. His instincts threw him into gear, and he charged the steps. A glimpse into the bedrooms proved no one was there. He banged on the bathroom door.

"Maeve, it's Lock. Are you okay?" He took a deep breath to slow his heart. He didn't want to picture her lying on the floor with blood around her.

"Fine." The door muffled her voice. "Don't come in."

"Did you fall? I heard a loud crash. I'm trained to help with first aid." Why did he say that? She knew he was trained. Or did she? He wasn't thinking straight.

"No. No. I didn't fall. I only knocked something over. All good here." Silence fell between them.

Zeke pounded up the steps behind him. "Maeve, open the door."

"Go away. Both of you."

Zeke shook the knob. "Open up. It sounded like the whole sink came down in there."

Lock put a hand on Zeke's shoulder and shook his head. "Dude, she might not be decent."

"I said. Go away."

"You heard her. The queen has spoken. She doesn't want our help." Zeke trudged back down the steps, but Lock was hard pressed to go.

Maybe she had fallen off the toilet and didn't want anyone to see her in a compromised position. That kind of thing happened all the time with guests on the ranch. Someone became dizzy, and they fell over.

"Ouch."

"*Ouch*? Maeve, please open the door."

The door swung open. Maeve tugged on the hem of her oversized sweatshirt. The pale blue material came almost to her knees, and he recognized it at once. She still wore his shirt. From the first time he had helped pull it over her head to cover her naked body from the chill, he only wanted to see her wearing that.

Her dark brown eyes were wide, and her face had lost some of its natural bronze she had inherited from her mother, as if someone had diluted her skin tone. Her cheeks were sunken, but her dark hair still shone as it curled past her shoulders like corkscrews.

"Hello, Lock. Did you need the bathroom?" She offered him a smile that didn't quite reach her eyes but still tugged at his low belly because he always thought her slightly crooked front tooth was adorable.

Zeke yelled up the steps. "What dropped?"

"Oh, that. Sorry. I broke the glass with your toothbrushes in it. You'll want a new one. I cleaned up the glass on the floor, though." She held up her finger with a drop of blood on it.

"Looks like you need a bandage," Lock said. "I have a kit in my truck."

What was he doing? She didn't need his help. That cut was barely a scratch.

"We have some in the kitchen… Uh, well, we had some in the cabinets, but now they're in a box somewhere. Maybe the garage." Zeke said from his spot at the bottom of the steps.

"It's not a big deal. I'm fine. Sorry for upsetting you all." She gripped the side of the doorway and squeezed her eyes shut.

Lock grabbed her elbow to keep her from falling over. "Maybe you should sit down. Let's get you some water." He shot Zeke a look. "That means you. Go get it."

"Right. Sure." Zeke disappeared.

"Do you want to go in one of the rooms?" He led her to what had been her old bedroom when they were kids. He hadn't been upstairs in years, but he still remembered she had the one at the front.

The room hadn't changed with its light purple walls and pictures of famous actors. She had a bookcase filled with books too. Maeve sat on the edge of the bed covered in a white ruffled comforter more suitable for a teenager than this woman who had taken the movie business by storm.

"You don't have to fuss over me." She looked up at him with glassy eyes. "I just have a headache."

Zeke returned with a glass of water and handed it to Maeve. "Are you sick or something?"

"It might be jet lag. I took something on the plane to relax. Thanks for this." She brought the glass to her lips.

"Well, if you're okay, I'm going to go back to working on the kitchen," Zeke said.

Maeve nodded.

Zeke handed Lock his keys. "I think you were looking for these. You good with showing yourself out? No rush. I'm just saying I need to finish some stuff."

"Yeah. No problem." He pocketed the keys.

Zeke bolted down the steps.

Maeve's gaze drifted toward the window.

The room closed in on him. He didn't belong there, and he didn't want to stay where he wouldn't be wanted. He should have insisted someone else bring that tray of food over here.

"Okay then. I'll be heading out." He turned away but turned back. "I'm sorry about your dad. He was a good man."

Her full bottom lip trembled. She worked it under her teeth, and heat broke out over his body with such a simple move. Maeve Barnes was not for him any longer. Stirring up old attractions didn't pay.

"Thank you. I don't mean to be rude, but I need to put my head down. Could you go?"

"I was planning on going." He jangled his keys in his pocket to prove his point. Even though he was about to leave on his own, her ushering him out stung.

"I didn't mean it to sound the way it did."

"It didn't sound like anything." He only wished he had left when he thought to and not turned around to tell her how sorry he was. She wasn't looking for any comfort from him.

"Thank you for your concern today. It was very nice to see you, though."

"You too. Take care, Maeve." He turned before he

said something he shouldn't—like did she ever regret her decisions—but he could probably guess her answer from her reaction to him.

"Goodbye, Lock." Her words, flat and hard, were a push against his shoulder.

Lock hesitated by the front door. Zeke was in the kitchen banging away at something and creating a racket. How would Maeve get any rest?

Not his problem. He was turning into his mother, meddling in the lives of others like a hen. He pushed out the front door and into the bright sunshine.

His Backwater Pathfinders needed him. His ranch needed him now. Maeve had made her choice all those years ago, and that was that. No time for regrets.

And yet, as his truck followed the long drive back to the road, he couldn't shake seeing the pain in her eyes. He'd witnessed that deep hurt plenty of times when she didn't get a part or when she was missing her mother. Hell, he had even noticed it when she ended their relationship.

Something more was going on with her than a simple slip in the bathroom. But saying what it was would be up to her. Maeve Barnes wasn't his problem anymore.

****

Maeve pushed the curtain aside and made sure Lock's truck went down the driveway. If she hadn't been sweating before, she sure was after laying sights on him. He'd taken up so much space in her small room she could barely breathe. He had smelled like leather, refined. Not an actor in Hollywood could hold a candle to his good looks. The sun had textured his skin to rugged perfection. The lines around his eyes had deepened over the past six years, accenting his ability to laugh at life. He'd been so good at that.

Her body had not forgotten their past. When he held on to her elbow to help her across the hall, her every nerve had piped up, wanting more. But she had sailed that ship, and she couldn't turn around. Now with her life in shambles, she wondered if that had been the right move after all.

If she had stayed with Lock, she wouldn't be broke and pregnant at forty-one. But she also wouldn't have had the last six years to live her dream either. She had touched stardom for the briefest of moments, and the electricity of fame and success burned through her. Just as her body still desired Lock, her ego wanted more and more of the crowds chanting her name. Neither would be hers again.

In her relationship with Michael—or whatever his real name was—she had believed he loved her, doting on her every need. He followed her around to every special event, happy to be on the sidelines. What she had mistaken for love and support was truly only observation and calculations.

How had she been so gullible? He had lived in a beautiful home in Malibu overlooking the water. He had claimed to have sports clients. When all he had was the façade of a real life. All she had to do was look behind the curtain, but she had never thought to question him, believing his words held truth. Because another man in her life had only told her the truth and she had assumed all men were like him.

And now she was pregnant. Well, she wasn't about to tell anyone until she figured out what to do. She had options. She didn't have to keep it. Every time she looked at this child, she would see the man who had betrayed her in a horrible way.

A baby would be difficult with her work schedule once she found a way back. If she found a way back. She would have to go on auditions and stay in shape, which meant time with a trainer. Whether she brought the child on location or hired a nanny so the child could stay home, it was a losing situation. A child did not fit into her life.

She sat on the edge of the bed and dropped her head between her knees. This couldn't be happening.

One thing at a time. The test could be wrong. False positives happened. Maybe she'd get lucky.

But the queasy stomach and the repulsion to smells. The dizziness. Who was she kidding? The two lines told an entire story. She was pregnant.

She was broke.

She had been canceled by a viral video filled with untruths.

She didn't have a partner.

Her father had just died, and her brother was playing crazed demolition man.

She was a mess and in no shape to take care of a baby.

She also couldn't stay in this dust-infested house. She grabbed her purse and headed for her car. The first thing she would need to do was find another place to stay. And figure out how to tell Zeke she was leaving without telling him the truth.

She was on her own. And that was that.

Chapter Four

Maeve stared at her phone. This was impossible. She had pulled into the municipal parking lot behind the library to search for places to stay. Backwater didn't offer a whole lot of choices. It was either the Ryker Ranch or the Hartman Bed-and-Breakfast. Or a few vacation rentals she found through the rental app.

The other option was to go outside of Backwater, but she didn't want to do that. Even if she didn't stay at the house, she did want to go there to help pack up their dad's things. She wouldn't leave all of that to Zeke. Staying out of town would mean too much time on the road.

All the vacation rentals were booked. Sadly, so was the bed-and-breakfast. That left the Ryker Ranch. According to their online reservations, they had an entire guest cottage available.

Her appearance there would raise too many questions. She didn't want to risk running into Lock every day. He wouldn't want her on his ranch. He had been buttoned up like a priest's collar earlier today. She didn't blame him. Lock was a man of honor, and she had abused that by leaving him for a career. He had wanted to do the long-distance-relationship thing, but she hadn't wanted to be tied down. She hated herself for having thought this, but she hadn't been sure Lock would fit into the Hollywood scene, and she hadn't wanted to be held back or judged by having him as a partner.

The sun slowly cooked the inside of the car until sweat slicked her skin. She lowered the window and allowed some fresh air to cool her off and settle her nerves. Out of options on places to stay, she filled out the ranch's reservation form online, but the website wouldn't load to the payment section. Backing out of the page, she tried again. Her cellular service worked fine. She could get on other sites, but something must be wrong with the ranch's website.

She'd have to call, which she dreaded because anyone could pick up the phone. The family owned and ran that ranch. Once someone realized she was on the other end, if they weren't parting with condolences, which she had heard enough of, they would be asking questions she would have to dodge. Or worst of all, they would tell her to stay away because of what she had done to Lock.

Liking none of those possibilities, she hit the call button and held her breath. Ringing began on the other end of the line. She could still hang up and just stay at the house with all the dust and dirt. Or she could sleep in the car.

"Good afternoon, Ryker Ranch. How may I help you?" The male voice coated with a layer of gravel interrupted her runaway thoughts and vibrated deep in her soul.

Her tongue stuck to the roof of her mouth. She tried to swallow and force the words to come, but they wouldn't.

"Hello? Ryker Ranch. Is anyone there?"

She gnawed her lip and jumped in with her eyes closed. "Hello? Hi. Um, I'd like to book a room, please."

She should have said it was her. He was going to find out as soon as he asked for a credit card. *Hang up, Maeve.* This was a bad idea. Why did Backwater have to be such a small town? Why had her brother decided now was a good time to destroy the inside of their home? If she kept all the windows open, would that be better for the baby?

"Sure. When did you want to check in?"

"Today, please." He probably asked that question a million times without ever thinking about who was on the other end. He had no idea it was her and no reason to suspect she'd call. Only a couple of hours ago, he had stood in her room while she gave him the stink eye.

"Maeve, is that you?"

She froze, wishing she had prepared a script before making this call. Improv was never her thing. "I…um…yes. Yes, it is. Hello, Lock."

"Well, you can't stay here. And why do you even want a room?" His voice turned stone cold.

"I can't be at the house without my dad, and your place is the only one with an available room." She hoped she sounded more confident than the frantic palpitations in her chest suggested.

"Maeve…this isn't a good idea, you and me in such close quarters.

She wanted to agree with him. Seeing him around every corner would torture her. She had never stopped loving Lock. She had only wanted to take a different path than the one he'd been on. She had tried to make him understand that it wasn't him, but she had been helpless to avoid hurting him.

"I promise to keep my distance, Lock. I wouldn't do this if it wasn't important."

He didn't say anything. Clicking keys echoed in the

background instead. She let out the breath she was holding.

"I've got a guest cottage."

"The cottage is fine." She wouldn't want to stay in the main building, too many chances to bump into someone else. She wanted to be alone while she figured out what to do next with her life.

"How long will you be staying?"

She hadn't thought about how long she would need to rent space. Clearing out her dad's things could take weeks, or they could just dump everything into garbage bags and call it a day.

"A week?"

He let out a long and heavy breath. "Are you sick?"

"What?"

"Are you sick? Is there something wrong with you? Is that why you don't want to stay at the house with all the mess?"

How easy would it be to come clean? Lock didn't allow his emotions to get in the way of much. When she would be passed over for an acting part and drowning in tears, he would remind her that getting the role was out of her control. He would say she had won simply because she had taken the chance. And even though she wanted to deck him at those times, he was logical. He would give her good advice now, but how could she tell him she was pregnant with some other guy's child? She couldn't do that to him, especially if she didn't keep this baby.

A car turned into the lot and found a place to park. The driver hopped out and looked in her direction. She sank down in the seat, pulled her sunglasses off her head, and put them on. The woman halted, did a quick double take, but went into the building.

"Maeve, answer me."

"I'm not sick. I just can't stay there. Will you give me the room or not? Because if you won't, I have to find another place."

The clicking returned. She took that as a good sign. His answering her question would be a better sign.

"Your room is booked," he said.

"Don't you need my credit card?"

"I don't want your money."

"I can pay my own way." She didn't want or need his charity because her father had died and Lock cared about her once. He couldn't know about her work problems because she doubted he spent one second on social media or reading the entertainment section of…well, of any outlet.

"I know you can. You have plenty of money, if your career is an indicator. But I don't want you to. Not you. Not here."

"Lock—"

"Forget about it. You don't owe me anything. What I just did doesn't mean anything except that I want to do this. Let me have it, okay?" His words grew weary.

"Is this because of how we ended things?" She regretted that last argument. She had approached him at the wrong time, only thinking about how excited she was to finally have a shot. She hadn't thought about what her careless words would do to him—or her.

"I shouldn't have said what I did, and you wouldn't let me apologize," he said.

"You left me ten messages." She had said things, too, that would have been better left quiet and alone in the recesses of her mind. She hadn't meant them.

In all those messages, he had asked her to forgive

him for saying she was selfish. The saddest part was that he had been right. She had been too stubborn to call him back, thinking if he hated her, it would be easier for him to move on.

A soft chuckle met her across the line. "Yeah, I did. I was trying to make a point."

"You often were." She settled against the seat and pressed the phone closer to her ear, as if she could get closer to him. Her insides purred a little from just one softly spoken sentence. Maybe they could at least be friends this time.

"In case you forgot, we don't serve dinner. You'll need to pick something up or go out. I'll see you soon." His tone sharpened and cut off thoughts of friendship cold.

"Okay. Thanks."

He ended the call.

****

Lock stared at the phone for a second. She was coming here. The idea sat in his gut like too much fried dough. He couldn't turn her away even though seeing her on his ranch might kill him.

He had wanted her to go after her dreams. When she came to him, thrilled she had won that reality show contest, she threw herself into his arms, wrapped her legs around his waist, and hollered into the sky. His heart nearly burst free. Her dark eyes shone as if the sun lit them up from inside her. He never imagined in that moment she would do it without him.

They had a good thing going. She understood his need to hike into the woods or ride his horse and the hours he might spend sitting by himself in the fields. He understood her need to be the center of attention and gladly took a step back for her.

He considered a life with her. Hell, he asked Gage to go with him to a jewelry store in Bozeman. When he saw the price tags of a ring worthy of her, he left. He needed more time to save, but she didn't give him time. She'd told him she had to do this alone, without the pressure of him waiting for her back home. She wasn't coming home again, and he wasn't invited for the ride.

He shoved the unwanted memories aside and hurried outside to meet the five fifth graders who were eager to learn about their progress in advancing to the next Pathfinder level.

The Backwater Pathfinders promoted community, friendship, creativity, and love for the outdoors. Lock had been a Pathfinder when he was ten until he was about fourteen or so. His Flock Leader had been Mr. Finnegan.

Knowing that John Ryker had died in his field, working himself to death, Mr. F took Lock under his wing. Lock might have had three older brothers, but Mr. F was a decent stand-in from time to time. But by the time Lock was settled into high school, he lost interest in the Pathfinders and earning merit badges. After that, he only saw Mr. F when he passed him in town, but he had left a lasting impression on Lock and was probably the main reason he became a Flock Leader himself.

The sun warmed up the day. Birds sang into the sky. He inhaled the scent of freshly cut grass. The kids already sat at one of the picnic tables on the side porch. The overhang kept the sun off them and offered a great place for guests to enjoy breakfast or lunch. He had built those five picnic tables from repurposed wood, and that project was still a proud moment for him. Jett couldn't tell him no to outdoor seating once he showed his brother what he had in mind. His mother had decorated the space, adding touches like lantern chandeliers. Yes, he loved this ranch.

Mia Yearwood's mother—Lock could never remember her name—waited at another table, tapping away at her phone. Her eyebrows twisted together, and the tip of her tongue protruded out of the corner of her mouth as if she were deep in thought or deep in anger. He couldn't tell which.

A breeze caught her long beige sweater and revealed exercise clothes that looked as if they'd never seen a gym. He didn't understand why women got dressed up to work out. She lifted her gaze from the phone as he approached.

"Mr. Ryker, I've been waiting for you for almost ten minutes now. You're supposed to be here when the children arrive." She pushed off the bench and hurried over to him.

"My apologies." He was often late to most things. It wasn't personal. The kids were safer on this ranch than in other places. Mia's mother had no idea how many eyes watched.

"You don't seem sorry." She glanced at her phone again with a huff, then shoved it into her sweater pocket.

He wanted to ask if all her huffing meant she landed on the waiting list at the gym, but he kept that to himself. "I assure you my apology is sincere. Thanks for waiting. I can take it from here."

"Are you certain you don't need help with these children?" The lines on her forehead crinkled, then snapped back into place like a rubber band.

"We've had this discussion before." He had hoped for the last and final time, but apparently not. "The kids will earn their badges on time."

He hoped for this too.

"I don't see how you're qualified to ensure they complete the tasks. I'm not implying because you're a man."

"That's good to hear." But he wondered. Mrs. Yearwood had been overheard more than once claiming she never wanted to hear a man's opinion. How did Mr. Yearwood feel about that one?

She shot him a glare. "You're a very busy man, running this business. And what do you know about writing a play?"

He knew absolutely nothing, and that had him worried. But he would never tell Mrs. Mia's Mom that. The group had attempted the play last year but hadn't succeeded, and they weren't allowed to advance to the next Bird level.

He would figure out how to help these kids construct a play on friendship so they could earn their Friendship Badge. He wouldn't let them fail—again.

"We're going to be fine. If I need anything at all, I'll text. I promise." He crossed his heart and tried to offer her his most charming smile.

She glared at him again. "See that you do."

She glanced over her shoulder to the group of kids, talking among themselves. Except for Bodie Finch who sat on the ground with his back against the building.

"I don't want that Bodie Finch anywhere near Mia."

He stifled the groan forcing its way over his lips. This woman had been gunning for Bodie all school year. "Why is that?"

"You've heard about that boy's situation. Moving from foster family to foster family. He must be trouble.

Mia has a bright future ahead of her. I don't want the likes of that child getting in her way or getting in the way of the Friendship Badge." Demon Mother from Hell pointed a finger at him and marched off toward the parking lot. Her sweater flapped behind her.

He wanted to remind Mia's mother—the uptight housewife whose husband had just been fired from his big corporation job outside of Backwater, which she thought no one knew about, but the whole town did—that Mia was only ten and nothing other than her overly determined mother would get in the way of her daughter's future.

But Lock never ruffled the feathers of guests or the parents of his Pathfinders. The Ryker reputation was always first on his mind. Sometimes being the family everyone knew and expected something of was a lot to carry around, but he did it willingly.

He was worried about Bodie Finch, though. Something was up with him, but not what Mrs. Yearwood implied. Bodie was a good kid whose parents had suffered from addiction and lost the battle. Bodie had an aunt who had refused to take him in and sent him to foster care. Lock knew a little about the families Bodie had lived with because of his role as Flock Leader, but he didn't have the details. Why Bodie had been moved around often was a mystery.

"Hey, everyone." He gave a wave, hoping to grab their attention. "Why don't we sit together? Come on over, Bodie." Lock stood at the end of the table with his back to the view of the mountains in the distance and Mrs. Yearwood driving away.

"I want to stay here. I can hear you." Bodie ducked his chin, and his hair flopped over his eyes. The kid could use a good haircut.

"You can hear me if I yell. Come on over. We're a team, and we have to make decisions as a team."

Mia made room and patted the seat beside her. She gave Bodie a big smile. That girl was the complete opposite of her mother.

Bodie rolled his eyes and blew his hair out of his face with a huff, but he pushed off the ground and sat beside Mia. Nothing like the right look from a pretty girl to change a man's mind. Lock laughed to himself. He'd had a crush at about that same age once. He wasn't sure if Bodie was crushing on Mia, but it would serve Mrs. Yearwood right.

He pulled over a small bench and sat. "Okay, let's get down to business."

William Katz raised his hand but didn't wait to be called on. "Mr. Lock, guess what happened today?"

He held up a finger to ask for a minute, but he needed to remember these kids wanted to share their days with him before they did any Pathfinder business. They had stories filled with pets, homework, playground antics, and sometimes unhappy parents. His niece had been the same way at that age.

"William, I want to hear all about what happened, but let's do some work first." He had no idea how anyone handled being a parent. He only saw these kids once a week, and his nerves could be rattled until his whole body vibrated. Having to do it every day, all day? Not for him. He'd stick with animals. Horses were easier.

William's body deflated. Lock's heart sank. He definitely wasn't cut out to be a parent. He gave props to his brother Gage for raising his daughter alone.

"I promise, buddy. We'll all do a check-in when I'm

done."

"What's a check-in?" Emma Sharpe picked at the scab on her skinny knee. Her curly hair hung down her back. Her face was dotted with freckles. She already wore braces.

He wanted to hang his head but held Emma's dark brown gaze instead. "It's what Mr. Jett and I do every morning before we start working on the ranch. We sit down together and go over all the jobs for the day. It's a very important part of running a ranch this size. You guys are old enough to learn how to do it too."

All their faces lit up. Even Bodie leaned in a little closer. At least he had their attention before moving on to the bad news. "We have three badges left to earn before June to go from Downy to Flicker. One badge is the Forest Badge. We have to—"

"I know what the Forest Badge is," Nolan Adams interrupted. Nolan was the overachiever in the group. There was always one. But Nolan was a well-behaved, polite kid that Lock liked.

"Okay, Nolan. Tell us."

Nolan stood, tugged his T-shirt into place, and pushed his glasses back up his nose. He was tall like his father, but he had little interest in sports the way his dad had back in the day. Lock had gone to school with Ted Adams. Good guy.

"The Forest Badge is one of the last two badges a Downy must earn before advancing to Flicker level. Each Pathfinder must spend a day in the woods foraging for living plants like mushrooms and berries. They must fish in a lake and build a fire with sticks." Nolan's face broke out in a wide smile.

"Well done. The other badge is the Kindness

Badge." Lock put up a hand to stop Nolan, whose mouth was poised to offer up more knowledge he had memorized from their handbook. "That one is self-explanatory. But the last one is the Friendship Badge."

"Why can't we just do something nice for another person? Why do we have to write a play? We're horrible at that." Mia slapped the tabletop.

"Great question. But the top brass of the Backwater Pathfinders wants you to develop creativity, and that means writing a short play that shows good friendship."

"This stinks," Bodie said.

Lock wanted to agree. He had asked on more than one occasion if the Pathfinders Board would amend the rule. Pathfinders were about wilderness. Friendship could be shown in a thousand other ways. They could help each other build a tent or cheer for each other on an obstacle course. Every time he asked for another option, the board turned him down—probably because parents like Mrs. Yearwood would not change their minds once they were made up.

Or he could stop behaving like a child and suck it up. He didn't have to like writing. He didn't like brussels sprouts. Why was this any different?

"I know writing the play isn't any fun, and we've had a hard time in the past. But this is our year. We're going to pull our strengths together and do it."

"Mr. Lock, no offense, but you can't write. You're terrible at it. We need someone who knows what they're doing," William said.

"I'm not that bad." Granted, writing wasn't his strongest suit and they'd been unable to finish their play last year. They struggled to come up with ideas or to execute. But, hell, he had to have some skills.

"Can you find someone to help us? I could ask my mom," Mia said.

That wasn't going to happen. "Okay. Okay. I'll find us an assistant coach on this, but I'm still in charge here. Start thinking about ideas for the story. Next week we'll hash them out. Once we get started, we're going to have to meet more than once a week. I've emailed your parents about the schedule."

He was met with a couple of cheers and a groan from Bodie. Lock checked the time on his phone. They still had enough time left for a quick walk in the woods. They could catalog some plants for the Forest Badge.

He had no idea who would assist him on this play thing. He didn't know any storytellers. But he did know an actress who was in town. He would never ask, and she would never agree. Having her on the ranch was enough of a challenge. He didn't need to be in her company on a daily basis too. Besides, she wouldn't stick around. Hollywood was waiting.

He would just have to do it alone. And that was that.

Chapter Five

"What do you mean you're moving out? You just got here."

Maeve repacked the few things she had unpacked while Zeke paced the bedroom. He clenched his fists tightly enough to turn his knuckles white. A vein pulsed in the side of his neck, and his breath was short and ragged. She hadn't expected him to take her announcement poorly.

"I'm not sure why you're so upset. It's not as if we've lived together in years. And I'm not leaving town. I'm just moving over to the Ryker Ranch. I'll come back to help with Dad's things." She had to get out of the house and hoped she could come back. In the few short hours she was gone, he'd demolished the wall between the kitchen and the dining room. The dust was now upstairs too.

"You left town for Hollywood and never came back. Why is that? What is so wrong with Backwater?"

"I never said anything was wrong with Backwater." She had never known him to react in such a dramatic way. Like their father, Zeke rarely spoke of his feelings. She'd hardly noticed he had any until this trip, and she only suspected he was upset because he had torn the house apart.

"You don't have to actually say the words out loud. You stuck your nose up at this town and what Dad did for a living long before you ever left. Now you're sticking your nose up at me. You've always been a self-absorbed snob."

"What are you talking about?" She chucked her blouse into the suitcase without folding it. "I am not a snob."

She had wanted more than the small life of running a farm in the middle of nowhere, Montana. She had dreams and goals, and they didn't include this town. Having wishes and dreams didn't mean she didn't love her father and her brother. She'd needed to find a way out, and when the only opportunity presented itself six years ago, she'd taken it and run. Passing up the chance of a lifetime to stick around and grow vegetables had been out of the question. Did that make her selfish? What was wrong with wanting something for herself, something bigger?

She placed a hand on her belly. Having a child was selfish.

She'd had to leave Lock back then too. He would have held her back and not on purpose. He had supported her dreams through it all, but if they stayed together, she would have always worried she wasn't spending time with him or asking him to live a life Lockwood Ryker would have hated. All the lights and cameras, the parties and events that required a suit or tuxedo, the lack of privacy. The man didn't even have a social media presence. He would never have lasted with fans coming up to him during a meal out.

"Oh, come on." Zeke threw his arm in the air. "You always thought you were better than me and Dad. You either buried yourself in acting books, the plays you were in, or the music you blared. When you did that summer theater in New York, you came back with a New York accent. What the hell, Maeve?"

If his face weren't blooming red, she might laugh at that last statement. She had returned that summer, trying on a new persona. New York City Actress was a good role to practice.

"I don't think I'm better than you. You've lost your mind, Zeke. What is going on with you? All this demolition? I know Dad dying is throwing you for a loop, but I'm concerned about your erratic behavior since I've been back."

"What do you know about my behavior? You're never here to see it. You don't check in with us. You didn't even know Dad was sick until I called you."

"He didn't tell me. I'm not a mind reader. I would've come right away."

"Would you have? Ask yourself that. Because you didn't ask Dad the right questions. You're selfish and always have been. You think the world revolves around you and your famous career and all that money you have. It's a good thing you never had a kid. They would suffer at your hand." He stormed out.

His words sliced her in two. She loved her father. He knew that. Didn't he? When she found out, she had offered to pay for the best medical care. What she hadn't known was Michael had spent all her money.

Would she make a horrible mother? What if Zeke was right? She had been debating with herself whether she could put her child's needs above her own. He had just voiced her concerns.

And what about how she'd handled that child actor on the movie set? She had lost her temper, and someone had recorded her. If she had been a patient person, maybe someone with motherly instincts, she would have responded differently.

People on social called her a poor excuse for a woman because she overreacted and upset a child. What they didn't know was how well that child could upset all the adults in her path. Maeve hadn't been the only one. She had been the only one who was videoed.

The room began to spin. She sat on the edge of the bed and gripped the mattress. Closing her eyes, she tried to suck in deep breaths and count to ten. She needed to get out of this house. With each breath, she was certain the plaster dust coated her lungs and the lungs of her baby. Did the baby even have lungs yet? She knew little about what was happening to her body.

She would need to find a doctor soon, regardless of her decision to be a mother or not. In the meantime, she had to get to the ranch and settle in there.

Pulling herself together, she finished packing and went in search of Zeke. The first floor was quiet except for the dripping of the kitchen faucet. She pushed out the front door. His truck was gone. She couldn't believe he had left and hadn't said goodbye.

How long had he felt that way? She always thought they got along well. He seemed happy for her success. How could he accuse her of not being proud of their father and him, for that matter? She wasn't ashamed that her father had been a farmer.

At least, not once she'd matured. When she was a teenager… But what teenager wasn't embarrassed by their parent? Probably not the Ryker boys. Their mother ran a guest ranch by herself. She had employees, but she didn't dig in the dirt and walk around all day with manure on her boots.

Maeve tossed her suitcase in the trunk of the rental. Comparing her small family and their farm with the Rykers wasn't fair. She sent a text to Zeke.

—*Where did you go?*—

She waited a few minutes, but he didn't respond. He could be driving, but more likely he was still mad at her and ignoring her. She forced the hurt back down her throat. He would come around. She would try to explain. He hadn't seen the video. If he had, he would have questioned her, but like Lock, he didn't care about pop culture.

She cast another glance at the tired old house, once the place where she'd dreamed of a bigger life filled with a career in a city whose lights could be seen from the sky. She had wanted to leave Backwater. No matter how hard she had tried, she couldn't make the town fit around her strange edges. This place was for someone who wanted dirt under her nails and hay in her hair. She was happier in a skyscraper and with concrete under her feet.

One more glance at her phone told her Zeke had not replied.

"Oh well." She placed her phone in the cupholder.

No matter what he thought, she cared enough about the life inside her to move out of that dilapidated thing. Until she had her mind made up, she would care for this baby the way it deserved to be taken care of.

Her house was in her rearview, and the road stretched out before her. The sun dipped over the treetops. Its long rays swirled between the leaves. She'd be at the ranch soon and hoped she didn't see Lock. Too many of the old feelings wanted to surface, and she couldn't figure out why that was. Hormones, maybe. Or the loss of her dad.

She had enough heartbreak to last her. She didn't need Lock figuring out her career was in the toilet and she was flat broke because she allowed herself to trust a man who wasn't him. He might feel the way Zeke did about her anyway, thinking she was too big for her own britches. He had never said it, but the hurt in his eyes when she said her final goodbye had haunted her on many nights.

She drove through Backwater on autopilot until night seeped into the sky like spilled ink. She pulled into the Ryker Ranch and found a place to park by the main building. The air whipped around her, chilling her heated skin, as she pushed out of the car. She pulled her sweater closed and shivered. Spring was as unpredictable as her period, which was probably another reason she ended up pregnant. Missing her period wasn't a huge concern because it happened all the time.

She climbed the stairs to the wraparound porch decorated with planters of azaleas, forsythias, and crocuses. Wooden rocking chairs faced the setting sun, inviting her to take a seat and forget for a while. No time for that luxury. She pulled open the oversized door instead.

The lobby area sprawled into a main room on the left with a large stone fireplace that sat quiet at the moment. The comforting smell of woodsmoke greeted her. She always associated that smell with Lock and warm nights under the covers with him.

No one waited behind the registration desk. Her hammering heart drowned out any sounds except the pang of the bell when she announced her arrival.

Doors on the right swung open. She held her breath. She wasn't ready for this. Why was she even here? She had to be out of her mind trying to close the physical space between her and Lock. Her feet refused to listen to the command from her brain to run screaming.

"Welcome to Ryker Ra... Maeve Barnes. What are you doing here?" Kace Ryker smiled at her, his teeth bright against his darker skin. He smoothed a hand over his head.

"Hello, Kace. It's nice to see you again." Was it really? Her head hurt. Of course, it was. This was one of Lock's older brothers. Kace had been in school with Zeke. She had enjoyed Kace's company on many occasions. He was much rowdier than Lock ever was, which made Kace a lot of fun, but she had craved the quiet stability Lock offered. She had needed it many times in her short career.

"I'm sorry about your dad. How are you?"

"I'm doing okay. I'm here to check in." Her loss pressed against the backs of her eyes, threatening to explode in a fit of tears. Grief was unfair like that, sneaking up when no one was looking and stealing all the breath from everyday moments. She missed her father and wanted to hug him one last time.

She also wanted to change the subject and find her room or cottage or whatever it was before her emotions took control. This man didn't need a weeping woman at his reservation desk, and she needed to hold it together for a little longer. She could break down when she was alone.

"I don't usually check in guests, but no one else is around. I should be able to handle the computer." His easy laugh was a contradiction to the furrow between his brows.

Somehow she doubted Kace's incompetence, but at

least Lock wouldn't be walking in here to do the honors. Hopefully, this went quickly and she could get on with her night. The longer she stood here, the worse her chances of avoiding him became.

Kace tapped on the keyboard. His brows furrowed farther. "The computer isn't working."

"What does that mean?" So much for quick.

"Can you hang on a second? I'll be right back."

"I can come back later." Or never. She could suck it up and get a room out of town. The drive back and forth didn't have to be a big deal, if she didn't make it one. Her head throbbed more.

"Don't do that. This won't take long. I promise. Sorry for the inconvenience. We just switched the program, and I haven't learned it yet."

"Okay." She wanted to say it was not okay.

He hurried back through the doors. How was she going to stop him anyway? She had nowhere else to go. It was getting late, and her body ached. She wanted to put her head down.

She made her way into the main room and ran her fingers along the rough stones of the fireplace. A warmth filled the room from the hardwood floors to the wide planks on the walls. Large windows invited the outside indoors. In the daylight, that view would be the kind on postcards. Too bad the idea of walking among the giant pines made her skin itch.

The leather sofa called her name. She dropped down and sank into the downy softness of the couch. She would close her eyes for a second.

"Maeve." A hand gripped her shoulder.

She blinked a few times. Lock stood above her, looking at her with something like worry on his handsome face.

He stepped away. "You okay?"

She pushed to stand. "I'm fine. Sorry about that. It's been a long day. Was I out long?"

"Not sure." He shoved his hands in the back pockets of his jeans.

He wore a green Ryker Ranch T-shirt that stretched across his chest and bunched above his biceps. The wire-rimmed glasses perched on his nose surprised her. She had almost forgotten he wore them, but how could she ever? They added another layer to his charm.

When she'd first learned he wore glasses, she couldn't picture this man who rode horses, chopped wood, and hiked in the woods wearing glasses that made him look more like a professor than a rancher. But in no time at all, she would ask him to leave his contacts behind and wear his glasses for her instead. He rarely did, not because she had asked, but because he didn't want to break them.

"I'm sorry you had to wait," he said.

"Kace mentioned the computer wasn't working." She could do this sort of living-near-each-other thing if they kept the conversation on the practical. As long as they didn't travel back in time to their life together, she could juggle this stay with all her other problems.

Lock shook his head. A smile teased the corner of his lips. She missed his smile. It appeared she would have trouble staying in the present moment. Her mind tripped on every chance to look behind.

"Kace doesn't know how to work a computer unless it's attached to a car." He returned to the reservation desk and typed away with ease. "You're in guest cottage number three. You'll need to drive over. I can give you a map."

The room spun again, and sweat broke out over her face. She gripped the edge of the desk to keep upright.

"Hey, are you okay?" Lock's large hand covered hers.

His heat swept over her, making her sweat more. She liked having his rough skin against hers more than she should.

"I think I need to sit." She must be coming down with something, or battling flu-like symptoms was part of pregnancy. She had no idea what to expect for the foreseeable future. Trying to have a baby by herself seemed like a daunting task.

He led her over to the sofa, and she went with the hope of not being sick all over the floor.

"Do you want to lie down?"

"I'm good like this." She put her head between her knees and closed her eyes, forcing herself to take slow breaths. She would worry about how embarrassing this moment was tomorrow. For now, she was grateful not to be alone.

Alone. That word again. She might have had the career she dreamed of with all the opportunities that came with it. But when she came home at night, the emptiness of her apartment echoed until she couldn't stand the sound of it any longer.

Right around this time, Michael showed up in her life, sophisticated in expensive suits, waving around platinum cards and making her laugh. He had seemed like a good fit. But then, what did she know about how well things fit her?

"Maeve, did you hear me?"

She met his gaze with effort. "I'm sorry. I didn't.

What did you say?"

"I could call a doctor for you. Or Zeke."

"No calls. Can you point me in the direction of the cottage? I think some sleep will do me wonders." The day had attached itself to her like a cinder block tied to her ankle. She couldn't shake the weight of it. That was all. In the morning, with a good night's sleep, she would feel more like herself and ready to tackle at least one of her problems.

"I'll drive you."

"That's not necessary. The cottage is close. I'm assuming." She hadn't been on the ranch in years but knew the layout. They were always updating something and adding something else—she'd followed the ranch on social media while she was gone—but nothing in this town ever changed that much.

"It's not far, but you don't look like you should drive."

She acquiesced, too tired and nauseous to argue with him. One ride wouldn't hurt anything. They both could survive that.

He kept his hands on the wheel. She kept her gaze straight ahead. No one spoke.

He carried her suitcase into the cottage, and she let him do that too. On any other day, she would have put up a fight. She didn't need him or want him to do things for her, or to give him the wrong idea, but her stomach was about to turn inside out, and he was chivalry on a stick.

She sighed with joy over the living space with a stone fireplace. The two leather chairs—*lots of leather on this ranch*—faced the fireplace and looked as if they might swallow her up when she sat in one. She couldn't wait to grab a fleece blanket and do just that. The small kitchen was pristine with dark cabinets, a granite counter, and stainless-steel appliances that winked at her.

"It's cold in here." She went looking for the thermostat more to have something to do than worry over the room's temperature. She wasn't ready for the awkward goodbye that was about to happen. She found the thermostat and two bedrooms down a short hallway with a bathroom that matched the sleek kitchen.

"I can start a fire to warm things up."

She should stop him, tell him to go, but she didn't. She didn't want to be alone right now, and no other person would come over here and sit with her. She had done a bang-up job of ending most of her friendships. If she had to choose between an audition, a meeting, or especially rehearsal, coffee with an old friend never ranked.

She pressed the buttons on the thermostat, and the screen turned an angry red. She hit them again, but the red remained. Even she knew that couldn't be good.

"Lock, I think I broke it."

He turned the corner, and a smile broke out across his face. Little things never flustered him. If something broke, he used to fix it. If someone were late, he would shrug and move on. The big things, though, could drive him to the edge. Lying. Or breaking his heart. Those were nonnegotiable for this man.

He pushed up his glasses. "Needs service. I'll check the furnace. I can do it now if it's not too much of a problem. Or I can come back in the morning."

"I'll be fine until morning. I don't want to bother you. I'm sure you're done working for the day." Having him so close sucked up all the air in the hallway. She wouldn't need the heat running as long as she could look into his eyes.

"I'm never done working. People need us twenty-four seven around here. You know what it's like to be committed to your job."

The statement stung. He was still mad at her. She supposed she deserved some of his anger.

"I wasn't implying your job was less than important." She edged past him and back to the living room. She couldn't have this conversation now. She wanted to lie down. They'd had the work talk years ago, and it hadn't turned out well.

"I never said you did. That's your guilty conscience talking." He followed close on her heels.

"I had nothing to be guilty about." She spun to face him but turned away. The fast movement took the room with her, and she needed something to hold on to before she fell on her face. "Whoa."

"Hey, what's going on with you?" He gripped her arm.

"Stomach bug. I think." She flopped onto the chair that faced the fireplace.

"Can I get you something?"

"Lock, I can't handle you being nice right now. We were just about to have a fight. Let's leave it, okay? You've done enough today. Come back tomorrow and fix the furnace."

"I'm not here to fight with you. Our past is just that. The past. My job is to ensure my guests have a pleasant stay. I'll start a fire and come back tomorrow to fix the furnace. It's in the attic. You can be here or not. It's up to you."

He began building a small pyramid of twigs from

the wicker basket by the fireplace. Her spot in the chair gave her a full view of his strong back. Nice view, but she had better think of something besides his rugged masculinity.

Flames took hold, and he pushed to stand. With those broad shoulders and thick thighs, the man was built for strong work. She never had a problem soaking him in. Especially when he had no clothes on. Sex had always been good with Lock. Better than good. Great. And there she was thinking about exactly what she shouldn't be.

"Gage is in the first cottage if you need anything in the middle of the night." He interrupted her thoughts about fantastic sex.

And what the hell was she thinking anyway? She was carrying some other man's baby. For now, at least. Why would Lock want to be saddled with some guy's kid? He could have any woman he wanted, one he could put his own baby in and add to the legacy of this family in the right way.

"I won't be bothering Gage." She would close her eyes and sleep off whatever this was. She hoped it wasn't from the pregnancy. Morning sickness was supposed to be in the morning, and she hadn't had any yet.

"It won't be a bother if you get sick and need help. Gage takes care of everyone in town."

"I don't need any help." That sounded like a very difficult job for Gage, and one she would not be good at, but Lock's brother was good at everything.

"Stubborn as ever." He held her gaze with a knowing in his. He had seen all sides of her, the good and the not so good.

"I prefer determined." Determination was what had gotten her where she was and what would bring her back.

"Same difference."

His laugh was soft and landed against her cheek like a butterfly's kiss. This man should not have any effect on her. And yet...

"I will take that blanket on the back of the sofa, though."

She reached out for it, but he unfolded it and covered her. She snuggled in and let the warmth of the fire wash over her. Coming here wasn't all bad. She had a warm place to stay that wasn't covered in plaster dust. The ranch was full of caring people who helped one another. She could get lost in the ranch's vastness while she was in town and maybe figure herself out.

"Can I get you anything else?"

"Thank you for being so nice to me."

"Even though you said I shouldn't be?"

"I don't deserve your kindness after what I put you through." She should have ended the relationship when her chances started looking good on the reality show, not after she was headed to LA permanently. But she had been so caught up in what was happening to her the time flew by and the right chance to tell him goodbye never seemed to present itself. A chance of a lifetime had dropped into her lap, and she couldn't pass it up or be tied down to anything that might interfere.

"I treat all my guests with kindness."

Guests. What had she expected? That he would sit down and gossip with her about the last six years? Tell her all his deep secrets?

"Do you make your guests a cup of tea?"

"You want tea?" He arched a brow over the rim of his glasses.

"If there's any here. I'm not asking you to go out

and get something. I think tea would settle my stomach."

And give her a chance to get him to talk a little.

He moved around the kitchen as if he'd done it a million times, grabbing a box of tea from the cabinet next to the stove. The guest cottages must come stocked with a few essentials.

He looked inside the refrigerator. "No milk."

"I don't use milk."

The silence grew as they waited for the water to boil in the teakettle. Lock remained in the kitchen with his arms crossed over his chest.

"Can I at least ask what you've been doing with yourself? Are you happy?" She wanted to know everything she had missed in his life. He deserved love and happiness even if it wasn't from her.

"I work the ranch." A quizzical look crossed his gaze.

"You're not going to make this easy, are you?"

"I don't see the point in trying to start a friendship. You're going to leave soon. We're too different. Being polite is enough, isn't it?"

Not for her and not with him standing there all adorable in those glasses.

The teakettle screeched, startling her and ending their conversation. He placed the mug on the table beside her, denying her the chance to touch his fingers.

"I'm sorry." She had said it all before, but maybe she needed to say it again.

"Nothing to be sorry about. You don't feel well. You're away from home."

"Not about this. About us."

"We don't need to talk about that."

"It seems like we do if the scowl on your face is any

indication." She cupped her hands around the mug for its warmth. Did she want him because she was alone and pregnant and he was familiar?

Or did she still love him?

"I'm not scowling."

"Yeah. Okay. We dated for a long time. I know your facial expressions." She remembered that annoyed scowl, but she also remembered the bright smile that exploded in his eyes and the lust that passed over his face when he took off her clothes. Hard to forget that one. Michael had never looked at her as if she were the only person in the room. She should have paid better attention to the signs.

"That was more than dating." He turned away from her, taking her ability to read his expression with him.

"You know what I mean." She hoped to joke him into some light banter.

"I don't suppose I do. I'll let you get settled."

She tossed the blanket aside and swung her legs over the front of the chair. "Wait."

He hesitated by the door.

"I've had a terrible day. I know I shouldn't ask, but could you stay a little while longer? Talk to me for a bit? I could use the company."

He removed his glasses and wiped a hand over his face. His exasperation was evident in the crease of his brow and the set of his jaw. She held her breath.

"What do you want to talk about?" He came farther into the room.

She sank back into the chair, taking his decision to stay as a good sign. "Tell me something I don't know about you."

"It's been six years. You don't know plenty."

"What do you do besides work on the ranch? Do you have any hobbies?" The question sounded like something from a job interview, but she couldn't think of anything else.

"I'm a Flock Leader with the Pathfinders."

"You're kidding?" She hadn't thought about that group in ages. All the boys had been in it when she was a kid. Even some of the girls. But the outdoorsy group wasn't for her. She had tried to go out with a flock once as a sixth grader and ended up lost in the woods. The troop leaders had searched for her for hours. She had spent the entire time crying, getting mud on her new sneakers, and stressing over missing out on the hot chocolate.

"Is that so surprising?" That dark eyebrow took another trip over the top of his wire-rimmed glasses.

"No... I mean...I just didn't think a single guy without kids would want to babysit a bunch of ten-year-olds."

"I like the kids. They're fun. I'm giving back. And honestly, it takes care of my fix for children. After an hour with them, I'm good for the week. I'm not cut out to be a dad like Gage is. Gage is the best father I've ever seen. Hell, even Kace or Jett make better dads than I would."

"I didn't know Kace and Jett had children." She hadn't often asked about the people from home when she spoke with her dad, and he hadn't kept track of the town gossip.

"Both are more like stepdads because of their girlfriends. Well, Jett is engaged. Kace isn't, but I think they're trying to have a baby."

"What about you?"

"What about me?"

"Why don't you see children in your future?" She placed a hand on her belly, as if to protect the little seedling from his response.

He regarded her for a minute. "Maybe I'm too selfish. Too stuck in my ways. Unable to adapt to a different life. Isn't that what you said to me once? You might have been right, and I didn't know it until now when I said it out loud."

She wished she had never said those words, and having them thrown back at her turned her stomach. Fear had dictated her speech, not truth. She had been afraid of losing the tenuous dream she had achieved. Ironic, since she had lost that delicate career all by herself anyway.

"What if you fell in love with a woman who had a child from a previous relationship? Wouldn't you try to love that child too?"

"Well, hell, of course I would love someone else's child, if the right woman came along. But I don't do the whole fall-in-love thing anymore. Relationships require work, and this ranch is all the work I have time for. You showed me that too. I think you said it was easier to travel light. Wasn't that it?"

She wanted the floor to swallow her whole. Zeke had been right. She was selfish.

"I didn't mean all those things to sound the way they had. I wish I could take that back." Or explain herself better.

"No regrets. You got what you wanted, and in the end, so did I. I'll be back in the morning to fix the furnace around nine if you prefer to make yourself scarce while I'm here."

"Why would I want to do that?"

He headed for the door again. "Stay here while I work or don't. It's up to you."

"Lock."

He turned to her, but the coldness of a last goodbye was in his eyes. She had missed her chance with this man. She had turned him away when she was on top of the world. Now that the world sat on her chest, crushing her, she had no right to ask him for another go-round. And if she decided she wanted this baby, he might reject her this time.

"What's up?" he asked.

"I'm hoping we can be friends."

He pushed his glasses up on his nose. His face remained stoic. Her mind hurried to catch up to her frantic heart. He said nothing.

"Is that a no to friendship?"

"I'm not looking to make friends. I have enough of those and no real time anyway. Take care, Maeve. I hope you feel better soon."

He let himself out, and a chilly breeze swept in after him.

Chapter Six

Lock was called to the principal's office. He truly didn't understand why he had been the chosen one, but when Alessandra Gomez said it was important and it was about Bodie Finch, he ended the sunrise archery class on the ranch early and headed into town.

He pushed through the glass doors of the elementary school, pressed the intercom, and waited to be let in.

"Hey, Lock. I heard you were coming. I need you to sign in here." Mary-Pat Reinhart sat behind the security window and handed him a clipboard.

Mary-Pat had moved to Backwater about five years ago after she and her husband retired. They wanted a quieter life, and she wanted something to do during the day. She had stopped in the sheriff's office to get her fingerprints taken when she applied for the job at the school.

Gage had wanted to hire her for his office on the spot, but his assistant at the time, Phyllis, had said no. Mary-Pat was too soft, Phyllis had said. But Mary-Pat had fooled Phyllis. She was tough as nails and could hit a target at twenty feet.

"I'll call down to Ms. Gomez's office and let her know you're here. Can I get you anything?"

"I'm good. Thanks." He wanted to hurry this along, figure out his connection in all of this, and get back to work. He still had to head over to Maeve's cottage and fix that furnace. He wasn't looking forward to that. Being in Maeve's company proved more difficult than he had imagined. After all these years apart, he'd assumed she would have no effect on him. He had assumed wrong.

Mary-Pat pressed on the desktop and heaved herself out of the chair. "That adorable brother of yours was here earlier. In fact, I think he still is."

He couldn't think of a reason why Gage would be here except for maybe an assembly. "Mary-Pat, you know I'm the best-looking Ryker brother." He enjoyed the banter they had acquired over the years whenever they bumped into each other in town. She was fun and reminded him of his aunt Winnie, Grandpa Ryker's sister who had passed away when he was about eleven.

"Come now. You are sweet on the eyes, but nothing tops Gage in that uniform." She winked.

"Hard to argue with the uniform." Women hung over Gage all the time, wondering if the perpetual bachelor could be caught and reeled in like a blue marlin. The ladies had backed off some when he and Calista became an item, but that didn't deter everyone. Nope, some women liked the challenge of fishing for the hardest catch.

Lock wasn't envious. His brother could have the attention. Lock preferred to fly under the radar. That allowed him to come and go as he pleased without the hassle of attachment. He had been committed, and that hadn't worked out. He didn't need to be hit over the head twice.

Mary-Pat ambled down the hall in her white pants and printed pink top while he paced the small lobby. The minutes ticked on as if pulled by a snail before he received the okay sign to go into the principal's office.

Alessandra Gomez met him with a smile. She was a tall woman, almost as tall as he was, with shiny black hair to her shoulders. The plain straight dress that hit above her knee gave her an all-business look, but he wondered whether its red color was her way of protesting just a little. He'd seen her at the Local Band Night at Kennedy's Pub. Ms. Gomez had a mean two-step and a penchant for bourbon.

"Thank you for coming in, Mr. Ryker." She held out her hand.

He shook. "You can call me Lock."

"I think we should keep this formal, if you don't mind. Why don't you have a seat?" She indicated the chair with a sweep of her manicured hand.

Seeing he had little choice, he did as she requested, if only to move this along. She took her time, though, settling into her big leather chair behind the mahogany desk that was mostly clear except for a computer monitor and a picture frame with its back to him.

"How can I help you?" He adjusted in the seat, trying to find space for his legs instead of bumping up against the desk.

"As I mentioned on the phone, we've had an incident with Bodie Finch. He was changing in physical education, and one of the other students noticed the bruises on his torso. That student informed the teacher who then approached Bodie."

Fire burned in the center of his chest. He leaned forward. "Who did it? Was it another student?"

"It appears, at least according to Bodie after some persuasion to get him to tell, that his foster father has hit him several times. Bodie didn't want to say anything. He was afraid of getting into trouble. We assured him that would not be the case."

"The foster father hit him? Was he arrested?"

"A warrant has been issued for his arrest. I believe Deputy Pearce is delivering it."

"Where is Bodie now?"

"He's in the guidance counselor's office with Sheriff Ryker."

"Why is Gage with him?" He now had an explanation for his brother's presence in the building, but Lock didn't like the circumstances.

"Unfortunately, the county counselor who handles this type of situation can't get to town until tomorrow. Sheriff Ryker is the backup in cases like that. We're removing Bodie from the foster home immediately. He won't be sent back there no matter what the foster parents say. The bruises on Bodie are all the proof we need."

"That's good news. Can I see him? Give him some kind of Pathfinders' pep talk?" That must be the reason he was called in for this. He knew Bodie well. He could make him feel comfortable going with Gage to another family. Hell, he'd ride in the car if that would help.

"Bodie asked to see you, actually." Alessandra's smile pressed into a thin line, but she held his gaze with her steely one.

"He did? That was nice of him." Bodie was a good kid beneath all those problems, and that was exactly what he had tried to tell Mia's mother the other day. If he had to admit it, he'd say Bodie was his favorite in the Flicker Group.

"Mr. Ryker, to spare the child any further emotional distress in emergency situations, sending the child to a familiar home until a suitable foster family can be located is the best thing."

"I agree. Bodie deserves to be with someone who cares about him." If he knew his brother, Gage would take Bodie home to live with him, Calista, and Izzy until a foster family was found. Maybe that was why Lock was here, to tell Bodie going home with Gage was cool and he could visit later tonight since he lived on the ranch too.

"Bodie asked to live with you."

"What?" He moved to the edge of the chair to make sure he heard her correctly.

"Bodie asked to live with you temporarily. I'm asking you if you'll take him for a night or two at most."

"Isn't there some kind of protocol for this? I mean…I'm not licensed or anything. Just because I volunteer with the Pathfinders… I have had my background check done. Several times, as a matter of fact. My brother is the sheriff, but—"

"Mr. Ryker, Lock," Alessandra interrupted him. She folded and unfolded her hands on the desk and stared at him with wide eyes. "Take a breath. Gage and I are making an executive decision here. Personally, I want to find that jerkwad of a foster father and wring his neck until his head falls off his shoulders, but for obvious reasons I can't. What I can and will do, and Gage is on board, is find a good place for Bodie to stay in the meantime so that poor little boy doesn't have to go to some orphanage in Bozeman all alone, hurt, and frightened. Will you or won't you step up and help out?"

With all her pretenses down, Alessandra Gomez was a force. The fire in her eyes said all he needed to know. She would protect her student at any cost, and she wanted him to help because Bodie had asked for him specifically.

He didn't know the first thing about taking care of a kid. And not a kid who had been hurt like that. Honestly, he wanted to find that father, too, and snap his neck.

"There's no one else?" Someone else had to be a better fit than he was.

"Unfortunately, no. That's why he's in the system to begin with. If you don't take him, he'll be sent to a children's home outside of Backwater. I'm asking you as a favor and as an upstanding member of our community, and because that little frightened boy asked for you personally. Will you or won't you step up and do it?"

Alessandra didn't look as if she would take no for an answer, and Gage was in on this, which meant his brother had put in his endorsement too.

"Okay. I'll take him."

"Excellent. Follow me." She led him down a hallway and turned right. She knocked on a closed door, then opened it.

The window behind Gage and Bodie looked out onto the parking lot. They sat at a round table, playing a card game. It looked like Go Fish. Another man sat at a desk covered in papers, folders, and coffee cups, working on his computer. The nameplate read *Mr. Springs, Guidance Counselor*.

Mr. Springs turned to them. "Hello. Thank you for coming." He stood and held out his hand. Springs was a skinny guy with frizzy hair pulled back in a messy ponytail. "Ms. Gomez, I have that meeting. Feel free to use my office for as long as you need to. Bye, Bodie. See you tomorrow." Springs left the office and closed the door behind him.

Lock turned to Gage. "Hey, man. Good to see you." And it was. If he had to become an instant parent, he was glad to have his brother in the room while it happened.

"Same." Gage gave him a nod and picked up another card.

"Bodie, Mr. Lock is here," Alessandra said. "Do you want to say hello?" She stood near the boy, but not too close.

Bodie didn't look up from the cards. He bowed his head and shook it.

"Hey, pal, it's okay." Gage put the cards down. "You can say hello later."

Lock, unsure of what to do, knelt beside Bodie. "How's the card game going? I bet you're beating my brother but good."

Bodie continued to look at the table.

"He sure is. He's one tough player," Gage said.

Lock searched Alessandra's and Gage's faces, but all that came back to him was confusion twisting their brows.

"Bodie, Mr. Lock came to the school for you just like you asked," Alessandra said.

Bodie put down the cards but didn't say anything.

Lock didn't know what to do. If Bodie had asked for him, why wasn't he talking?

"You can go with him now. Are you ready?" Alessandra grabbed Bodie's backpack. He had pinned all his Pathfinder badges to the front.

Lock sucked in a breath. He had been meaning to ask at the meetings why the badges had not been put on his uniform, but Bodie never showed up in any part of the uniform like other kids did. And now that he knew for sure Bodie wasn't being taken care of at home, the badges on the backpack made sense.

Bodie slid out of the chair. His gaze remained on his shoes.

"Wait a second. You don't want him to finish the school day?" This was all happening fast. Asking questions seemed out of place at the moment. He needed to appear as if he knew what he was doing. Kind of like the first time he held a Pathfinders' meeting. He could find out what he needed to know later. Gage would have an idea. Lock hoped.

"I think Bodie should take the rest of today off. He's earned it. I've spoken to his teachers. He has some homework in his backpack, if he's feeling up to it, but don't worry about getting it done tonight," Alessandra said.

That was a relief. He had no idea how to handle homework. His instincts wanted him to run out of the school, give this responsibility to someone else. But all he had to do was look at Bodie, folding in on himself, and something deep inside Lock made him stay.

"Does he have other belongings?" He took the backpack from Alessandra and swung it over his shoulder.

"I'm going back to the house to get them," Gage said. "I'll bring them by in a couple of hours. Bodie, do you know if all your things are in your room?"

Bodie only shrugged.

"I'll make sure to look around. If I missed anything, you can let me know. I'll go back."

Bodie nodded.

"Okay, then I'm heading out now, unless you need me for anything else here?" Gage asked.

"I'll send the reports to your office," Alessandra

said.

"Great. Can I get a high-five, Bodie?" Gage held up his hand, but Bodie only looked at the floor. Gage squatted down to Bodie's level. "You take good care of Mr. Lock, okay? He needs someone to look out for him. He's always making a mess." Gage turned his gaze on him and winked.

Gage made everything seem so easy.

Bodie nodded. The tightness in Lock's chest loosened a little, but he was still concerned about how the next few hours would go. What time did this kid go to bed? And what would he do about tomorrow?

Gage gave a final wave and took leave. Lock wanted to call his brother back.

"Lock, I took the liberty of writing down the school day schedule for you." Alessandra handed him a piece of paper with the answer to one of his questions as if she could read his thoughts. "You can put him on the bus in the morning. One stops just outside the ranch. I checked and marked it down. I also let the bus driver know that Bodie would be on this bus for the time being. Or you can drive him. Whatever is easier for the two of you."

"Great. Thanks." He put the paper in his pocket. "Okay, pal. You ready?"

Bodie didn't say a word but slipped his hand into Lock's. Bodie's hand was much smaller than his, getting swallowed up, and for a second he pictured pummeling the butt wipe who had hurt this little boy. No more. That was certain.

They left the building hand in hand. He helped Bodie climb into the cab of his truck and closed the door.

He stepped toward the back of the truck and leaned on the tailgate to catch his breath. In a matter of minutes, he'd become a stand-in parent. If this predicament had been with any other kid, he might have said no way. But here he was, like a trained horse set off in the wild. He sneaked a peek at Bodie, sitting inside the truck. He had leaned his head against the passenger door.

This poor kid had been hurt and needed someone to take care of him, but Lock had told Maeve just last night that he wasn't up for the work of raising a child.

Alessandra had said he would only have to watch Bodie for a night or two, but what if it was longer? He didn't want to mess things up further for this kid by making mistake after mistake. Bodie had enough strikes against him. Getting lassoed to Lock might not be for the better.

Chapter Seven

"But, Kristen, what did the director say? Did he say it's a definite no?" Maeve walked back toward the guest cottage. She had woken up feeling better than the night before and had decided to take advantage of the nice day, proving to herself evergreens were as lovely as skyscrapers.

The day warmed up some, coaxing her sweatshirt from her shoulders so she could tie it around her waist. Activity bustled around the ranch's main building. Guests with smiles on their faces were out and about, enjoying their vacations. Who wouldn't relish time spent on this expansive ranch? They had everything from hiking events to classes on how to make fire and workshops on taking photos of nature. If this were a vacation for her, she would attempt to do everything and then relax by the firepit in one of those rocking chairs. Why hadn't she enjoyed this type of living before? Because she'd grown up on a farm.

Now she was on the phone with her agent, begging for an answer she already knew but wanted Kristen to say.

"I'm sorry, Maeve. He's going in a different direction. I know this is hard to hear, but you're going to have to wait this scandal out." Kristen's smoke-coated voice scratched its way over the line.

Her agent had been in the business for thirty years

and was one of the toughest talent agents to come out of Los Angeles. A lot of good it was doing Maeve now.

"I didn't do anything wrong." When were people going to understand that?

"It's all about perception. That video makes you look like a deranged child hater."

"You know I'm the furthest from that." Her hand went to her belly.

"I know that. Your closest friends know that, but the video makes you look bad."

"Why doesn't anyone care about the truth?" That video hadn't shown everything, especially not the child's part in the altercation.

Kristen croaked out a laugh. "Truth? In this city? There's no such thing. Look, if you had children of your own so that other mothers could stand up for you, maybe this would pass over, but you don't, and the viewers are always looking to catch someone doing something wrong. This time it's you."

She hated Kristen's argument, and yet she was right.

"Hollywood is unfair, fickle, and unpredictable. If something comes across my desk, I'll let you know. I have to grab this call. Sorry. I'll be in touch soon." Kristen ended their conversation.

Maeve wouldn't be deterred and sent a text to Dennis Leary, the director she'd worked with on the Bright Lights series six months ago. The part had been small, and she only worked one day, but she and Dennis seemed to hit it off. Maybe he wasn't influenced by cancel culture and had something, anything, for her.

Kristen would most likely drop her. In this business, no one could afford to be tied to anyone whose career was in the toilet. And if she kept the baby, parts for a pregnant woman were scarce. Getting her career back would be the equivalent of climbing out of a muddy hole with her fingertips. She didn't know if she had the strength.

Her quads ached with each step, and a sharp pain shot up her big toe. Was she that out of shape? She was barely over forty, and her body was falling apart too. It couldn't break down just yet. She needed more time. But how much more did she have? This baby was coming if Maeve didn't start making decisions.

Somehow, in all the walking and talking with Kristen, she had gotten herself turned around. She must have taken the wrong turn back at the fork and was now in front of the employee cottages. They didn't look much different than the guest cottages with their logs for walls. They were smaller, and they sat in a horseshoe shape. Still nice. And one cottage had planters of flowers on the porch.

A pickup truck pulled into a driveway, not the one with the planters, but next door. The black vehicle had Ryker Ranch logos on the doors. She wanted to duck behind a tree, but it was too late. Lock unfolded, stepped out of the vehicle, and lasered her with his gaze.

"Everything all right? I wouldn't expect to see you back here. Guest activities are either by the main building or on the trails." He didn't have his glasses today. She liked him with them.

The dusty remnants of their conversation last night stuck in her mind. He didn't want to be friends. While she was on the ranch, he would tolerate her. That would have to be enough.

She was never satisfied, always wanting the thing she couldn't have—a life off her family's farm, her mother to still be alive, the career of her dreams, freedom from her responsibility to Lock, and now to have him back.

"All good. I went for a walk." She offered a wave and turned to go before embarrassment strangled her tongue and made her say something stupid.

"Did you get lost?" He came around the back of the truck, shoving his hands in his jeans pockets.

She wanted to deny it because getting lost made her look incapable of navigating her way around, but what other reason could she have for being here when this was clearly not where the other guests were? It would look as if she had stalked him. She stifled a groan.

"Kind of. But I think I know where I made the wrong turn."

The passenger door opened, and a gangly boy hopped out. His hair hung in his eyes, and he tipped up his chin to send the locks back into place. His thin arms stuck out of his shirt and dangled by his side. He wore shorts that exposed scraped knees. This adorable boy looked between her and Lock.

"Oh." Lock hurried over to the boy. "This is my friend Bodie. Bodie, this is Miss Barnes."

Bodie just stared at her.

"Hello, Bodie. It's nice to meet you." She took a step forward with her hand out, but Bodie backed up and into Lock.

Was wanting to shake hands wrong, or had no one taught this young man yet? She wasn't good with kids. She didn't know the first thing about how to handle children. This was exactly why she wasn't suited for motherhood. She would mess up the whole thing.

Lock held Bodie's shoulder and leaned near the

boy's ear. "It's okay to say hello. She doesn't bite." Lock's words were playful, and a small smile tugged at Bodie's lips.

Bodie turned to Lock. "Is that Maeve Barnes the actress?"

"You know who she is?" Lock said with a look of shock.

She had to admit she was a little shocked too.

"Yeah. My foster mother always watched that movie she was in with that man that Audrey, my foster mom, thought was dreamy. She said 'dreamy' with her eyes all glassy. I don't know what 'dreamy' is except what you might dream about. He didn't look like anyone I would dream about. Anyway, Maeve Barnes pretends to be his girlfriend in that movie, but they don't like each other until the end when they do and they really want to be boyfriend and girlfriend. I think it's dumb. There isn't one scene with a car chase, but Audrey watched it all the time."

Lock turned to her. "Is that you?"

"Sounds like it." The movie was *The Truth Is*, and she starred with George Jason, who had landed on *People's* Sexiest Man Alive list three times. He was a box office golden boy. Women everywhere experienced hot flashes when his dimpled smile and boy-next-door good looks came on screen. She had overheard countless conversations from women and men who had him on their hall pass list. She thought he was a bit of a dick.

But the movie did well, and it was the only fake-relationship role she had taken on. So Bodie here was correct. And she was impressed.

Bodie crossed the space between them. "Are you friends with Mr. Lock?"

She glanced over Bodie's head. "Mr. Lock?"

He shoved his hands in his pockets and tipped his shoulder. "The kids in the Pathfinders call me that."

"Well, Bodie, Mr. Lock and I have known each other for a very long time. Do you think that makes us friends?" She couldn't resist a glare in Lock's direction since he had said he didn't want to be friends with her.

"I guess so. I've known Robert since the first grade. We're friends." He returned to Lock's side and leaned against him. Compared to Bodie, Lock was a lot like a tree.

"Makes good sense to me. Are you visiting today?" She liked Bodie and his gangly arms that swung a little when he stood still. His cheeks were still round with baby fat that gave him an extra innocence.

"He is." Lock answered for him, and Maeve wondered why. "Bodie, do you want to go inside and get a soda or something?"

Lock was probably trying to end this conversation as fast as possible, and sending Bodie inside was a good way for Lock to do just that.

"Okay. Can we get lunch soon? I'm starving. I didn't have breakfast this morning." Bodie blew his hair out of his eyes.

"Sure thing."

Bodie turned away but then turned back to her. "Can I ask you something?"

"Of course."

"Since you're a famous movie star, do you know about scripts?" He tipped up his chin to get his hair out of his eyes again.

"I do." In fact, she had been mulling script ideas around in her head for a while, hoping for a chance to explore the ideas further. Maybe even write one of her own someday.

"Can you help my Downy group write a play?"

"Downy group?"

"It's what we are in the Pathfinders. Flicker comes next. If we don't write a good play, we can't get our Friendship Badge and move up to Flickers. We really want to, but Mr. Lock isn't very good at writing. We need help. Would you help us?"

"Bodie, she's too busy to help us, and she isn't staying in Backwater for very long."

"How long are you staying?" Bodie's question was simple curiosity. She had to answer him.

"Maybe a week or two." Just long enough to decide if she wanted to keep her baby and what to do with her life. Nothing too big or important that needed time.

"She can't do it, Bodie. She's busy. Right, Maeve? Didn't you tell me how busy you are?" Lock shot her a glare over Bodie's head.

"Oh, okay." Bodie's shoulders slumped, and the hair fell into his eyes again. "Grown-ups are always busy."

Her stomach hollowed out. She couldn't let this little boy down. She didn't know why he was here with Lock on what would definitely be a school day, but he seemed forlorn, and only after he recognized her did he brighten a little.

"I'll do it."

Lock rolled his eyes. When Bodie turned to him, Lock replaced the disdain with a high-voltage smile. "Looks like I was wrong, kid."

"We have a chance now." Bodie cleared the space between them and threw his arms around her middle. "Thank you, Maeve Barnes."

Her brain took a second to catch up to what was happening and tell her arms to move around him. She hugged him back but eased from his grasp, not because she didn't want to show him affection, but because something told her this boy needed love. She didn't have the power to give him what he needed. She had a number of questions—like where were his parents?—but for now, she would go along for the ride and ask questions later.

"You can just call me Maeve. Maeve Barnes shoved together in one breath sounds kind of funny, doesn't it?"

"Miss Maeve," Lock added.

Bodie looked up at Lock. "Miss Maeve." He looked back at her. "Thanks for helping us. I had a really bad day, and now it's better. Mr. Lock, can I get that soda now even though it's still morning?"

"Sure. Grab your backpack. The front door is open. I'll be inside in a minute."

Bodie grabbed his backpack from the floor of the truck's front seat. He bounded up the steps and let himself into the cottage.

"What did he mean he was having a bad day? Did he get suspended or something?"

"It's a long story. Look, you don't have to do this. I can explain to him that you checked your schedule and this won't work."

She could easily back out. How could she be around children while she tried to figure out if she wanted to be a mother? Her inability to be a parent would burn them like a poison if she made the difficult choice to end the pregnancy.

Spending time with Lock was not something she was excited about doing at the moment either. She could do without the tension while she worked through her long list of problems.

"Bodie seemed glad for the help. I can't let him down. He's a kid, and from what little I can tell, adults might disappoint him. He mentioned a foster mother. Where are his parents?"

"Deceased."

That sweet little boy had no parents to keep him safe, to cheer him on, to snuggle with and tell him stories. She couldn't bear the thought. Growing up without a mother had been difficult enough, but to be his age and to have lost both parents? She couldn't imagine the long road ahead of him. He would need plenty of people in his life who loved and cared for him.

"Recently?" Helping with a little play wasn't exactly a hardship for her. Lock would have to agree to her help.

"A couple of years, I think."

"I'm so sorry. All the more, I have to do this. I know you don't want me to. I could tell from the look on your face, but you're going to have to put your dislike for me aside for a couple of weeks. Can you do that?"

He tilted up his head and stared at the sky. "Doesn't look like I have much of a choice." He returned his gaze to her. "Okay. For the kids. They need this, and I can't allow our past to get in the way of their advancing."

"Or your pride."

"This isn't about my pride."

"It's always about your pride. I'm glad you agree, though. It won't be terrible working together. Will it?"

Karen Ryker pulled up in a golf cart and hopped out, interrupting them. "Lockwood, I got your message and came right over." She hurried to her son and gave him a hug. Then she turned.

Maeve's question about his feelings got tangled up in the wind and taken away. They'd have no more discussion of what working together would be like for him.

"Maeve, what are you doing here?" Karen flashed a warm and welcoming smile.

She wanted to believe the smile was genuine, and maybe it was, but Maeve had done a number on Karen's son, and even though that woman could put a good face on most things, Maeve had to wonder if Karen preferred Maeve was anywhere but the ranch.

"Went for a walk and got lost. I'm heading back to the cottage now."

"I'll be by later to fix the furnace. If for any reason I can't get there, I'll send someone else," Lock said but didn't move.

She wished he would hug her too, but she might as well wish for wings and a portal to take her back to her old life. "Fine. Thank you. Good to see you, Karen."

"You too. Let me know if there's anything I can do for you."

"I'm good. Thanks." She turned to go because tears had sprung up and she didn't want to shed them. The rush of emotion surprised her. She wasn't used to random acts of weeping.

Maeve missed her mother something terrible. She wished she could tell her all her problems. Mom would have sliced her lemon-blueberry cake, poured her a glass of iced tea, and sat and listened as Maeve shared about the things that had her off track.

Mom had been the best at that. She'd always put down whatever she was doing if Maeve or Zeke came into the room and demanded her attention. Maeve wished she had told her mother how much she appreciated all she had done so Maeve could be happy.

She peeked over her shoulder. Karen and Lock climbed the steps to the small front porch. Karen's hand was on Lock's arm. They both laughed at something.

The tears fell anyway.

Chapter Eight

Lock put clean sheets on the bed in the extra room. He used this space mostly to store the hiking and fishing gear he didn't want tangled up with the stuff the ranch used. When it was too cold to sit outside, he came in here at night to read. He had put a recliner in the corner with a small table and lamp years ago. The bed never got used.

His mother was in the kitchen making Bodie a snack. They chatted on about Maeve helping the Pathfinders with the play. Their voices drifted down the short hall and landed all around him, giving him no escape from his conversation with the woman he had loved once.

Maeve had asked him if it would be terrible to work together. *Terrible* wasn't the word he would use. *Uncomfortable* described it better. *Foolish* came to mind. For the sake of the two of them, *pointless*. For the kids, probably *fantastic*. She knew more about storytelling than he did. They deserved to have the help.

He wrestled with the fitted sheet that popped off from one end every time he pulled another corner. Did the bed need this sheet? He yanked it off and tossed it on the floor.

"Do you need some help?" His mother appeared in the doorway.

"I think I have the wrong size sheet. I'll have to get new ones."

"Mind if I give it a try?" She didn't wait for an answer and shook out the sheet. With an expertise he didn't possess, his mother fluttered around the bed, pulling, smoothing, and arranging.

"How did you do that? I would've sworn those sheets were too small."

"Practice. I'm also not dealing with the responsibility of watching a child for the first time while having Maeve Barnes on the ranch. That's a lot for anyone."

"Especially me."

"I didn't say that. But you don't like things complicated, Lockwood. You've always allowed your brothers to handle the tough stuff for you."

"Mom, please, no lectures, okay? I don't shirk my responsibilities. I'm just not Jett or Gage."

"No, and I wouldn't want you to be. But you, Kace, and Ajay all had a wilder streak than the other two. Ever since we lost Ajay, you decided life was too short to get bogged down."

"It is. Can I ask what the point of all this is?"

"Give yourself a chance with Bodie. He's a good kid. He needs someone to love him."

"He's only here temporarily. A night or two at most." Lock wasn't the one to give Bodie the kind of love he needed from a parent. He would just be a solid support system. That was a kind of love, and one that often worked well.

"You have the chance to change the life of a young man. That's not a temporary thing." Mom fluffed the pillows.

"I'm just some guy passing through. In a few years, he'll forget about me."

"And that, my dear son, is where you're wrong. You are much more than some wanderer. Maybe now you'll figure that out. As for Maeve, I think the thing that upset you the most was she left before you could."

"Mom, enough. It's been a long day already, and it's barely noon. I still have a ton of work to get to. Jett has texted me ten times. Then I have to figure out what to do with Bodie." Maeve had said he allowed his pride to get in the way too. Had his pride broken when she left? He wasn't sure about his pride, but his heart sure as hell had broken.

"Tell your brother you aren't working today. Kace is on the property. He can help out. Spend the day with Bodie. Take him fishing or something. If you want, you two can come over for dinner."

"I have to fix Maeve's furnace."

"Jett can do it. Or Juan. We do pay Juan to take care of the maintenance. Unless you want to see her again?" Mom folded the blanket, keeping her gaze away from his.

"You know what? That's a great idea. I'll send Juan. Thanks, Mom." He kissed the top of her head and brushed past her.

This conversation was over for him. He didn't want to think about three steps ahead, Maeve, or his pride. Right now, he needed to deal with the boy in his kitchen.

Bodie sat at the table with his face in his phone. His hair fell over his forehead into his eyes. A plate with apple slices and peanut butter smeared on the edge sat to the side. The soda had been swapped out for milk. Lock could thank his mother for that one.

"Looking at something good?"

Bodie's slow gaze found his. "Just scrolling. Am I

in trouble for using the phone?"

"No way. You can't get in trouble with me." He suspected this kid was scared most of the time. Whoever took Bodie next was going to be interviewed by him first. No one was going to scare this kid anymore.

"You're the first adult to say that."

"Okay, boys, I'm heading out." Karen blew into the kitchen like the tornado she was. "I'll have dinner ready at six. Don't be late." Karen hugged Bodie, who gripped her and squeezed his eyes shut.

"Thank you for the snack, Miss Karen."

"You're welcome, sweetie. My pleasure." She turned to him. "Lockwood, please bring dessert. I've already asked the family to join us."

"Already?"

"Your mother is a good texter." She waved her phone in the air.

He stifled a groan. He wasn't up for a Ryker family dinner with everyone wanting to ask questions about Bodie and how Lock would take care of him. His brothers would think he couldn't do it.

He wouldn't refuse her invitation. She would never let him hear the end of it, and she had come right over when he called her. "Sure thing. Thanks for stopping by."

"Here if you need anything. Either of you." Karen let herself out.

Lock grabbed the chair beside Bodie, flipped it around, and straddled it, facing Bodie. Bodie looked back at him with wide eyes.

"I meant what I said. You can't get in trouble with me. You might only be here a couple of days, but if it goes on longer, just always tell me the truth and we'll handle whatever is going on together. Deal?" He put his fist out.

Bodie looked at him as if he was trying to determine the truth behind his statement. "Deal," he finally said and fist-bumped him.

"Good." Should he ask about the foster father and what happened, or should he wait for Bodie to bring it up? He'd have to ask Gage what to do.

"Did you get enough to eat?" He made a plate of apple slices and peanut butter for himself.

"Yeah." Bodie pointed to the almost empty plate as if to explain the obvious.

"You know you can talk to me about anything, right?" He dipped an apple slice in the peanut butter and took a bite.

"I guess so."

"Do you have any questions about what happens next with you?"

"If you don't want to keep me, then another foster family will be forced to take me." Bodie eyed the apple slices.

Lock pushed the plate toward him. "Whether you stay with me or not isn't about me wanting you."

Bodie took an apple slice but didn't say anything.

"I'm not allowed to have a foster child. I haven't applied." Those words sounded hollow to him. They must sound worse to Bodie, but they weren't an excuse.

"So, if you were a foster parent, you would keep me?"

"Sure." The word slipped out in haste. He couldn't allow this kid to be hurt again. But Lock wasn't a foster parent and wasn't ready to be any kind of parent. He could make sure Bodie was placed with a good family this time, one that would treat him well, and Lock could be like an uncle.

"Then apply."

He opened his mouth to say *it's not that simple*, but he closed his lips over the words. To Bodie, it probably was that simple. "You're going to be fine no matter what happens."

"That's what the social worker said. What did she know?" Bodie slid off the chair. "Can I go to my room?"

"You don't have to ask." He wanted to keep Bodie talking but didn't know how to drag out this conversation.

"I did in the last house."

"My house isn't the same as the last one."

"They're all the same."

****

Maeve splashed cold water on her face. She had felt fine when she returned from her walk, but then—*bam.* The morning sickness rocked her entire body until she thought her insides would end up on the outside and all over the bathroom floor.

Was it going to be like this the whole time? She wouldn't last. She wiped her mouth with a towel and dragged herself to the kitchen. The cabinets revealed white dishes and cups, enough glasses for four. Silverware and serving utensils filled two drawers. The kitchen was void of food, and right now she would kill for some crackers and jelly or a simple piece of toast.

She needed to get some groceries if she was going to stay here for the next couple of weeks. That would require her to leave the cottage and go into town, which was about as appealing at the moment as having her bikini line waxed.

Mustering what little energy she had, she grabbed her keys. The main building where they served breakfast and lunch was bound to have something. She wouldn't have to drive as far as the grocery store. The main building wouldn't have much of a selection, but it would do.

She also wanted to stop by her dad's house at some point today and check on Zeke. Had he demolished any more walls? Was he mad at her? He still hadn't responded to her last text. But food first, then she could tackle her problems with her brother.

The ranch bustled with activity. Guests sat on the grass, drinking from to-go cups and taking advantage of the warm day. An archery class was in full bloom. The rockers on the front porch were occupied with smiling faces, and a group stumbled off the hiking trail a little dusty.

As she climbed the front porch steps, eyes turned her way and the lively chatter dwindled to hushed whispers. They had noticed her, the crazy actress who'd screamed on the viral video.

She tried to avoid the burning gazes for fear of what she would find, but a deep-seated need to know what people thought swarmed her. When they realized it was her, any expressions of awe in finding a celebrity in the wild had turned to disgust. She wanted to shout that they didn't understand, that the video wasn't the entire truth, but the shouting would serve little. She had been tried and convicted in the eternal court of social media.

"What is she doing here?" someone said in a poor excuse for a whisper.

Maeve didn't dare turn to look. The front doors seemed to grow farther away instead of closer with each step. Sweat left a hot trail down her back. If she kept her head up and shoulders straight, she would be inside in no time and these gawkers would be behind her.

"Take her picture."

"I don't want her picture."

"Good thing she doesn't have kids of her own."

She stumbled over her own feet and threw her arms out to brace herself. The porch reached up and smacked her palms while her knees slammed into the wood. The impact shook her, rattling her teeth. The doors swung open and nearly collided with her head.

"Oh, dear." Karen lunged forward. She gripped Maeve's arms and helped her to her feet.

The woman was strong for her size.

"Maeve, are you okay?"

"I think so." She inspected her hands and knees. Everything seemed intact except for her pride, which had once again shattered into a million pieces.

She gathered the nerve to look around. The guests had returned to their private conversations as if she hadn't appeared at all. Not one of them came to her rescue, but she was pretty sure someone had either snapped a photo or taken a video. Her haters would enjoy seeing her make a fool of herself yet again.

"Did you scrape your hand?" Karen turned her palm over. Tiny droplets of blood dotted her skin. She hadn't noticed before.

"I'm sorry," Karen said. "The wood is so rough by the door. We always sand it down during the off-season, but the traffic can be hell. Come inside. I'll clean you up."

She didn't protest, wanting to be away from prying eyes. Karen led her through the kitchen and into an office. The desk was cluttered with papers and a couple of coffee mugs. A baseball cap hung from the corner of the computer monitor.

"Have a seat." Karen pointed to the office chair behind the desk.

"I can stand." She didn't think it was her place to sit at this desk.

"You look a little pallid, if you don't mind me saying so. Sitting might be a good idea. I don't need you passing out and banging your head."

"I'm fine, really. If I could just wash my hand." The scrape only stung a little.

Karen regarded her for a moment. "How are you getting along? You've had a few bad blows recently."

She flopped into the chair after all, too worn out from everything and no longer sure she could stand. Tears fought their way to the surface. She had to suck them back down. She wanted to share her anguish with someone, but how could she burden Lock's mother? He wouldn't want her to lean on Karen for support.

"I'm hanging in there."

Karen pulled the other chair from the front of the desk and sat near her. "It's okay to say you're having a hard time. With your dad gone and something going on between you and Zeke."

"Did Zeke tell you that?"

"He didn't have to. I've known that boy since elementary school. He practically lived here the entire sixth grade. He's struggling, too, with Ray being gone. I know he's torn that house apart. I don't blame you for moving out while you settle your dad's estate."

"The dust was awful. He's mad at me, and I don't know why." She had an idea, but to say it out loud would make it real.

"He's just mad at the world. Give him time. You can stay here as long as you like. I changed your check-out date to a month from now." Karen took a first-aid kit from the bottom drawer of the desk. She dabbed a cotton ball with a cleanser.

"You didn't have to do that." Maeve took the cotton ball and patted her scrapes.

"I know. But I can do what I want. If I don't take advantage of being the boss some of the time, what fun is that?" She giggled.

The giggle was contagious, and Maeve found the relief of laughter on her lips. "Thank you."

"How are you handling what happened on the set of your movie?" Karen opened a latex bandage and covered the scrapes that maybe didn't need to be covered, but Maeve soaked in the attention.

"You know about that too?"

"I follow your career." Karen pushed up her glasses and shrugged. "I keep an eye on all my children."

That did it. The tears spilled in uncontrollable waves. She tried to catch them in her fingers, but they slipped past and down her wrists. Karen handed her a box of tissues.

"Why are you being so nice to me?" Maeve blew her nose.

"Because I like you." Karen laughed. "What happened between you and Lock doesn't change how I feel about you. I understand why you ended things with him even if he didn't."

"You do?" She blew again, then grabbed more tissues from the box.

"I never dreamed of running a guest ranch as a little

girl. But I put my dreams on hold for a while, then I met John, and we married. Gage was on the way faster than I thought, and when I wasn't looking, the years raced away, taking my husband and my dreams with them. At that point, I had to buckle down and take care of my children. Five boys... And this ranch." She blew out a long puff of air. "I don't regret my choices. I adore my boys, but if I could tweak a few things, maybe I'd be something else."

"I never wanted to run my father's farm."

"You had your own closet of dreams to go after. When your chance came, you didn't want to worry about what was waiting for you here, possibly distracting you, maybe even making you feel a little guilty."

No one had ever understood her before. "I never meant to hurt him."

"You thought you were sparing him." Karen patted her uninjured hand.

"I did. But he hates me now." And she couldn't bear it.

"I doubt that. Give him time. Maybe someday you can be friends."

"He doesn't want to be friends."

"Well, maybe you two can learn to get along. That's a good place to start. Let's get you cleaned up."

Karen walked her to the bathroom, where Maeve washed her face for the second time in an hour. She was grateful for Karen. She only wished Karen had said that Lock would love her again. Karen would know.

Karen waited for her in the hallway. "Lunch is being served if you're hungry."

The idea of food turned her stomach. "Do you have some crackers and ginger ale?"

Karen narrowed her eyes. "We do. Come with me."

The kitchen was inviting with its dark cabinets and wood floors. The stainless-steel appliances gleamed. Guests ate in the dining room, not in the kitchen. The kitchen was reserved for the family, and the long table that could seat them all still waited under the window for its occupants to settle around. She had been to many a family dinner here.

Karen grabbed a canvas grocery bag and filled it with ginger ale, crackers, a loaf of fresh bread, and a jar of jelly.

"You don't have to give me all that. I'll go out to the store later today."

"You might need it." Karen handed her the bag.

The back door swung open, grabbing her attention away from the bag. Autumn Archer floated in wearing jeans and a black Henley. Her hair was pulled back, and her face free of makeup. Her silver hoop earrings dangled near her neck, but the glittering stone on her left hand that reflected the light from the window was what Maeve couldn't take her gaze from.

"Oh my goodness, it's Maeve Barnes." Autumn dropped a pile of magazines on the table and crossed the room. She threw her arms around Maeve and pulled her into a hug. Autumn smelled like honeysuckles in the sun.

"Hi, Autumn." She wished her eyes weren't puffy and her face all red from crying or that she was still wearing the exercise clothes from her walk this morning. For a reunion, she would have liked to be better prepared.

Autumn held her at arm's length. "It's so great to see you. You have not changed one bit. Jett didn't mention you were on the ranch. Are you filming here?" Autumn turned back to Karen for the answer.

Karen only tipped a shoulder and rubbed her hands together. "Ladies, I have to dash. Maeve, if you need anything at all, just call me. Anything. I mean it."

Maeve tried to read the look that moved across Karen's eyes, but she couldn't.

"I brought those magazines for you to look at," Autumn said to Karen.

"Great. Can you put them up in my room? I don't want them to get lost in the office. I'll call you later." Karen gripped Autumn's arm. She hurried from the kitchen, leaving them alone.

"When did you get back in town?" Autumn moved around the kitchen. She pulled a salad out of the fridge and sat at the table. The move was effortless and assured, as if she'd done it a million times. "Did you want some? I'm sorry. I wasn't thinking. I have about thirty minutes before I have to get over to the construction site, and I'm running around like that chicken we all seem to see without a head. I want to hear all about what's going on with you."

She and Autumn had always gotten along when they were younger. Living in this small town made it impossible to be invisible. But after Autumn and Jett broke up and Autumn married Trent, she and Autumn had drifted apart. Autumn had been very caught up in her life and raising her daughter. By the time Maeve and Lock got together, Autumn and Jett had been just part of the family lore.

Based on that huge diamond on Autumn's hand, Maeve assumed something had changed.

"No, thanks on the salad. I'm not staying. Well, I am staying on the ranch for a few days in one of the guest cottages."

"Really? How come?" Autumn dug back into her food.

"Long story. Are you working here now?" Her curiosity had the better of her and maybe that little green monster lurking in dark corners. She needed the whole story.

"I guess so." Autumn laughed. "I don't really think about it as working. I've never had so much fun in my life."

"That's great." Work used to be fun for her too, but the last movie had riled her nerves in ways she didn't know possible. "Are you and Jett back together?" Might as well jump in with both feet and just ask what she wanted to know.

Autumn's face brightened. Her cheeks turned pink. "We are." But she didn't flash that ring. Maeve was intrigued. Everyone in her circles would be flaunting their newest piece of fancy jewelry for everyone to *ooh* and *aah* over.

But not Autumn Archer. She was the same woman she had always been even with an engagement to the very successful and desirable Jett Ryker.

"That's great news. Congratulations." Maeve glanced at the magazines on the table. Bridal. What else would they be? She beat the green monster away. Maeve's life was torn apart, and Autumn had returned to the family everyone wanted to be a part of.

"Thanks." Autumn jumped from the chair. "What was I thinking? I'm so sorry. My head has not been screwed on straight lately. I swear if I didn't know any better, I'd say I was pregnant. I was so absentminded when I had Quinn. Anyway, I'm terribly sorry about your dad. I couldn't make the funeral, but I know the family was there. How are you?"

Autumn's words shook Maeve. To be pregnant with Lock's baby would have been something she never dreamed of before she was pregnant with Michael's. Every time she thought of him, she wondered who she had really shared a bed with. And was he off somewhere laughing at her expense? How many other women had he done the same thing to?

Deep down she knew Lock would be an amazing father, showing his child all the things he loved about this ranch and how to work with his hands. Lock's child would have the entire Ryker clan around to keep him safe and loved. She only had Zeke now, and he didn't seem to want her anymore. Who would love her baby besides her? And would that be enough? Could she even consider allowing another family to raise this little person growing inside her? Would that be better for everyone?

"It's an adjustment without Dad, but I'm okay." She didn't want to talk about herself at the moment. The conversation could too easily turn to her career or the spectacle of it all over social media. The nausea wanted to make a comeback as well. "You seem to have it all going for you, Autumn. I'm so happy for you. You deserve it."

"Thank you. I had a lot of tough years. Finally, my ship came in. Or I should say 'my rancher.' "

As if on cue, the back door opened and Jett Ryker sauntered in. He looked so much like Lock she had to hold her breath. Why did these men all seem to have been stamped out of the same mold?

"Hey, babe." Jett kissed Autumn on the cheek. "Hello, Maeve. I'm sorry about your father. He was a good man. We did a lot of work with him."

He didn't move to offer a hug or even a handshake, but she didn't mind. She preferred it. The tenderness would feel wrong.

"Thank you." The room was suddenly too small and suffocating her. She needed some fresh air.

"Lock mentioned you were on the property. Is the cottage to your liking?" Jett asked.

"The cottage is lovely. I think I'd better be going. Nice to see you both." She only needed to last a few seconds, then she would be gulping down a cool breeze and settling the grumbling in her stomach.

"We should grab a coffee," Autumn said. "Unless you're really busy with stuff."

"I won't be in town long, and I have to help my brother. Maybe next time."

Autumn's face fell, and it was all Maeve could do not to backpedal and say she would love to get together because she would. She didn't have many friends and could use one about now, but to befriend a future Mrs. Ryker would require a strength Maeve doubted she had at the moment.

She offered them what had to be a watery smile because the tears threatened again, but she turned to go.

As the kitchen door swung closed behind her, she could have sworn she heard Jett say "She had better stay away from my brother."

Chapter Nine

Lock folded the instructions from Alessandra Gomez and shoved them in the back pocket of his jeans. The school bus was due in fifteen minutes, and Bodie still wasn't ready to leave.

"Hey, Bodie, man, you okay in there?" He spread peanut butter and jelly onto bread. Bodie had said that was his favorite and the foster parents never made it for him. Luckily, Lock had those exact ingredients in his fridge.

The house was small enough that he could yell from his spot in the kitchen, though he would have to go and see what was taking Bodie so long. Lock didn't want him to miss the bus. That would mean he would have to drive him to school and lose close to an hour. He was already behind schedule today.

Bodie hadn't talked much after Karen left last night. Overall, their first night together seemed okay. He wondered why Bodie was dragging his feet this morning. Maybe Lock had let him stay up too late.

He and Bodie had watched a movie, and after Bodie went to bed, Lock had been up reading in his room, now exiled from his recliner in Bodie's room, when Bodie called out. The scream had surprised Lock, causing him to drop his book and run into the bedroom.

Bodie sat up in bed, his hands shaking, and big fat tears fell from his eyes. The blanket pooled around his slim waist. The shirt he slept in was pushed up on one side, and from the light in the hall, Lock witnessed some of the bruises.

"Bad dream?" He stood at the door, not knowing if Bodie needed space or not.

Bodie only nodded.

"Do you want to talk about it?" He took a cautious step into the room.

Bodie only stared up at him.

Lock waited for Bodie to say something, and when he didn't, Lock tried to offer a hug. Bodie only shrank back. Unsure of what to do, Lock left the door ajar and the light on in the hallway.

Lock climbed into bed, ready to let sleep take over after a very long day, when Bodie knocked on his door.

"Can I sleep in here? I could sleep on the floor." Bodie held a blanket and pillow. "I won't bother you. I promise. That bed is too lumpy. I can't sleep on it."

That mattress was brand new, but Lock didn't point that out. He wondered what this child had been through in his short years after losing his parents in a car accident.

Lock had lost his dad, but he never experienced fear growing up. His mother had tried to fill every void she could with plenty of love and a dose of discipline. She had five boys to wrangle. Sometimes they got out of hand.

In the spots she couldn't fill with a mother's love, his three older brothers did. He was lucky to be so far down in the birth order. Gage had taken on the role of father figure, and Jett became his second-in-command. Kace had shown Lock how to have fun, and he'd had Ajay behind him to cause enough trouble.

"You don't have to sleep on the floor." Lock moved

over to the edge of the king-size bed. He didn't know what was right or wrong in this scenario, but Gage had done this very thing for him a hundred times growing up.

Bodie had burrowed under the covers and fallen asleep. Now Lock couldn't get him to come out of the guest bedroom and go to school.

He pushed the door open wide. Bodie sat on the edge of the unmade bed, staring at the hardwood floor. The morning sun laid streaks across the wall and over Bodie's face like prison bars.

"Hey, you need to put on your shoes. The bus will be here soon. I made your lunch. I think you'll like it."

"I don't want to go to school." Bodie held his chin in his hands and rested his elbows on his knees.

When Gage dropped Bodie's things off last night, he had said to expect this. "I get it. But it's important you go today."

"School is dumb."

"It can be. I didn't always love school, but it's your job to go, like it's my job to run the ranch. And I don't want to be late for work."

He was already late. The horses needed tending first thing before the sun was even up. All the guest activities had to be set up for the day. He checked in with the maintenance and housekeeping departments as well, before guests had a chance to rise and shine their displeasure about not enough towels, low water pressure, or noisy neighbors. He hadn't even checked on Maeve's broken furnace. He had to assume Juan had taken care of it.

"Can I come to work with you?" Bodie's eyes were hooded, and he looked a lot younger than his ten years.

"Sorry."

"Why? I'm a good helper." Bodie started making the bed as if that would prove his point.

"I know you are. But I don't have the time to train you today. All you would do is follow me around and get bored." And slow him down.

"No, I wouldn't."

"Yeah, you would. What I do isn't fun unless you're actually doing it. Another day." He handed Bodie his shoes.

"I'm not going." Bodie turned away.

"The school is expecting you. Let's not let Ms. Gomez down, okay? She's doing you a big favor by allowing you to stay with me." If this was how every morning would be, he would have to figure something else out for Bodie. Lock could not argue each day about going to school when many people and the ranch relied on him to be efficient and timely.

"I don't care. I can only stay for a day or two anyway. So why can't I miss school for two days? What's the big deal?"

He checked the time on his phone. Two minutes to the bus, and no way they'd make it to the ranch's entrance in time. He was about to do something he didn't want to do.

"If you don't go to school, you can't come to the Pathfinders' meeting today, and you'll miss out on Miss Maeve."

"She's coming?" Bodie's face lit up. "I really like her. She's nice and pretty."

Lock couldn't argue with any of those statements, though he might if someone pushed him to admit it. "Then put on your shoes, and I'll drive you."

"Is she really coming?" Bodie narrowed his eyes.

"Would I lie to you?"

Bodie considered him for a moment. "I don't think so."

"Good. Get your shoes on. I'll be waiting at the front door." He turned to go.

"Mr. Lock?"

Lock turned back. "Since we're living together, why don't you drop the mister and just call me Lock, okay?"

Bodie's smile doubled in size. "Lock, what if the kids make fun of me?"

"For what?"

"For what happened to me." Bodie dropped his gaze to the floor. His hair fell over his face.

Lock put a hand on his shoulder. "Bodie, look at me."

Bodie did as he was told. His lips trembled. Lock squatted down to be at his height and met Bodie's gaze. If he ever had the chance, he would get this foster father alone in a dark alley and scare the living daylights out of him for what that scum had done to this innocent boy.

"Anyone who is dumb enough to make fun of you for living a tough life is a jerk. You're the strongest kid I know. Be proud of yourself for being strong."

"But what do I do if they say something or bully me?"

"I won't stand for bullies. If they bully you, as long as they don't touch you, you just walk away with your head high, then tell me, and I'll take care of it."

"What if they do touch me?"

"If they put their hands on you without your permission, you have my permission to deck them."

"Isn't that the same thing as what Steve did to me?" A tear fell from Bodie's eye.

Lock gripped his shoulders. "Not even close. Steve is the worst kind of bully. He took advantage of his strength against you. He is a coward, not a man. A real man doesn't lay his hands on a child or a woman. Do you understand?"

Bodie nodded.

"Good. If anyone at school punches you, pushes you, shoves you, or tries to hit you with something, you can retaliate. I'm saying it's okay."

"We get in trouble at school for fighting."

"You won't get in trouble with me." Gage had taught him the very same thing when he was about Bodie's age and some kids at school decided they wanted to steal his books. Gage had told him he was never to start a fight for any reason, but if someone put their hands on him, Gage had given him permission to swing. Gage had said the same thing to his daughter too.

"Okay." Bodie slipped his feet into his sneakers. Lock hadn't noticed they were dirty and torn along the worn-down rubber before now.

"After today's meeting, I'm getting some clothes. I need new sneakers. Do you want to come?"

"Sure. That would be fun." Bodie pushed the hair out of his eyes.

"Yeah, it will."

****

Maeve put the prescription for prenatal vitamins in her purse. The day was warming up nicely for May. The breeze tickled her skin as she walked across the parking lot to her rental. The morning sickness had given her a break today. Maybe it was over.

Considering she had been nearly in tears after leaving Autumn and overhearing Jett, not to mention the rumination into the night of her life's mistakes, she had slept well. She was wrong for Lock, but did Jett have to say it out loud? She shouldn't have yelled at that child, but she wasn't perfect and hadn't pretended to be. Why did her worst moments have to be recorded? Who needed that kind of reminder?

She had driven out of Backwater this morning to a new ob-gyn in the next town over, minimizing her chances of running into someone from Backwater. She had used the alias she often used to make the appointment and keep her identity a secret for as long as possible. No one in the waiting room had recognized her with the simple disguise of a baseball hat and glasses.

Being grateful for that was an understatement. When she had checked social media this morning, she was still trending as the worst woman in Hollywood. Becoming famous had taken forever. Becoming a pariah had taken seconds, and it wasn't even the whole truth.

The doctor had confirmed what she already knew but still wanted Maeve to take a blood test to be medically certain. She had prescribed the vitamins and wished her luck. She was due in December. A Christmas baby.

She had asked about her options if she didn't want the child. The doctor told her she didn't terminate pregnancies but could connect her with someone who did, if that was the route Maeve chose. Her time to decide was running out. She wished she had someone to talk to about it, not that she had that kind of a friend. Her friends in LA were superficial. Most people sized others up to find out what they had to offer and how they could benefit from it. The smart celebrities moved out of LA.

She drove back to town at top speed because she

didn't want to be late for the Pathfinders' meeting. She had actually looked forward to this all day. Doing something for these kids gave her a purpose, and she truly liked Bodie and wanted to help him in any way she could. Lock hadn't given her details, but losing his parents was enough suffering for one person. Seeing Lock could be good or bad. She hoped for the first and expected the latter.

After the meeting she would go over to her father's house and corner Zeke into talking to her. They needed to clear the air between them.

She had no plan in place to help the kids write a play on friendship. She would keep it simple, pulling on basic messages. She didn't think it mattered if it was full of cliches. This was a ten-minute production for a Pathfinder badge, something that would end up in the back of most of these kids' closets five years from now.

She pulled onto the ranch's driveway and parked near the main building. Lock had texted to tell her they would be on the side patio and to meet them there. She had tried not to get too excited when she saw the text. He was all business, but it did give her a chance to save his number in her contacts.

The group of five children sat around a picnic table with a red-and-white gingham cloth spread over the center in a diamond shape. Lock typed away on his phone, and a woman stood off to the side with a look of repugnance twisting her otherwise attractive facial features.

Maeve took her time getting to the group. She recognized Bodie immediately. He seemed to be in deep conversation with another boy beside him. The two girls had their heads together and wrote in a notebook.

The woman made eye contact and hurried over to her. Maeve smiled as she always would when approached by a stranger, because she never knew if the person was a fan or not, but that smile was met with a murderous scowl.

Maeve stopped in her tracks.

"You are that vile actress who attacked that poor child on the movie set. I saw all the videos with you screaming at that innocent girl over nothing and bringing her to tears. There is no way you will be working with my daughter now or ever. I'm reporting you to the Pathfinder Board Council, and I've asked Sheriff Ryker to issue a restraining order against you."

Shock shoved Maeve back a few steps as if the woman had placed both hands on her chest and pushed with all her might. This lady wasn't a big person, but the fury in her blue eyes and the baring of her teeth would make any surly bouncer at any trashy bar pause.

"I didn't attack anyone." Defending herself would do no good. She should just allow this hag full of icy wind to blow out and disappear. But Maeve's hormones were in full gear, and having to be near Lock threw her off balance. She had only wanted to come home, deal with her dad's leaving, and lick her wounds alone. She didn't want to be the brunt of someone's ill-founded anger or even Lock's Pathfinder buddy.

"Do I need to pull up those videos?" The woman reached for her back pocket.

"I've seen the videos. You shouldn't believe everything you see." She tried to step around her, but the crazy lady blocked her path.

"I know what I saw. I know what's been circulating on every media outlet. If there was an ounce of a lie, someone would have come to your rescue by now."

This woman knew nothing about how Tinsel Town worked. Maeve had become the outcast, and like any good middle-school playground, the outcast was left alone to fend for herself. Standing up in the face of career loss in an industry that knew little of forgiveness and much about one-upmanship took a rare person. Maeve hadn't been in the game long enough to have those kinds of allies. She was still the woman who had won her place through a reality show. She was expendable.

She had wished someone from the cast or crew would have spoken up on her behalf, but they had all remained quiet, including her costar. The child actor had influential parents who had been in the business for decades. Maeve hadn't stood a chance.

"Ladies, the kids are watching." Lock stood between them. His jaw was set, and his eyes held a warning.

"I don't want her here. Mia told me this woman was going to help them get their badge. If that happens, I'm pulling Mia."

"I've asked Maeve to assist with the play. She's skilled, and we need the help." Lock held his stance.

"I'll help you. How hard can it be to write a short play?" Helicopter Mommy threw her hands in the air and didn't bother to keep her voice down. One of the kids looked over but went back to what he was doing.

Lock clenched his jaw. He shifted on his feet and glared at Cranky Pants. "Mrs. Yearwood, this is my group. I have everything under control. It might be best if you waited in your car until the meeting is over."

"I will do no such thing. I'm going to take my daughter out of this useless group. She can earn her badges on her own."

"That's a mistake," Lock said.

"She goes, or Mia does." Mrs. Yearwood pointed a well-manicured finger at Maeve.

Maeve wondered what Mrs. Yearwood would do if Maeve snapped that finger.

"I can't make that choice. You'll have to decide for yourself, but removing Mia will only hurt her." Lock clasped his hands in front of him, ever the picture of calm.

Maeve wanted to cheer—not only because he had defended her, but because he had put this overbearing mother in her place. She hoped her face remained as neutral as Lock's.

"Mia, get your things. We're leaving."

Mia looked up from what she was doing with her friend. Her face went slack as if she tried to process what her mother had said. "Mom?"

"Let's go. Hurry up." Mrs. Yearwood waved her arm in a frantic "come here" motion.

Mia didn't move. Her gaze dashed from one child to the other. No one else moved either.

"Now, Mia Michele. I will not wait another second or tolerate your belligerence."

The other kids continued to stare with wide eyes. Bodie's face paled.

"You're making a mistake," Lock said.

"This mistake is yours, Mr. Ryker. You'll be hearing from me again." Mrs. Yearwood marched away. Mia juggled her books and backpack and hurried after her mother.

Lock leaned in close. He smelled like wood and leather with a hint of heat. Maeve wanted to rest her head against his shoulder and allow his warmth and comfort to seep into her bones.

"Sorry about that. She's a giant pain in the butt." He stepped away.

She missed the nights she could climb into bed after a long day and he would be asleep. She would curl against his warm body and breathe him in, knowing she could finally relax. She hadn't experienced that since she left. She only wished she hadn't thought about it now.

"She's difficult, all right. Thank you for coming to my defense. I appreciate it."

"Do you have a few minutes after the meeting?"

"Sure." She couldn't imagine what he wanted to talk to her about, but just that he wanted to was a good sign. She was still hoping they could be friends.

"Thanks. Are you ready to get started?"

"I am."

Lock introduced her to the group. They talked about themes they wanted in their play and who wanted to do the acting. A couple of the kids shied away from the idea of a speaking role, but Lock made it clear they all needed to have a speaking part or they couldn't earn the badge. The kids included a part for Mia too.

"Will you and Mr. Lock be in the play?" a boy named Nolan asked.

"Oh, I don't think so." She was only there to assist from backstage. No more limelight for her for a while. Other parents might feel the way Mrs. Yearwood did. Maeve just wanted a chance to redeem herself by helping out behind the scenes, nothing more.

"Not me," said Lock. "I'll leave the acting to the experts."

"Please," said Bodie. "It would be fun."

Lock looked at her. She didn't know what to say, but

it wasn't her place to decide. This was his group, and these children clearly respected and liked him.

"If Miss Maeve agrees, then I'll do it too."

He'd surprised her twice today, by coming to her rescue and now including her in his event.

"Please," the children said in unison.

Bodie came over to her with a bright smile and cheeks turning pink. His hair fell over his eyes, and he pushed it out of the way. "Please, Miss Maeve. It would make my day. And I need to pile up my good days."

This young man seemed to know how to charm her. The other children looked on in wonder. Lock pressed his lips together and held up his palms.

"Okay, okay. I'll do it. But a small part. One line. No more than that. This is your show."

They all cheered in tandem.

Air stuck in her throat. She had to blink away unexpected tears. She cursed these hormones and their control over her. Something as simple as praise from a group of ten-year-olds knocked her on her butt. Talk about surprises.

"Looks like it's settled, then. Your parents are here, so you can all leave. Next time we start writing." Lock waved to each one of them as they headed to the parking lot to meet their parents.

Only Bodie stayed behind. He must still be staying with Lock.

"Bodie, do me a favor. Go inside to the kitchen and ask my brother Kace to get you a snack. I told him you'd be coming in at this time." Lock checked his phone.

"How will I know it's him?"

"They all look alike," she said before she could stop herself.

Lock choked out a laugh. "Miss Maeve is right. He looks like me, but not as handsome." Lock tugged on the collar of his shirt and squared his shoulders.

She could not argue. Bodie hugged her goodbye and ran into the building.

"Can you sit a minute?" Lock said.

"What's up?" She took the seat opposite him at the picnic table.

The sun began its final descent as if encouraged by the new breeze pushing up the corners of the tablecloths. Woodsmoke tickled her nose. The nostalgic smell surrounded her with comfort and warmth, much like Lock used to. She could not stop thinking about their past together. The pregnancy hormones made her crazy. She couldn't explain the obsessing any other way.

"I should have asked you this sooner, but I didn't get a chance with Bodie and his excitement to have you help us."

She braced herself for what was about to come. Ideas of comfort blew away in the breeze. "Okay. Ask."

"I saw the video of you and that girl. What really happened?" Lock held her gaze.

He would expect the truth. Anything less would be unacceptable to this man. Honor was a top priority for him. She owed him that much, but she had a question of her own.

"What tipped you off? I didn't think you followed social media or entertainment news."

"Were you going to hide it from me?"

"I'm not hiding. I'm not. I swear. I was hoping you would find out later rather than sooner. That's all." Her worst moment on display embarrassed her. She wished the videos would go away and allow time to heal those involved. She had apologized for her behavior. When could she move on?

"My soon-to-be sister-in-law mentioned the video."

"Autumn?" Autumn had shown no indication she knew from their conversation the other day in the kitchen. Had she been a better actor than Maeve?

"Calista. What happened on that set?" He leaned forward on his forearms as if he were about to tell her a secret instead of waiting for hers.

"I did lose my temper." Admitting it still hurt. If she had only taken a deep breath...

"I could see that. Why? That behavior wasn't like the woman I knew. You love kids. That was evident today. But I need the whole story because I doubt Mrs. Yearwood will be the only parent questioning my judgment."

"We can't have that." Her words bit with a sarcasm she didn't mean to season them with.

"Give me a break, will you? This isn't about us." He sat back.

It wasn't, and she needed to remember that. This was a business arrangement, and when she was done helping, he would gladly see her go. "I'm sorry. I shouldn't have said it that way."

"Apology accepted." He smiled, setting the mood back on its feet.

"I shouldn't have yelled at Ivy. That's her name. Ivy Julia Longfellow-Simon."

"That's some name."

"Do you know who her parents are?"

"Nope."

Of course, he didn't. Lock wasn't someone who paid attention to pop culture. "It's not important except that they are Hollywood royalty. Ivy is a very entitled little girl. She has a bigger entourage than her mother, who has won three Academy Awards, a Tony, and an Emmy."

"Are those important?"

"Are you serious?"

His face scrunched up and turned red as he laughed with the ferocity of a hurricane. She shook her head. Leave it to Lock to make a joke at an unexpected moment.

"I should've known with you."

"Gotcha." He wiped his eyes. "Okay, go on. Ivy with too many names is spoiled. What else?"

"It's not just spoiled. It's crazy spoiled. Whatever she wants. If she wants brown M&M's and there aren't any on set, she will throw herself down on the ground and scream as if she's in pain until they appear. I've never seen anything like it."

Every adult around her jumped whenever Ivy snapped her fingers. Each morning, her staff would review the list of items Ivy had asked for the day before and would have them on set by five o'clock in the morning to avoid the high-voltage temper tantrum.

"This got on your nerves?"

"Wouldn't it for you?" She had tried every way she could think of not to react to Ivy's behavior. She had even consulted a meditation coach, but nothing worked. Maeve's life had been falling apart with her father getting sick and Michael stealing all her money. Her fuse had been short and lit.

"Probably, but when we have guests with obnoxious children, we have to hold our tongues. Jett might shoot me if I didn't."

"Jett would never shoot you." This joke was an obvious one. His family was as tightly woven as burlap. Jett might shoot someone who harmed Lock, but never Lock. Maeve slipped out of her jacket. Her skin broke out in a sweat, and the woodsmoke lost some of its pleasantness.

"He hasn't yet." He smirked.

"I had been watching what I said and did for weeks. Our shooting schedule was behind, we were costing the studio a lot of money, and nothing and no one could stop this child. She halted filming for an entire afternoon because she decided she needed ice cream from a shop forty miles away."

Maeve had lost another acting opportunity because the film had been held up. The new director couldn't wait for her to finish and went with someone else. Parts weren't always easy to come by, and she never liked losing a chance to work, especially over ice cream.

"Are her parents on set?"

"Actually, no. They both have very busy schedules of their own. Ivy only needs a guardian with her, and the parents have assigned one. A useless one, I might add." The guardian spent more time running around taking selfies than paying attention to Ivy.

"So Ivy is without supervision of any kind."

"You're getting it. Anyway, I just wanted the whole ordeal to be over with. It was our last day, and I would never have to see her again. We had to film two more scenes. It was late. She was tired, as was I, and she decided she didn't like the outfit the costume designer had picked for me." Maeve still couldn't believe the decibel of that screech when Ivy had decided Maeve needed a costume change. Maeve had argued against it to no avail. She had no power on that set. No one listened to her because Ivy held all the cards.

Maeve's mouth went dry as she sat with Lock. Her stomach churned like battery acid. She hoped the morning sickness hadn't decided to make an evening visit.

"Did you like this costume?"

"Could I help myself to one of those bottles of water?" A small table placed against the building held a few bottles Lock had brought out during the meeting.

"Sure." He glanced from her to the bottles and back again.

She gulped down the water. Her stomach behaved some, and she was grateful. "Honestly, I had liked all the costumes or outfits picked for us. But Ivy's dislike of mine wasn't the only problem. The big problem was our CD refused to change my clothes because Ivy thought they clashed with hers and her skin tone. The CD was right, by the way, and also extremely tired of dealing with this child." She had wished Courtney had said something in her defense, but Courtney was barely thirty and desperate to be in the business. This was her first film, and she wasn't going to rock that proverbial stupid boat.

"So what happened?"

"Ivy demanded a twenty-minute break after arguing with Courtney. We took it. Ivy returned, but the director decided to retake a different scene between Ivy and another actor. I went into my trailer to change and found several of my sweaters—sweaters I owned—cut up into little pieces and thrown around."

"She cut up your clothes?" Lock's eyebrows shot up to his hairline.

"And believe it or not, she never touched the outfit for the scene. Either she didn't see it or changed her mind mid-meltdown." Maeve had never asked. Afterward, the reason hadn't seemed important. She and Ivy had never really connected during the entire filming process, which made pretending to be her mother who loved her a true challenge. She wasn't sure she had risen to that challenge, but the critics would decide if the movie studio released the film.

"So you lost it."

"I did. I'm not proud of myself. I came charging out of my trailer with guns blazing. I couldn't see straight. Everyone pulled out their phones, including the devil's offspring." The breeze chilled her sweaty skin. Maybe the water wasn't such a great idea. Her stomach protested again.

"Also known as Ivy with too many names."

"Exactly." A bubble of laughter spilled over her lips. He could always take the steam out of her. If she had been paying better attention six years ago, she would have realized making it work with Lock would save her in the end. Even then she had been impatient to get on the road and live her dream. She really was selfish.

"People posted those videos out of context, and you got canceled," he said with conviction.

"So you understand now?"

"I do. Thank you for telling me. I thought you might not want to, or there was more truth to the story than I wanted to hear. You're human, Maeve. Life happens." He stood.

"I'd like to stay and help you with the play." She followed his lead and stepped away from the picnic bench even though she could use a few minutes longer to sit. He was ending their conversation, and she would go along with it.

"The kids and I are fine with you helping. We'll have to see what Mrs. Yearwood does, though. If the council comes down on me, I'll have to think about whether I can keep you or not."

"I understand." She didn't. She wanted him to continue to defend her, but he owed her nothing. His group was the most important thing here.

Her stomach flipped again. A wave of nausea crashed over her, and more sweat coated her skin. Her head spun. She gripped the side of the table to keep the world steady and sucked in air through her nose. If she remained perfectly still, she might be able to keep down whatever wanted its way out of her.

"Are you okay? You look green." Lock stood too close, using up all the air around her.

"It's something I ate for lunch. I've got to run." She didn't wait for Lock to say anything else. She needed to get out of there as fast as she could, but hurrying made the waves crash harder. She tried to slow down, but that didn't help either.

The car seemed farther than she remembered. She quickened her pace again and took a quick look behind her. Lock was gone. She held on to the car door and begged for this not to be happening.

With a sigh of relief that at least Lock wouldn't see her, she vomited in the grass.

She was quickly learning that dignity had little place in a pregnancy.

Chapter Ten

Maeve turned onto the drive for her father's house. The field stretched out to the side, empty this year. Her father always rotated crops so they would grow better, but this year he hadn't the strength to use this field. Her heart ached. She missed her father.

If he were here, she would tell him that she was pregnant and listen to his advice on how to handle it. He would have loved the idea of being a grandfather, but without him to be there for her along this scary journey, did she really need to become a parent now? But would she ever have the chance again?

She needed to get herself together and figure out her career situation. If she was going to be a parent, she would be doing it alone. Unless she stayed in Backwater, and she wasn't sure that was the right answer either.

Zeke's truck was parked alongside the house that begged for a good paint job and a lot of tender care. If it were up to her, she would sell the house and the farm. Farming was hard enough and wouldn't get any easier. Zeke had little help and never really wanted to become a farmer.

Maeve let herself in the front door, which of course wasn't locked because no one locked their doors in this town. Music blared from the back of the house.

"Zeke, are you here?"

The inside was in the same shape as when she'd left

it a few days ago. Dust still covered all the surfaces. The house smelled like an old trunk stuck in the attic for decades. The furniture had filled the rooms since her childhood but had grown tired, waiting to be relieved of duty. At least he hadn't torn down a bearing wall. Banging from the kitchen drew her farther into the house.

Zeke stood on a short ladder, attempting to hammer a cabinet into the wall. The cabinet pitched sideways, fighting Zeke's attempts to permanently attach it. The cabinet won.

"Zeke?" She raised her voice over the music.

He dropped the hammer, and the cabinet crashed onto the counter. The racket rattled her teeth.

"What the hell?" He spun around. "Shit, Maeve. What are you doing coming over here and doing all that yelling?"

"It's nice to see you too." She ran a finger along the grit on the counter but had nowhere to wipe it except on her pants.

If he had bothered with a shirt this morning, it was gone now. Sweat slicked his torso. His head was covered in a blue bandana. She could assume to keep the sweat from running into his eyes. His faded jeans hung loose on his hips. He hiked them up as his gaze took her in.

"I wasn't expecting you." Zeke turned off the music. He leaned against the counter and crossed his arms over his chest.

"That's because you won't answer any of my texts. With me here, you can't continue to avoid me."

"I don't have anything to say." He turned his gaze out the window.

"How about you tell me why you're so mad at me?" She never liked fighting with him even when they were kids. She would do anything he said just to keep him happy. When she left six years ago, he hadn't understood and took her departure personally. He'd been cold ever since.

"If you don't know why I'm mad, then I don't see the point in talking. I have a lot of work here. Can you go?"

"No, Zeke. I will not go. You're my brother, and we're going to work this out for Dad's sake."

"There's nothing to work out. You picked your career over your family and left us here. Dad got sick, and you didn't care enough to come home. You're only here because no one in Hollywood wants you anymore." He turned back to the cabinet. "Damn thing. I'm going to have to fix it now."

"That's not the reason I came home." It was one of the reasons, but she would have come for her father no matter what. She hadn't known he was sick because he didn't tell her. As soon as she knew, she'd returned. The timing looked bad. Everything in her life looked bad at the moment.

"Whatever, Maeve."

"I'm not leaving town anytime soon. I want to help you around here. You know, pack up Dad's things, stuff like that." She could manage to stick around until they had settled all of Dad's affairs. At least in Backwater, she was familiar with the surroundings and not everyone was sorry to see her. Karen Ryker had treated her with kindness, and Bodie was her biggest fan. The irony was that a little boy would be the happiest with her in town when she couldn't decide whether she wanted to be a mother.

"You moved out of here as fast as you could. The

funeral was barely over."

She debated telling him her real reason, but the words stuck in her throat. "You have torn the house apart. I don't even know how you're living here."

"This is my home. It's the only place I've ever known. And where else would I go?"

And that was the real problem. The real reason Zeke was angry with her. She had set off for a different life, and he had been stuck in Backwater as a farmer. How could she make him understand that their choices were different, that she had to see the world the same way she had to breathe?

"All this dust isn't good for you." That wasn't going to convince him of why she left. She was being a coward.

"I'll be fine."

"You could've left, Zeke. Dad would've understood." Okay, a little closer to an honest conversation.

Zeke tilted his head back and laughed. "You really think it's that easy. If I hadn't come back home after college and helped Dad, this farm would've been sold a long time ago. Dad would've been left trying to save his land alone. He couldn't do it, and I couldn't abandon him."

"You weren't abandoning him. He would've hired someone."

"He barely had the money for that back then. I built this business. Dad was great with the crops, but the business side of things wasn't his strength. Besides, the Barneses aren't the Rykers."

"What does that mean?" She had never heard Zeke say a negative thing about the Rykers and didn't know why he had now.

"Look, Lock is my best friend. He's like a brother I don't have. But they sit up on that mountain, and everything works out for them. Sometimes I wish it was us."

"I get it. They have each other."

"All four of those guys working together, plus their mother, have made that ranch what it is today. Here it was just me and Dad. You didn't even want to help out, like ever. Now it's just me."

"Are you worried about what's going to happen to you?"

"Damn straight I am. Look at me. I'm in my forties. I don't have a wife or a family of my own because I've been working the land. I'm married to this farm."

"You don't have to be. You could sell it. Start over. I would help you with that."

"No, Maeve, I can't sell this land. Then I would have nothing to show for my life. I will fix this house up and turn it into one of those vacation rental places. There's money in that."

"But in Backwater?" Sure, the Ryker Ranch offered the kind of atmosphere people wanted for their vacations, but an old, renovated farmhouse not near town? She doubted it.

"Why not Backwater? Did you know the Hartman Bed-and-Breakfast is booked all through the summer? Other than the lake, what does it have that we don't? You had only two choices of places to stay after you ran out of here. That was what gave me the idea."

"I don't know if renting out our house is a good idea."

"It's a great idea, and I'm doing it. The place is in my name. I don't need your permission." He returned to his hammering.

She tried to call out to him, but he paid no attention. If the farm was in his name, did that mean she had no inheritance? She didn't want anything except her father back, but if they did sell this place, she would at least have a little nest egg, which would come in handy at the moment.

"Zeke." She tried again.

He turned to her.

"Did Dad leave me anything?" The dreaded tears threatened again. Her father hadn't had much, but had he wanted her to have something of his to remember him by? Something she could give a grandchild one day when she told stories about her dad.

"Take whatever you want that was his. Take it all. I don't care. The land and the house are in my name. Dad signed it over to me a few years ago. I'm sorry if he didn't tell you, but you weren't around much, and it was my hard work that saved the place. I guess he didn't think you'd mind."

She didn't know how to feel about being left out of the house and land. On one hand she could understand that she had no right to it, but on the other hand she needed proof her father loved her as much as Zeke.

"I'm pregnant." The words slipped out before she could call them back. She hadn't said them to make him feel guilty, but now that the truth was out there, the pressure lifted from her chest some.

"What?"

"I'm having a baby. Well, I think I'm having it. I don't know." She leaned against the wall, too tired to hold herself up. She had juggled so much on her own lately, and the weight of it all wore her out.

"Wait a minute. Michael's baby?"

"Yes." She hated to admit it. To anyone else she would deny it.

"Does he know?"

"I don't know." She couldn't look at him. The shame ate her up, destroyed her. She would forever ask herself how she could have been such a fool to believe he had ever cared for her.

"What do you mean?"

She had started this truth ball rolling. She owed Zeke more of the story. "He stole all my money and disappeared. His number isn't in service. My emails bounce back. He's long gone. A scam artist of some kind. A very good one who had incredible sales skills." And a few other good skills. Convincing her that he was in love with her was at the top of the list.

She had fallen for it without much effort. Michael had been charming and attractive. He had taken pictures of her with the camera he carried with him and showed them to her one day when they were together. She had looked beautiful in those pictures, and the rest was history, as they say.

"Ah, Maevey, I'm sorry about that. Why didn't you tell me?" Affection replaced the anger in his eyes.

"Because I was too embarrassed. Look, you can't tell Lock, okay? I don't want him knowing what a screwup I am." She couldn't face Lock's judgment of her choices. He made it a habit to let others live their lives their way—he certainly did—but when it came to her, he would question her decisions, not because he was a judgmental person, but because she had let him down in the worst way possible. She had rejected him.

"You're not a screwup, but I won't tell him. Did you

go to the police about the money?"

"I did, but there isn't anything they can do. I'm an idiot, Zeke. Now I'm pregnant with this man's baby. I don't even know if I want to be." A tear slipped free, and she swatted it away.

"It's going to be okay. I'll help you in any way I can." He wrapped her in a hug.

"You're a good big brother." Her heart swelled. Zeke was always there for her. She hadn't reciprocated enough, but that would change.

"I know. I'm the best." His laugh cackled.

She pushed out of his embrace. "You're all sweaty, and you stink. And put on a shirt."

He tossed a balled-up paper towel at her. "I mean it. I'm here to help you through whatever. I can lend you money, or I can take you to the clinic."

"Thanks. I don't need either at the moment." She would never take money from Zeke. She had plenty of credit to live on for now. Hopefully, a job would come along that paid enough to cover her bills. If it didn't… She couldn't think about it. She'd cross that bridge later. As for the clinic… She couldn't think about that either.

"If you keep the baby, I can help you raise it. You could live here with me." Zeke's face lit up for the first time since the funeral.

"How can I do that if you're renting the place out?" But the idea held some merit.

He narrowed his eyes. "I didn't think about that. No matter where you live, I'll be the best uncle."

"Even if I live in LA?"

"I hate that place, but if you go back, then I'll come visit. I promise this time."

Zeke had stayed away as much as possible. He had

come out for her first movie premiere, but that was it. Her dad had visited a few more times after, but the sounds and the pace of the city had been too much for a country boy like him.

She would have to think about the best place to raise a baby. Backwater had its advantages, but so did Los Angeles. "I would like that. There are so many things I wanted to show you over the years."

"Dad's lawyer has his will, if you want to see it." Zeke had effectively changed the subject about any visits to Tinsel Town.

She would take his cue and not push her brother to a regular travel schedule, especially when she had no idea what was going on with her life.

"Do you have his number?"

"I'll text it to you. Do you mind if I get back to this? I was hoping to have the cabinets hung by the end of the day. The project needs my focus."

"Sure. I'll leave you to it." She started to turn away but stopped. "Why don't you have anyone helping you with this? Or hire a contractor? What about Lock? Isn't he helping you?"

"I didn't ask him. He would come in a second, but right now I need to do this myself. And I don't want to pay anyone for something I can do."

She understood that. Zeke would want to prove he didn't need Lock to make this happen, and she had felt that same way six years ago when she left town. What was it about Lock Ryker that made the two of them believe they had something to prove? Lock had never treated either of them as if they were less than. Yet she still felt that she was. Because she was a farmer's daughter? A sad possibility.

"Don't you have to work the crops? Will you have time for all this work alone?"

"There are no crops this year. You saw the empty field. We didn't plant."

"Why didn't you plant?"

"Because it didn't seem worth it once Dad got sick." Zeke tapped the hammer's handle in his hand.

"But I thought you were doing okay." She had to believe that, or the guilt of staying away would strangle her.

"We are. I've socked away some money, but I don't want to be a farmer anymore. This is my chance to start over."

She couldn't argue with the desire to start over, and Zeke deserved that chance. She wouldn't get in his way. She had taken her new beginning without asking. "Call me if you want some help."

"Ask a pregnant lady to do this work? Not possible. Now I know why you moved out. You were right to. This isn't a place for you. I'm going to get back to it. I'll text you."

"Sounds good." She hesitated a second to watch her brother as he turned on his music and returned to hanging the cabinet. Hammering echoed again off what was left of the walls.

She pushed through the front door and back out into the fresh air, relieved to be away from the dust and the dirt. She had a lot to think about and no idea how to solve her woes.

Her stomach growled, reminding her she hadn't eaten all day. The bright afternoon faded into that colorless pause before night took over. A breeze shuffled in and chilled her skin. Spring struggled to take hold, but she should expect nothing less this time of year. Everyone and everything seemed to struggle.

Hopefully, Lock had fixed the furnace sometime today. She wasn't great at starting a fire. The idea she had earlier, of joining the community firepit, no longer held any appeal. She wanted to be alone.

Maeve turned her car around and headed down the drive. She would pick up something to eat on the way back to the ranch.

If someone had told her a year ago she would be back in her hometown, pregnant with a con artist's baby, blackballed from her dream job for something that wasn't the entire truth, and living on Ryker Ranch, she would have had herself a good laugh.

But the world laughed now.

Chapter Eleven

Lock stared into the wasteland that was his refrigerator. He needed to get to the grocery store but hadn't had the time. After he dropped Bodie at school this morning, he'd raced back to the ranch to take care of whatever needed his attention. He hadn't stopped until the Pathfinders were due to arrive.

The principal had called him around one to tell him Bodie was having a good day, but he refused to get on the bus to come home. Bodie claimed he wasn't comfortable with the new bus stop. Lock didn't believe him exactly, but he couldn't leave the ranch to pick up Bodie. Bodie said, in a small whisper, he understood. Lock's chest ached from the obvious sadness, and why shouldn't that boy be sad?

Lock found a compromise. Bodie took the bus to the sheriff's office, and Gage brought him in time for the meeting.

Considering Maeve was in attendance, distracting his thoughts, the meeting went well. He could smell her flowery scent every time the wind picked up and messed with his head. He didn't want to miss her in any way, but when Mrs. Yearwood started giving Maeve hell, he couldn't stand by and watch. Like no time had passed at all, he'd wanted to protect her.

He would fight to keep her helping the group too. Mia's mother had no right to push Maeve around. Now that he knew what Maeve's real story was, he'd take care of it. He stopped and closed the fridge door. He would not take care of Maeve. That wasn't his job any longer.

"When am I going to another foster family?" Bodie sat at the kitchen table, doing his homework.

He wasn't ready for this conversation. "I don't know. Ms. Gomez told me this afternoon that another family hasn't been lined up. We might as well plan on you staying for the week." Alessandra had told him she was vetting the families herself. The county's children services department hadn't appreciated her intervention, but Alessandra was the kind of woman who got what she wanted.

"We have to talk about the bus." And another conversation he would rather not have. He had spoken little in the last two days. Working with the animals meant he could remain silent. The way he liked it.

"I'll go on it tomorrow." Bodie kept his gaze on his notebook.

"Is that a promise?"

"Yes." Bodie erased something he had written and kept his gaze on the paper instead of looking up at him.

He wasn't sure if Bodie was blowing smoke up his backside or meant to hold to the promise. "Bodie, when a man makes a promise, he looks the other person in the eye."

Bodie took his time looking at him. "I promise."

"I don't take promises lightly. When you give someone your word, you have to stick by it. I can't come pick you up after school. Do you understand?"

"I understand. Your job is important. Adults always say that. You don't have to repeat it ten times." Bodie rolled his eyes.

He wasn't sure he was getting through to him. "Mr. Gage can't always leave work to come for you either. We got lucky today."

Bodie's gaze held his. "If you were my foster dad, would he be like an uncle?"

The wind went out of his lungs. He sat at the table as much to keep his legs from giving out as he wanted to be eye level with Bodie. Here he was talking about the bus, and Bodie wanted to know if he could get a family of his own. If he could give Bodie a family, he would.

"I can't be your foster father. I'm a single guy, living in a pretty small place."

"Your house is way nicer than where I just came from. That apartment was a dump. Here I have the whole ranch to play on. Over there you couldn't go outside alone. And my friend Joey—we met at an adoption day and stayed friends—he got fostered by a single dad. His dad is pretty cool. That was the same time I moved into Steve and Audrey's place. I wish Joey's dad had picked me."

Lock gripped Bodie's shoulder. "You're going to find a good place to live with a good family."

"Do you promise?"

How could he promise Bodie anything? Alessandra would do her best to find a good home, but the foster care system was far from perfect. He couldn't say that he would keep Bodie. That was too much for him.

"I promise." He pushed out of the chair, unwilling to continue to look Bodie in the eye with the possibility of a lie on his tongue. "Let's go up to the main building and see what there is for dinner."

"I haven't finished my homework."

"Bring it with you." After today's meeting, Lock

had run Bodie into town and to the general store to get him new sneakers and extra clothes. He had eaten away at their evening time and kept Bodie from his homework. He had no idea how parents did this on a daily basis.

They took his truck instead of walking to save time. The kitchen was shut down for the night. His mother always turned off the lights after she had cleaned up the dinner dishes.

"It's dark in here," Bodie said.

Lock flipped on a light over the island. "That's my mom's cue that she's done for the night. No guests in the kitchen, but if one of the family wants something, we have to get it ourselves."

"I wasn't allowed to eat after dinner."

"What do you mean?" He pulled out some cold cuts and rolls to make sandwiches. Ripe tomatoes on the counter with some crisp lettuce would be a good addition. His mouth watered.

"After we ate dinner, no more eating. I couldn't have a snack if I was hungry."

"Were you hungry?" He stopped what he was doing to pay attention to Bodie's answer.

"All the time. No one made breakfast. They didn't have time before work. Or there wasn't enough food in the house."

"Did you ever tell your caseworker?" He couldn't imagine allowing a kid to go to school hungry. That wasn't the house he grew up in, wasn't the house Gage made for Izzy either.

"I'm ten, Lock. No one listens to a ten-year-old."

Bodie was wise beyond his years, and Lock hated that was the case. Bodie should be concerned about playing sports or video games, how to build a fire or earn his Pathfinder badge, not where his next meal was coming from.

"They might not have listened before, but that's going to change now." He would see to it.

He spread mustard on the bread, found some carrots in the fridge, and placed the plates on the table. "There's chocolate cake for dessert. Do you like chocolate?"

"I guess so. Do you?"

"It's my favorite." He fist-bumped Bodie.

The kitchen doors swung open. His hand paused halfway to his mouth. Good thing he wasn't swallowing. He might have choked.

Maeve stood in the doorway. Her cheeks were flaming pink and her eyes a little wild. He would never get used to her in his home. She was supposed to be gone and stay gone. Seeing her at every turn ripped open old wounds he didn't want to revisit. She had made her decisions, and he had to make his.

She looked better than she had at the end of today's meeting—except for the giant stain down the front of her shirt and pants.

"Hi. Sorry to interrupt. I spilled my soup and was hoping for a towel or something to clean it up."

"Did it burn you?" He jumped up from the chair and grabbed a dish towel out of the drawer.

"Thankfully, it was still cold. I grabbed it from TJ's Pizza in town. Is that new? Anyway, it was in their refrigerator section. I thought I could heat it up back at the cottage. The container slipped from my hands and landed on me and all over the seat of my rental car. I should've not touched it until I got back to my place."

He handed her the towel. Her fingers slid over his, and his foolish heart sat up and took notice. He banished it back into his chest. That touch meant nothing except that her cold fingers were small against his. Everything about her was small, at least to him. She stood a foot shorter than he was. He could lift her with one arm. Even soaking wet—and he had seen her that way enough times he could picture it now—she weighed nothing more than a square bale of hay.

He shook the images away before he did something he would regret.

"Lock, are you all right? I asked if I could use this for the car. I think my clothes might be ruined, but I don't want to pay the fees to the rental company." She stared at him with wide eyes.

"Huh? Yeah. Sure. Here. Take this." He tossed her the roll of paper towels.

"Thanks."

She slipped through the doors, and he stood there, unable to move.

Bodie tugged on his shirt. "Lock?"

"Yeah?" He looked at Bodie, then back at the kitchen doors, trying to make sense of the sensations across his skin.

"Do you like Miss Maeve?" Bodie blew his hair out of his eyes.

"She's a nice lady."

"I mean, do you *like* her like her? You know, do you want her to be your girlfriend?"

"Where did you get that idea?" He returned to the table and their dinner, needing to distract Bodie from this line of questioning. Not only was this kid wise beyond his years, but he was also observant.

"Your face got all red. So did hers. You two look like one of her movies. Did you see the one—"

"I don't watch those kinds of movies." If his face was red, it was because Maeve was a finger splinter he couldn't pull out, but not because he had any feelings for her. And he could keep telling himself that all night long.

"What kind of movies do you like?" Bodie bit into his sandwich.

With the mission of another topic for discussion accomplished, he and Bodie ate their dinner discussing movies and television shows. He looked out the window but couldn't see Maeve's car from there. Either she was out there still trying to wipe up the mess, or she had returned to her cottage. Whichever it was, she was not his concern. So why did he keep looking?

He cleaned up their dishes and left the kitchen the way he found it. He didn't want to hear from Jett or his mother tomorrow that he'd left a mess. He did pack up two slices of chocolate cake for them to eat back at the house.

He took the long way back and drove past the guest cottages. Gage's house was lit up. Lock stole a glance in the window as he slowed. Gage and Calista looked as if they might be dancing. They smiled at each other.

Would he ever feel that way about a woman again? He sure hadn't in the past six years. But he never stuck around long enough to find out if anyone had the potential. He didn't see the point in having his heart handed to him again. Once was enough.

Two doors down, Maeve's rental was parked in the driveway. The porch light was on, but the curtains were drawn over the front window, blocking any ability to see what she was doing. Not that he cared. He just wondered if she managed to clean the seat well enough. Rental companies could be tough when it came to stuff like that.

He had a great fabric cleaner at the stables he used for horse blankets.

His phone rang. The screen in the dashboard read Alessandra Gomez.

"Uh-oh. Ms. Gomez is calling. Do I have to leave tonight?" Bodie scrunched up his face.

"I don't know why she's calling. It's getting late." He parked in front of his house. "Bring the cake inside. I'll take the call, okay?"

"I want to hear."

"I'll tell you what she said. Let me talk to her first." He leaned over Bodie and opened the door.

"Fine." Bodie grabbed the bag with the cake in it and went inside.

He hit the accept button on the screen. "Hey, Alessandra. What's up?"

"Oh good, you answered. I thought it was going to voice mail. I need your help."

"With?" He almost didn't want to ask, and with the long pause she took, he was fairly certain he should have waited to answer.

"I need you to apply to be a foster parent. Immediately."

Chapter Twelve

Maeve tossed her clothes into the washer. She was grateful the guest cottages came with stackable machines in a closet. She had saved the car. At least that was a win. Bumping into Lock and Bodie, covered in soup, had not been her finest moment. Admitting to Lock she was a klutz came in a close second for most embarrassing moment. At this point, she wanted to keep what was left of her dignity intact.

If she were being honest, and why not? She was the only one around. The washer wasn't going to give her away. She wanted to see Lock. His truck had been in the parking lot. Connecting the dots didn't take a rocket scientist. She hadn't been paying attention when she adjusted the soup. Her hand had slipped because she was trying to see if Lock was outside. Luckily, she hadn't gotten hurt or hurt someone else. The ranch had been quiet, and she was grateful for that.

The cottage's windows lit up white from the outside. Thunder rolled in on its heels. She wasn't expecting a storm and checked her phone. The app alerted her to a severe thunderstorm for the next couple of hours. She loved a good storm where she could hunker down with an excuse to read a book or watch a movie.

Lightning and thunder were nature's way of shaking up the world and reminding it who was in charge. Thunderstorms were also the breaking of oppressive heat as if they gave the day back its freedom. She loved the idea of having her freedom. She had run straight into it the first time she had the chance.

She wasn't hungry anymore. The pregnancy stole her desire to eat. A child would mean the loss of freedom. Was she ready for that? She didn't know what she was ready for, except for a cup of tea.

The minutes ticked by as the teakettle boiled water. Lightning and thunder played tag right outside her window. The lightning teased, and the thunder shook the little cottage in angry protest. She itched to go outside and watch as rain joined in on the game and pounded the roof. On the farm, lightning would strike the fields with all that open space. When a storm rolled in, her father would ring the bell hanging on the porch to let her and Zeke and anyone working for them know it was time to come inside. She always waited until the last second. She stood in the field with her arms wide and her face toward the sky as if to tempt the storm to find her, but she knew it never would. She was safe because her life was supposed to be so much more.

Her father would scream her name, and she would give up her stance with a laugh and fist to the sky. She had won. What happened to that girl?

She fell for a con artist, lost all her money, lost her temper and her job. Oh, and she got herself pregnant like a teenager who didn't know pulling out was a bad birth control method.

With her freshly made hot cup of tea, she settled onto the soft couch to watch a movie, but all she could think about was how this was no longer her career. Every movie she flipped through only made the longing in her worse. That life sped away from her, and she could not catch up.

No one had returned any of her phone calls. People she thought were her friends had ghosted her. All the party invitations had dried up. She was back to being a nobody. It wasn't fair. But life hardly was. Did she want to bring a child into this unfair world? What could she offer this little person growing inside her?

She debated on texting her agent but didn't see the point. If Kristen had something for her, she would call. The lack of calls meant there was nothing, or Kristen had parts but would never give them to her.

The lights flickered. The television went off. Darkness swallowed the room.

"Great. The power is out," she said to herself.

She hesitated a second to see if a generator might kick on and restore order, but the room remained cloaked. Hopefully, the Rykers stocked their cottages with flashlights or candles. She pushed off the sofa and grabbed her phone.

Someone pounded on the door. Thunder crashed into the house, shaking it and her to the core.

A scream leaked from her lips, and she dropped her phone. It clattered on the floor somewhere.

"Pull yourself together. It's just a storm." She had seen one too many horror flicks.

"Maeve, open up. It's me."

She hurried to the door and opened it. Wet wind whipped past her and left droplets on her feet. Lock stood on the porch, soaked through. His hair was plastered to his face. Rain ran down his cheeks and into the day's growth on his jaw. His shirt stuck to the muscles on his arms and chest.

"What are you doing?" She couldn't get her mind to

catch up to the image in front of her. What was he doing there in this weather?

"Can I come in?" His eyebrows shot up.

She didn't see as if she had much choice. Lightning broke open the sky behind him. Thunder slammed into the earth. "Yes, of course. I'm sorry."

He stepped past her but stood close, dripping on the tile floor. She pushed the door shut against the wind that pushed back.

"I'm leaving a puddle." He wiped a hand over his face.

"Let me get you a couple of towels. Wait a second. I need to find my phone so I can use the flashlight."

"Here." He handed her his.

She ran into the bathroom, grabbed a stack, then ran back. She had questions about his appearance at her door. She assumed her cottage would be the very last place he would turn to even in a storm.

"Thanks." He wiped his face, hair, and neck.

Her gaze stayed glued to the simple task as if she'd never seen anyone use a towel to wipe wet skin. But this wasn't just anyone, was it? This man could cast a spell on her, and she wouldn't notice.

"What are you doing out in this?" She shivered against the dampness now in the room.

"I went for a walk. One second it wasn't raining, and the next it was. I would've gone to Gage's, but no one's home, and he always locks his door. He doesn't appreciate it when I break in."

"You break into his house?" This conversation seemed unreal. Here she was, standing in the dark with Lock, talking about breaking and entering.

"Technically, it's the ranch's house. Which I guess

is his too. I've only done it twice. Once when he moved back home. Another time when Izzy was in the eighth grade and fell off her bicycle right outside the house. We were supposed to go over to the park together, but her knees were bleeding. And she didn't want to go with blood running down her legs."

"Can't say I blame her. I'd offer to throw your clothes in the dryer, but…"

"Do you mind if I just take off my shirt? That rainwater is cold." He didn't wait for her to respond and pulled his shirt off. He shook his head like a puppy coming in out of the rain.

She bit back a nervous giggle. Lock Ryker was in her house half dressed.

"I can start a fire if you'll hold the phone. We'll have some light, and I might be able to dry out."

"That would be great. The fire, I mean." Her tongue tangled around her teeth. What was wrong with her? The hormones. It had to be the hormones.

He slipped out of his sneakers and socks. One thing she could always say about this man was his complete comfort in who he was. She had seen him strip down to his underwear and jump into a lake without a second thought as to who watched. He would do the two-step with two left feet and laugh the whole time. She envied that in him. She'd spent years reaching a fraction of that comfort, and now she had fallen back to the beginning.

"Can you point the light over here?"

She hadn't been paying attention, too busy thinking about him. "Sorry."

"Come closer. I can't see."

She squatted down next to him, but her feet wobbled under her, and she tipped. He gripped her wrist and righted her before she landed on her butt.

"Thanks."

He kept his hand over her skin while his dark eyes soaked her in. His heat seared her clean through to the bone, but she couldn't pull away. The space between them fizzled like carbonation, and she wanted that bubbly effect all over her.

Her throat closed up. He was too close, but she couldn't move away without looking more awkward than she already must.

"The fire." The words croaked out of her dry mouth.

"Right." He broke their connection and returned to the task of building the fire.

The flames took hold as if they were fed by the sparks between her and Lock, or her imagination had clearly fallen off the rails. Without much effort, she could take this scene from *tension while building a fire* right to *hot lovemaking complete with soundtrack*.

She stood, needing air. "Why doesn't the ranch have a generator?"

"Only for the main building where most of the guests stay and the food is. The cottages, all of them, have to suffer through."

Rain continued to assault the house, so going outside was out of the question. Lightning and thunder fought all around them, and she was stuck in the dark, lusting after Lock.

"Have you eaten?" As soon as she said it, she remembered him and Bodie in the kitchen at the main house with plates of food in front of them. "Wait a second. Where's Bodie in this storm?"

"Back at my place. I had Gage come over and hang with him while I took a walk. I needed to clear my head and didn't want to leave him alone. That's why I was over on this side of the ranch." He sat on the hearth and poked the flames.

He must be uncomfortable in those wet jeans, but she could not imagine proposing he take them off.

"Are you having a tough time with Bodie?"

"Would you mind if I took off my jeans?"

"Excuse me?" This man must have read her mind. She was pretty sure she hadn't voiced what she was thinking.

"I mean, they're wet, and they won't dry while I'm wearing them. I could wrap myself in that blanket and let them hang from the mantel. Or would that make you too uncomfortable?"

Just having him here made her uncomfortable, but Lock in her little vacation house in nothing but his underwear? That might be more than she could take. And what if he wasn't wearing any? He'd been known to go around doing that too.

"Go ahead." She turned away.

"I can go in the other room."

"No, this is fine. I won't look until you're done." Not that she didn't want to. Her hormones salivated at the idea of watching him undress—or that was just her. *She* was salivating.

He rustled behind her, and she tried not to picture the wet denim peeling away from his long legs. She didn't think about the color of his underwear either, provided he wore any.

"Okay. You can look."

She turned with hesitation.

He had tied the blanket around his waist as if it were a towel. His jeans rested on the mantel with the pant legs hanging above the fire like some strange Christmas stocking. His shirt lay beside it. She swallowed hard.

"Is that better?" It might be better for him, but she might die.

"Much. Thank you for understanding. I don't want you to be uncomfortable around me."

"I'm not." She didn't think she ever could be. Being with him was like sitting under a giant weeping willow with a cool breeze wrapped around the warm rays of a setting sun. But she needed to stop thinking about him as anything other than a friend.

"Let's go back to whether you're hungry and then tell me if you and Bodie are having a tough time together." She made herself busy in the kitchen just to add some space between them. She had no idea what she would make with a candle.

"Do you have any dessert?" He returned to his spot on the hearth.

"Still with the sweet tooth."

He flashed his perfect smile at her. "What can I say?"

"It isn't fair that you can eat whatever you want and look the way you do, all muscular, and I have to do a thousand crunches for a crumb of a cookie." All the crunches in the world were about to be useless to her once her baby started to grow.

He flexed his bicep. "Ranch living."

"Hysterical. Unfortunately, I didn't buy any sweets. I have some chips and salsa."

"I'll pass. Thanks."

"Then tell me what happened with Bodie." She wanted to know and hoped things were working out for the two of them. Lock and Bodie were a strange pair visually—Lock so huge and Bodie just a wisp of a thing—but it said something so deep about the man Lock was that he took on the role of guardian for a little boy.

Lock moved to the sofa and stretched out his legs. The blanket separated and revealed his thigh. She dropped onto the kitchen chair with a thud. Lock arched a brow, probably questioning why she would sit far away when it would be warmer by the fire. Or was he questioning her lack of grace? Either way, sitting next to him would be too hot for her there.

"It's not Bodie exactly. Alessandra Gomez, the principal, asked me to fill out a foster parent application first thing in the morning. She can't find a suitable family to keep Bodie in the school. She wants to be able to monitor him and make sure he's well cared for.

"And that's a problem because…?"

"Well, for one, I wasn't planning on becoming a parent anytime soon. I thought maybe I'd have a wife first." He turned his gaze away.

The comment hit her center mass. She wasn't sure if he was implying she had messed up those plans, but he could have found another woman willing to marry him and have his baby.

"Wouldn't it take a long time to become a foster parent?"

"There's a process for sure. Alessandra can fast-track my application. She has contacts. The only thing stopping this from happening is me. Bodie is on board because she spoke to him at school today. He said he would like to stay with me for as long as possible."

"You're important to him."

"I'm his Flock Leader. I see him once a week."

"But for how long?" This man did not know how

valuable he was to others. He wasn't impressed with himself at all.

"Three years."

"That's a long time for a kid his age. You must've shown him you cared."

"How could I have?"

"Oh, come on, Lock. Bodie probably felt attached to you the first time he met you. You're the guy who includes everyone. You always make sure everyone is happy and comfortable. Who else in Bodie's life has done that for him since his parents passed?" The kitchen chair wasn't all that comfortable. She moved to the sofa but sat as far away as possible and tucked her legs under her to keep from accidentally touching him.

"I never thought about it. I volunteered for a job, and I did it."

"You're also the guy that never takes credit for what he does do."

"If I'm such a great guy, why did you leave me?" His eyebrows shot to his hairline. "Shit. I'm sorry. I shouldn't have said that. Forget it, okay?"

She didn't want to forget it. "How come you still don't understand?"

"I don't want to talk about it. I should go." He pushed off the couch. The blanket slipped. He caught it, but not before she could tell he was sans underwear. Her heart wasn't going to be able to take this.

"Where are you going to go in this storm?" As if to help her prove her point, thunder rolled over the house, and the rain pelted the window.

"I'll run. I'll be fine."

"Don't be ridiculous. No one should be out in this. The storm will blow over in an hour or two. Go back then. I don't want to be responsible for a tree falling on your head too."

He looked at her. His mouth opened and closed before he seemed to find the words he wanted. "I understood that you had to go to Los Angeles. I wanted you to do that. I even got that you should go alone. That place isn't for me. But I don't understand why you wanted it to be over." His tone remained indifferent, as if they were talking about the weather.

She would have preferred anger.

"Because I had to do it alone. I couldn't worry about what was going on with us. I needed to be focused. That was my one and only chance left."

"You didn't want to have to think about our relationship. You wanted to be free to do whatever you wanted with whomever. I was just some redneck from Montana that would slow you down."

"That's not fair. I never said that."

"You didn't have to. I might be all those things you said, but I know who I am. I'm also the Ryker brother most likely to take a dare, disappear for a day of fishing—an all-around good-time guy. I'm not my brother with his starched uniforms and his starchier rules, a born leader. I'm not Jett, and I'm not Kace. Kace ran in some of your circles. You should have tried to date him."

She did not want to tell him that Kace would have been the last man she would have dated. In his racing days, he was insufferable. And though Jett and Gage were good men with plenty to offer, she had only ever wanted Lock's ease and ability to live life to the fullest in everything he did. He made her laugh until her sides hurt. He protected her in his fierce and still-gentle way.

"I'm sorry you regret our time together." Her fingernails bit into her palms. She focused on the pain to keep the tears from spilling.

"It's not me with the regrets."

"I don't regret us. I don't regret taking a chance on my dream even if it did end in shambles. My only regret is I couldn't spare you the pain." In the end, the tears betrayed her. They leaked out of the sides of her eyes, giving away how she really felt. She wanted to look strong to the man whose strength rivaled an oak.

"You did what you had to do. I guess." He stood there with one hand on his hip and the other holding the blanket in place.

The storm did not let up. She wanted him to go to relieve herself of the guilt and the hurt at least for a little while. She had broken them because she wasn't willing to truly see her own flaws until her world fell apart.

"Would you have wanted me to stay behind with you instead of going to Los Angeles?"

He wiped a hand over his face. "I wanted to keep us together. That's all. If you had gone to Los Angeles, and we had decided together that it wasn't working, fine. If you had gone, and I had been a real insecure jerk to you, then you should've dumped my ass. But you said goodbye as you walked out the door. You never consulted me in your decision."

He grabbed his jeans and shirt from the mantel. His clothes still had to be wet. The storm howled on the other side of the walls. Being out there wasn't safe. For once, she had to protect him.

She gripped his arm and ignored the desire to pull him to her. "Don't go. Wait until the storm lets up some. Then call one of your brothers to come get you. I don't want you to get hurt out there."

"I'll be okay, Maeve. I can handle a little rain." He stepped away.

"Lock, wait."

He turned to her.

"Stay. Stay because I asked you to, not because of the weather. Stay because I'm sorry. Just stay."

His lips pressed into a thin line. He dropped his gaze. She wasn't sure if she imagined it, but he might have shaken his head.

She had her answer.

Chapter Thirteen

Lock used his phone as a flashlight and closed the bathroom door. He needed to get the hell out of this house before he kissed Maeve and truly complicated his life. He had enough on his plate with Bodie. He did not need to tangle with old feelings and the path of what-ifs. No good would come of looking back and thinking things would be different. He and Maeve were over.

She had asked him to stay, though. Something she had never done before, and he didn't believe she ever would. Was he reading too much into a moment laced with old feelings and a storm holding them in place? He could be seeing the situation through a fool's eye.

But the look in her eyes… He could still understand her. She said everything with her eyes even when her face said nothing at all. That was her flaw as an actress. He noticed it in her movies because he'd seen every single one. He never told anyone—not his brothers, not Zeke—that he had sat in a theater for hours on end to watch her.

Maeve could twist her face into whatever expression the scene required, but her eyes gave her away. Some of the better critics had blasted her for the lack of emotion in a scene, but they could never put their finger on why. They blamed it on her lack of experience, the strange way she entered their world, but they missed her eyes. They didn't know her the way he did.

He slid his leg into his jeans. The wet denim stuck to his skin. He did not want to put these clothes back on, but he also did not want to walk out there without them.

Hell, if Maeve wasn't in the other room, he would run home naked, but she was waiting for an answer from him.

He shot a quick text to Gage to see how he and Bodie were doing and to delay his decision to stay or go.

—All good. Should I come pick you up?—

—Don't come out. I'll be back soon.—

Even if some of his motivation was selfish, he didn't want Gage and Bodie out in this storm.

—Are you sure staying is a good idea?—

Remaining at Maeve's was probably a bad idea, but he might never have this chance again, and he didn't want to think it through for too long. If she didn't really want him, she would say and he would leave.

—I'll wait for the storm to pass. If Bodie needs me, call.—

—He's going to bed. I'll stick around until you get back.—

—Thanks.—

—What else are big brothers for?—

Lock didn't dare read into that comment. He'd owe Gage big time for this one, along with all the other times he owed Gage for something. Lock doubted he'd ever be able to repay that debt. He couldn't think about that either right now. Now was for what waited on the other side of that door.

He couldn't stay in this bathroom all night and pulled up his wet pants. Did he bother with his shirt or not?

A knock came at the door. "Lock? Are you okay in

there? You've been in there a while."

Had he? "Yeah. I'm good." He pulled open the door.

She stood before him in her brown yoga pants and that white T-shirt he could see through when she stood near the fire. Her long curly hair was pulled back. The curls spilled in spirals from the tie she used to hold it away from her face. She held a candle. Its flame flickered small shadows over her face.

Something was going on with Maeve besides the obvious tension between the two of them. Purple bruises like thumbprints hung under her eyes. The color of her skin reminded him of wax paper. She had been out of sorts after the last Pathfinder meeting too. He hoped she wasn't sick with something big.

Her gaze trailed up and down his chest and settled on his. He tried not to smile.

"You aren't finished dressing," she said.

"Looks that way."

"Does that mean you're staying?"

"Just until the storm lets up enough I can jog back. If that's still okay?" His decision had been made. He hoped he didn't regret it.

Her perfect smile spread across her beautiful face and gave him all the answer he needed. His control around this woman slipped. The air between them sizzled as if lightning struck where they stood. He took a step forward. She remained still.

He cupped her face, and she tilted up her chin. He had a million reasons to walk away, but he pushed them to the side. He only needed one reason to stay. And she had given it to him.

He blew out the candle. She startled.

"I don't want any accidents." He shoved his phone

in his pocket too. They didn't need any light. He could trace her body with his eyes closed.

"Always thinking."

He kissed her. He wanted to take it slowly, give her a chance to change her mind, but she opened her mouth to his and searched out his tongue. She kissed him back with a fierceness that hadn't been there before, as if she needed to believe this was happening.

She tasted like honey, and her kiss was full of spice. He no longer wanted to take his time. Too many years and too many regrets had gone by.

He placed his hands on both sides of her face to keep her close. She wrapped her arms around his neck and pressed against him.

"Your pants really are wet." She stepped back, laughing.

"What should I do about it?"

****

Lock Ryker had kissed her. And now he asked her if he should take off his pants. She could back out, and no one would be too embarrassed. They could pretend that nothing had happened. She could pack her bags and slink out in the middle of the night. Zeke would be happy to see her, if she survived the storm to get there. She could buy an air filtration system while she stayed at the house. If she avoided what was about to happen between her and Lock, she could leave Backwater with her heart intact.

Or she could take him to bed.

"Maeve, you okay?" Lock used his phone as a flashlight, pointing it toward her, but not in her face.

"You should save your battery." To offer him a real answer to that question would only dampen the mood growing like the storm seemed to be. She was great with the idea that they would have sex, but how would she handle it when she walked away?

"Probably, but I wanted to see your face. Should I be sorry that I kissed you?"

"Do you regret it?" She couldn't bear it if he regretted that one kiss.

"Regret it? Hell, no. Do I need to apologize?"

Her pride stitched itself back up. She could continue to face him and not want the floor to swallow her whole. "You did not misread me. I wanted to kiss you."

"But you don't anymore." He narrowed his eyes.

"I didn't say that."

"Then what are you saying, because I'm standing here half dressed. Do I stay or do I go?"

She needed to make a decision. If they kissed again, it would not stop there. She wouldn't let it. She wanted this man to make love to her, all night if possible. What would that decision do to her? And him? Did she need to think about why she wanted to make love?

"I want to kiss you and see where it goes, but I don't want to hurt you again. My life is broken, and I can't make promises beyond the next few weeks. This isn't forever. It's for now."

He ran his thumb over her bottom lip, sending ripples of electric currents over her. "I'm not asking for forever. I'm about to become a foster parent. My life won't make any sense to me for a while. I don't know if I'll have space for anyone else."

"You're going to do it, then?" Lock would be an excellent father. She wished she could see him in action, and a tiny part of her bristled against the idea that she wouldn't.

"I don't see as if I have a choice."

"You could say no."

"Like I said, no choice. I'm not built like that. Bodie needs someone to step up and do the right thing for him. That's me. But you don't need to be involved with a guy and a kid long term, especially if you aren't staying in town."

She opened her mouth to tell him she was pregnant. He should have that information if they were going to go forward, but if this was a one-night stand, her situation didn't matter. And he was right about her leaving. She wanted that career back, if she could get it. She only hoped her heart would be on board when it was time to go. She had said she didn't want to hurt Lock, but she should have included herself. She didn't want to end up in smaller pieces than she was now.

"Let's make the most of the storm," she said.

He extinguished the light on his phone, throwing them into total darkness. He took her hand and led her back into the living room. The fire had died down some, but the room was cozy with enough light from the flames to cast shadows on the walls. Rain and wind continued outside in no hurry to end, and she hoped that she and Lock were in no hurry as well.

He laid the blanket on the floor in front of the fire. She grabbed a couple of pillows and added them to this space he created. He stepped out of his jeans again and placed them back on the mantel.

He didn't bother to hide his excitement. Not that she expected him to. He was not a shy man.

He'd often slept naked when they were together, even if they hadn't had sex, which was rarely. She would at least need to throw on his shirt before crawling under the covers because she didn't possess the confidence, or maybe it was the carefreeness, he did.

Now she wondered if her belly had softened. Would he notice a change in her? Too many years had passed. Maybe he wouldn't remember.

"Have there been many women?"

He stepped closer and tugged the tie from her hair. Her curls tumbled over her shoulders. "I've been dying to do that. Watching your hair spring free like that... You are still the most beautiful woman I have ever seen." He ignored her question.

But the remark about her beauty landed square across her heart. "Thank you."

She placed a hand on his torso, wanting to touch him. The soft hair over his hard muscles tickled her fingers. He pressed her hand tighter to his chest. "You didn't answer my question. Have you been with a lot of women since I left?"

"Why does that matter?" He pushed the collar of her T-shirt off her shoulder and ran a finger along her skin.

His touch woke up parts of her that had been dormant for so long. She wanted to be naked beneath him with his hands everywhere on her body, not just her shoulder.

"I don't want you to compare me to them."

"No one compares to you, Maeve. No one." His voice dropped into a husky whisper, and he kissed her again.

She swallowed any doubts she had about herself in his eyes. The past didn't exist here in this room lit by the fire with the raging storm outside. She had waited for this moment longer than she realized.

His tongue swooped into her mouth, and a hushed

moan escaped her. He gripped her bottom and pulled her against him as the kiss went deeper. His hands were in her hair, down her back, and back to her bum.

She had even convinced herself for a long time that she didn't want him. How could she if she had made the choice to leave? But no matter how many miles and years she had put between them, Lock was woven into her life.

He was the song on the radio, the smell of honeysuckle in the spring, the fields of hay in the summer, the crystal on the surface of fresh snow. He was in her memory but would reveal himself in small spaces in her life, like when she closed the car door and engaged the locks because he had told her to do that once very long ago. Or when she found initials carved in a tree because he had done that for her when he had loved her.

She eased out of the kiss. He arched a brow.

"I need to look at you a minute to convince myself this is real," she said.

"I'm standing butt naked. I think it's real." He slipped her a sly smile. "But if you need more proof, touch me wherever you want."

She placed her hands on his broad shoulders, shoulders that had carried the weight of the world on them without effort. Weight she had added to. Her lips made a trail beginning at his collarbone. She ran her tongue down the center of his chest, but not all the way. She wanted to take her time with this.

Her insides shook with unexpected nerves.

Making love should be simple. They had slept together a thousand times, maybe more. But this time was different. The years had changed them. At least, they had changed her. She wanted tonight to be right because she might not have another chance to show him she loved him with all her heart and soul.

Her lips placed tiny wet kisses along his ribs. He put a finger under her chin and tilted her face toward him.

"Can you come back up here for a second?"

She stood to her full height, which didn't do much since he was over six feet. This solid man had been her protector once. She had been safest with him, knowing he would take care of her no matter what. How had she squandered that?

"I need to hold you." He pulled her against him and wrapped his arms around her.

His skin was warm, and she wanted to sink into him, his heat mixing with hers like a perfumed hot bath. She could stay like this all night. "Is something wrong?"

"This is the most perfect thing I've done in a long time. My heart is beating so fast I think it's going to come out of my chest."

She eased back to look at him, afraid to say what was on her mind, but she had to know. "Do you want to stop?"

"Stop? No way. I'm just nervous." His small laugh hesitated, as if he couldn't get it started or wasn't sure if he should set it free.

"To be with me?" She would never have guessed he could be nervous about anything, couldn't remember a time when he was.

"Is that so hard to believe?"

"Maybe just a little."

"Believe it. I didn't expect to be here. When I left the house a couple of hours ago, I thought I'd walk back home and get on with my night. Now I'm about to do something I never thought would happen again. I don't want to screw up."

"Screw up how?"

"Screw up what we're about to do. Screw up anything between us. I know I said I didn't want to be friends, but that wasn't true. I'd take friendship, if that's all I can get."

His honesty and tangible vulnerability opened her heart wider. She understood what it took for him to share that with her.

"I'm nervous too. Being with you now feels like the most right thing I've done in a while. But what if I don't know what's right any longer? I let a man I thought loved me steal all my money."

"What?"

She hadn't told him about Michael, and now didn't feel like the right time. Nothing felt right except being with Lock. But what would he think of her mistakes? If he looked at her with pity, she would never get over it.

"That's a story for another time." Another life, maybe.

"You don't have to tell me, but I promise I don't want any of your money. Your body, definitely. Your money, no." This time his laugh was full and hearty.

She couldn't help but laugh too, and that eased the nerves slamming around in her stomach like moths against a screen. Lock pulled her against him again, and she went willingly.

"I'd like this night to continue. But if you want to play it safe, I'll do that too." She didn't want to hurt him again and would watch him walk out the door, if that was what he needed.

He smiled at her and lifted her shirt over her head. She tugged at her yoga pants until they puddled on the floor around her feet. She stood before him in her sports bra and her thong. He helped her to the blanket, arranging them so she was closer to the fire. They lay facing each other.

He stroked her arm. "I could watch you all night. Just lying here like this with the fire behind you."

"Do we have all night?"

"We don't have to rush. Gage is with Bodie."

"Make love to me, Lock Ryker. I don't want to wait any longer." She removed the rest of her clothes, wanting nothing between them.

He kissed her until her head spun. His mouth found her neck while his hands, calloused from ranch life, explored the hills and valleys of her body. Each place he lingered increased the ache for him to touch her in the place that needed it most.

He took her breast with his mouth, and any thoughts except for what he did with his tongue scurried away, leaving her open for more. His lips placed claim on her body, and she was more than willing to give it over to him.

"Lock..." His name was a prayer on her lips. Her heart tumbled over a cliff's edge for this man. When it landed, it would break.

He answered with more kisses down her body. His hands and tongue moved in sync like a good love song only they knew the melody and lyrics to. With his finger, he entered her, and she fractured into brilliant pieces.

He returned his mouth to hers, possessing her. Their sweaty bodies pressed together. His fingers stroked the coil of desire inside her and brought her to glorious madness. She raised her hips to go higher and higher.

"Wait for me," he said against her ear with a chuckle but did not stop his exquisite torture.

She couldn't wait. Her body was not in her control. It demanded the release, except the ache built instead, defying her.

He pulled his hand away and met her gaze. "This may be bad timing, but I don't have a condom."

Her breath came in short spurts. Her heart beat to the rhythm of the rain pummeling the roof. She didn't care at all about condoms. What she wanted, needed, was this man inside her, filling her up and ending the longing.

For a half second, she debated again about revealing her secret, but the timing was definitely wrong for that conversation. She would tell him after. "I've got the birth control taken care of. No more talking."

She pulled him to her and quieted any more words. He went without a fight and kissed her hard.

She gripped the long length of him, placing him at her entrance, and wrapped her legs around his waist. Her invitation was clear, and he rewarded her with a slow, deliberate glide inside her, completing her.

He offered her his lopsided smile, and she cupped his face. The dusting of a day's beard prickled her fingers. He was the most handsome man she had ever seen. Better than any movie star she had worked beside.

Their bodies found their old dance as if no time had passed, returning her home. Their movements matched, growing with intensity until the final arc came and he thrust her into the incredible bliss that washed over her again and again until she was shaking and out of breath.

Chapter Fourteen

Lock tried to still his frenzied heart but couldn't. He had just made love to Maeve. He wasn't sure if that was the smartest thing he'd done—or the dumbest. Either way, he gathered her to him, needing to keep her close.

She wrapped her arm across his chest and settled against him. At least she wasn't running for the hills, though the storm might have something to do with that. He did hope all her excited noises were for real.

"That was wonderful," she said.

"It was." It was more than wonderful. Sex had never been like that with any other woman. And he'd had enough to compare. That was why he hadn't answered her question earlier. She didn't need that number in her mind while they were together.

When she first left him, he had tried to sleep his way through Montana in hopes of getting her off his mind. That hadn't worked. He'd decided that long-term relationships weren't for him. It was safer not to get too involved for any length of time. That had led to a trail of women who he hadn't satisfied and hadn't satisfied him either.

But Maeve was different. With her, long term had seemed like the only option. Now, he couldn't allow her to think he was looking for anything other than tonight. They had discussed it, and he had to agree with her. His life was upside down, and he didn't know if a relationship would fit with the addition of Bodie. Maeve didn't want to stay in town anyway, and he could never leave. They would always be the right love at the wrong time, though no one said anything about love.

"How soon before we can do it again?" She snuggled closer and ran her tongue along his side, leaving a trail like hot lava on his skin.

A laugh bubbled up in his chest. "Give me five minutes."

She pushed up on her elbow and looked at him. "That's all? I can wait." She kissed the spot by his temple, and his body began its climb out of its ecstatic slumber.

"Hey?" He brushed her hair away from her face. He loved the tight spiral of her curls and the angle of her nose. He loved her thick eyebrows and her naked body against his. Yeah, he was a mess.

"Hmm?" She ran her fingers along his jaw.

"There's something you should know." He stilled her hand.

She eased back farther but didn't pull away. "What's that?"

"I haven't had sex in six months. You don't have to worry about me, you know, having anything."

"You seriously haven't had sex in six months?"

"I wouldn't joke about that kind of a dry spell. I just haven't met anyone I wanted to do it with. That's all." Maybe he shouldn't have said anything, but he wanted her to feel safe with him.

She rested on his chest so their chins were almost touching and batted her eyelashes. "Lockwood Ryker, that is the sweetest thing any man has ever said to me."

"You can stop yanking my chain now." He tugged

on one of her bouncy curls.

She dropped a kiss on his lips. "You didn't have to share that with me, but I'm glad you did. And since we're being up-front here, I had myself checked out after Michael left town. He may have stolen all my money, but at least he didn't leave anything behind."

"Good to know."

"I thought you were going to tell me you had a girlfriend or something." Her finger made circles on his pecs.

He wanted her hands all over him. "Cheating isn't my style. But I thought you would know that."

"We don't really know everything about another person. Do we?" She lay on the floor beside him and linked her fingers through his.

"I don't know. I'm a pretty open book." He turned to face her but kept their hands clasped, wanting to touch her.

"Not everyone is like you." She didn't meet his gaze.

"What are you saying?" He wondered where she was taking this conversation, and he wanted her looking at him because her inability to face him scared him. Lying was a deal-breaker, even if Maeve was the one spilling the lies.

"I'm just saying I think most people have secrets. In fact, I heard on a podcast that everyone keeps an average of thirteen secrets from their spouse."

"That can't be right." He kissed the tips of her fingers, relieved this conversation wasn't any big deal. If she wanted to talk, he would, but with the hours they had left, he could think of better things to do, especially if this was the only night they'd get.

"What if it were right? What if couples were walking around keeping things from each other?"

"That might explain the high divorce rate." He moved from her fingers to her palm, intent on kissing every spot on her body.

She eased her hand away. "What if you found out your spouse had a secret?"

He sat up and took her in. Something was going on with her. "Are you okay?"

"Why wouldn't I be?" She sat up too.

"This strange line of questions. What are we really talking about here? Is there more to the story about you and that girl on set?" He couldn't figure out what her point was, but if she had a secret of her own and he was somehow affected by it, she had better tell him sooner rather than later.

"I told you the whole embarrassing story. I'm just curious about what you would do if you found out your spouse had a secret."

"Considering I don't have a spouse, I don't really know. I guess it would depend on the secret. Is she planning a surprise birthday party for me?" He tried to joke because he wanted to shake loose her smile and get back to the lovemaking.

"Not that kind of secret. What if she had a spending problem and didn't tell you?"

"Well, if my pretend wife was blowing through our money and not telling me, I'd be pretty pissed off. Is this about you and Michael? Do you want to tell me?"

"It's not about that. Well, maybe it is. I don't know."

"Maeve, what's going on?" His gut twisted, and he rarely ignored his instincts. Working with horses his whole life had taught him to trust that first warning sign.

When he didn't, he usually paid a price for it.

"Is there another blanket around here? The room is cooling down," she said.

He hurried and grabbed the blanket off the end of the bed in the second bedroom and returned with it. He also added more wood to the fire. The storm raged on outside. He wouldn't be leaving anytime soon, and he wondered whether Maeve was having second thoughts about them with this conversation she was trying to have. He would prefer she just come out and say what was on her mind. He preferred to shoot straight and get to the point so he could deal with whatever the problem was.

"Do you ever think about getting married?" She held out the blanket for him to climb under with her.

"Not anymore." Not since they broke up. He slid beside her and pulled her close. Her skin was cool against his. He rubbed her back to warm her up and did a good job of making himself hot. "Why all these questions?"

"The questions are bothering you." The tone of her voice suggested she wasn't asking.

Maybe they were bothering him a little. He wanted her to get to the point. "I don't mind answering you. I'm curious as to why you're asking, is all."

She eased out of his embrace and held his gaze with her intense one.

The knot in his stomach climbed into his throat. He wasn't sure he wanted to hear what she had to say. Whatever it was would affect him, and he couldn't imagine how or why. "Maeve—"

"I'm pregnant."

"Funny."

"It's not a joke. It's Michael's."

****

Maeve wished she had kept her mouth shut. The color drained from Lock's face. He stood up and shoved his legs into his jeans without another word. She hadn't expected him to react badly. Surprise was understandable, but the need to run from her stung.

She wrapped the blanket around her to ward off the cold shoulder in the room.

"Say something." She stood to take away some of his height advantage.

"What do you want me to say?" He looked down at her with hooded eyes.

"Anything. Tell me how you feel." She hadn't wanted to hurt him. She didn't know why she had told him. Maybe because she didn't want any secrets between them. Maybe because a small part of her hoped this night would happen again. At least while she was in town, and to do that would mean sharing the truth with him.

"It doesn't matter how I feel."

"Then why are you in such a hurry to get out of here?"

"I'm not. I just wanted to have this conversation with my clothes on." He dragged his T-shirt over his head.

She pulled the blanket tighter. "Are you upset?"

"That you didn't tell me before we made love?" He stepped over the spot where they had lain together, as if he might get burned, flopped onto the far edge of the sofa, and ran his hands through his hair.

"Yes." She took a step toward him, but the hardness in his stare stopped her.

"Yeah, I'm mad. You kept something pretty important from me when we just shared something that's special."

"How special can it be if the number of women you slept with is so high you don't want to mention it?"

"The number of women I've slept with is not the point. This is us. We're different. I…" He waved his hand in the air.

"I what? Say it."

He held her gaze but didn't speak. The pause stretched out until she thought he wouldn't say anything at all.

"You and me. That means more to me than the other women. You should have told me. I deserved to have the time to think about it." He jumped up and paced the space behind the sofa.

She regretted her decision to tell him. He wasn't ready to hear it. And since she wasn't even sure if she would keep the child, telling him held no purpose except to share her burden with him, forcing him to carry some of it too.

"I'm not asking you to raise it with me." That was a fantasy she didn't dare entertain for long. Michael was not a good man. Having his child would be hard enough, but asking Lock to love it as his own? That was too much.

"You're going to raise the baby alone?"

She turned away. She couldn't look him in the eye. "I haven't decided what I want to do."

"Have you asked the father what he wants?"

"I don't know where he is."

"I'm sure you can find him. He should have a say."

She turned back to face him. Shame burned her face. "He lied to me about who he was. His real name wasn't Michael. I don't know what his real name is or if he even has one. He's a con artist, and I fell for it."

She held her breath and waited for him to tell her she had been stupid or gullible, that she had brought this on herself and had no one to blame.

His face slacked. He must pity her. Poor pathetic Maeve had been taken advantage of by a guy way smarter than she. She couldn't look Lock in the eye and turned away. She pressed her fingernails into her palm to keep from crying.

"I'm sorry. You didn't deserve that." He put a hand on her shoulder and turned her to face him.

She was halfway in now. She might as well go all the way and let him think the worst. "The truth is I don't know if I want to keep it. I will be alone with a baby made not from love but by a man who was a liar and a cheat." Part of her did want to be a mother, just not this way.

He took her hands in his, and she almost crumbled from the relief that he wasn't disappointed in her. She had expected him to throw something or kick something or tell her she was at fault.

"Lots of babies are made for the wrong reason, but they come into this world and make it a better place. You'd be a great mom, if you want to."

What if she couldn't love it once it was born? Was that a fair life for a child? Look at what had happened to Bodie and that foster family. Bodie didn't get the love he deserved.

"I would be a lousy single mother. I'm a failure."

He brushed her hair away from her face. "You are anything but. Give yourself a break, Maeve. I think you've earned it."

The damn tears that continued to appear at the

wrong time couldn't be stopped. She bit her trembling lip, but it did little good. Tears spilled anyway.

"I'm sorry I didn't handle you telling me you were pregnant well. I don't know how I feel about your situation, but it's yours and not mine. What you decide has nothing to do with me in the long run. I guess I would have liked all the facts. That's all."

"I should have told you sooner. I was afraid you wouldn't stay, and I so very much wanted you to stay." Making love with him had been wonderful and a little selfish. She hadn't been cared for in that way in so long.

With Michael, sex had always been more mechanical. They knew where the parts went, and they moved around until—usually he—found his end result. But Lock had been tender and charming. He had made sure she was taken care of, because that was the kind of man he was.

How could she have been so foolish as to walk away from him when he had been hers completely? She had been blinded by the bright lights and big city and the dream of something untouchable here in Backwater. What mattered was the love and respect of a good man who only wanted what was best for her.

Her career had blown apart in seconds, and who was around for her now? Not one friend from LA, not her agent. No one returned any of her calls. But it was Lock who had listened to her story without judgment. It was Lock standing before her.

"I was so stupid, Lock. I'm so sorry I broke us up. If I could go back and change things, I would. I see what I did now. Do you think…" She had to swallow to summon the courage to finish. "Do you think we could try again?"

He wiped a hand over his face and didn't say anything. Her heart picked up speed, wanting him to answer her.

"I appreciate the apology. I do. And if this was even a month ago, I might have said yes. I don't know. But now with me about to become a foster parent, I can't be in a relationship. I have to focus on Bodie and what he needs. Tonight was incredible, a break from reality, but it shouldn't happen again. Let's try that friendship thing for a while, okay?"

It wasn't okay. Nothing was okay, but she couldn't make the words come out of her mouth to stop him from walking away. How had this night ended up so wrong? She wanted to go back to them lying on the blanket in each other's arms with hope still in reach.

"Is it the pregnancy? Are you freaked out about that?"

"I don't know." He scrubbed his face with his hands. "Maybe. If you decide to keep the baby, and I have Bodie, that's a lot to process."

"You can't love a baby that's not yours."

"I didn't say that. I just don't know. Give me some time. I have to get my head on straight." He opened the door. The wind and the rain swooped in, getting tangled in their fight.

"You shouldn't go out in that." It was the only thing she could think of to make him stay.

"I'll take my chances. I'll call you. Good night, Maeve." He stepped outside and closed the door behind him, leaving her with the remnants of the storm in her foyer.

She sank onto the floor, but this time she was out of tears.

Chapter Fifteen

Lock pushed into his house. He was soaked again. The rain had picked up, and he had to run the whole way from Maeve's to here. He had wanted to stay all night, holding Maeve, making love to her. But her big revelation had blindsided him. He wasn't sure why he was so angry about it.

Gage had fallen asleep sitting up on the couch. His mouth was open, and he snored like a backhoe. The television was on, but the sound was low. His cottage had a generator that he had installed years ago along with a generator for the main building. Lock stripped right by the door in the warmth of his home and wondered if Maeve would be all right in hers.

Gage groaned from his spot on the sofa. "When are you going to start keeping your clothes on? You're not five anymore."

"I thought you were asleep, and they're wet. What did you want me to do?" He gathered his clothes. They dripped on the floor.

"You can stop standing there and put some damn clothes on. Now I have to bleach out my eyes." Gage covered his eyes with his arm.

"You really are too uptight. I'll be right back." He dumped his wet clothes on the top of the washing machine and threw on sweats and a T-shirt.

"That's much better. Thank you." Gage stood at the

couch, arranging pillows in a symmetrical pattern.

Sometimes he envied Gage's need for order. The structure meant Gage was rarely surprised by others, his mistakes were kept to a minimum, and his life made sense to him.

Life rarely made sense to Lock. People always threw curveballs when he wasn't looking, like Bodie's coming to live with him and now this possible long-term foster parent thing. Growing up without a dad, losing his brother Ajay when Ajay was only eighteen and Lock only nineteen. Or like tonight when Maeve told him she was pregnant.

He had meant what he said. A relationship was out of the question at the moment. And he was not capable of dating her casually, knowing she could be with another man. He didn't share his women, especially not her. She was supposed to be the one. He often wondered if there was any such thing.

"How was Bodie?" It was better to stay focused on the here and now and what needed his attention the most. This thing with Maeve would have to wait.

"He did fine. When the storm came up and you hadn't returned, he seemed a little concerned, but we talked about it."

"What was he concerned about?" He went into the kitchen to make some coffee. The rain from the run over had chilled his skin. But he was cold before that. When Maeve told him her news, even the fire couldn't warm him.

"About you not coming back and him having to go live somewhere else." Gage came into the kitchen and leaned against the counter.

"What did you tell him about me not coming back?

You want coffee?" He held up a mug.

"No, thanks. I said you were too dumb to get hurt in a storm." Gage gave him a side glance.

"You did not."

Gage shrugged and shoved his hands in his pockets. "The joke made him laugh."

"So you do have a lighter side. Where the hell have you been hiding it?" He dumped some sugar into his coffee and decided he wanted chocolate cake.

"I can be easygoing."

"You do remember kicking my ass for not making my bed, right?" He had been eight and pissed off that Gage and Jett had all the good chores, like brushing and feeding the horses, and he had to make his bed and unload the dishwasher. He had protested until Gage threatened him, and when he told Gage to swing, he had.

"I was fourteen."

He checked the fridge. "Did you eat my cake?"

"Bodie and I finished it off."

"You didn't leave me any?" He had been looking forward to that cake.

"Sorry, bro. You weren't here." Gage punched him in the shoulder. "Ask Mom to make you another one. You're her favorite."

"Not me. You're her favorite, her oldest, the most responsible one." He shoved Gage.

"You're the one who always makes her laugh. None of us can compete with that." Gage shoved him back.

"Well, if it's not me and you think it's not you, then who is her favorite?" Lock never thought his mother played favorites. She spread her love and attention across all of them as equally as she could. But joking around with Gage was fun, and he needed to lighten his mood right now.

"It's Kace. He's really her favorite. She pays so much attention to him because he's the middle child," Gage said.

"You're right. No middle-child syndrome for him."

"Not an ounce."

"Hey, can I ask you something?" He had been going to Gage his whole life with questions and when he needed advice. Their mom was great and always listened, but there were times, like now, he wanted to know what his big brother would do. Gage had been the bar he tried to reach his whole life.

Gage had always been there for him with his thought-out answers and deliberate decisions. Gage rarely lost his temper and could always see someone else's point of view—unless it involved his daughter. He was a typical overprotective dad. Lock had no idea where he would be today if Gage didn't always have his back.

They were lucky to have each other even when they didn't get along. Bodie deserved to have people in his corner for the first time in his short life. Lock didn't know why he ever doubted what he needed to do for that boy. He would step up and give Bodie what he always had in his brothers.

"What's up?" Gage waited for him to answer.

"If you were dating someone, would you want to know if they were pregnant before you slept together?" He pulled a box of cereal out of the cabinet. Cereal wasn't chocolate cake, but it was better than nothing.

"Strange question. Why do you ask?" Gage took the box. He grabbed a fistful and handed it back.

"Can you answer it?"

"Not really. I've never been in that position. But if I

wanted to get serious with this person, I suppose I'd want to know she was pregnant beforehand. A child is a huge commitment, and now I'd be a part of his or her life. But if I was just trying to get laid…I don't know if I would need to know or not."

That wasn't the answer he hoped for.

"Why do you ask this? Did you sleep with a pregnant woman?" Gage's eyes widened. "You slept with Maeve, didn't you? Is she pregnant?"

His brother was too smart for his own good. Nothing got past Gage and his detective skills.

Lock could lie, but Gage would see right through him. Maeve's situation was her business and not his place to tell. If he were in a serious relationship with Maeve, he wouldn't have said a word until she was ready to say what she wanted.

"This isn't about Maeve." He forced himself to hold Gage's gaze.

Gage's eyebrows pinched together. "Okay, if you say so. This hypothetical has nothing to do with Maeve or the fact you walked back in a storm when you had basically said you'd sit it out at Maeve's after I asked if it was a good idea."

Sleeping with Maeve had been a good idea at the time. "Can you just answer the question without the I told you so?"

Gage crunched on the cereal. "I stand by my answer. If I was going to be in a long-term relationship, I would have wanted to know before we had sex."

"You wouldn't have sex with someone you weren't in a long-term thing with."

"That isn't true. When Izzy was young, I looked for companionship. I wasn't interested in a relationship back then. I didn't have time. But sex…well, sex is different."

"It's hard to live up to you. Do you know that?"

Gage pushed off the counter. "Don't try and live up to me. I screw up all the time. Be yourself, Lock. If this so-called woman we can call Maeve didn't tell you she was pregnant and it bothers you, live by your own choices."

"Thanks." He didn't know what those choices were. She had asked for another chance with him. But he wasn't ready to trust her again while she was about to have some other guy's baby. Being involved with her while she carried someone else's kid shouldn't bother him, but it did. Maybe because she had left him and the way she walked away still stung. She expected him to just pick up where they left off, and he wasn't sure he could.

"You good?" Gage shrugged into his windbreaker.

"Why wouldn't I be?"

"You're about to become a parent, and the woman you loved lied to you all in the same day."

"I don't love Maeve." He had, long and hard for years.

Gage shook his head and patted him on the shoulder. "I didn't say 'love.' I said 'loved.' Get some sleep. It's late, and Bodie will be up early. I'm here if you need anything."

"Thanks." He closed the door behind Gage and leaned against it.

Did he still love Maeve? Not the same way. Gage didn't know what he was talking about. So why did it bother him so much that she was pregnant?

Not wanting to get too close to that answer, he dumped his coffee in the sink. He wondered again how

Maeve was doing in the storm and whether she was warm enough without power.

He could text her and tell her to come and sleep on the couch. He would go and get her. But then logic set in, and he climbed into bed. He couldn't rescue her anymore. She didn't want him to do that. And he had a child who did need rescuing.

Lock pounded his pillow, trying to find a comfortable spot.

He couldn't find one.

Chapter Sixteen

"Lock?"

Someone shook him. If it was one of his brothers, he might punch them. He had just put his head down on the pillow. What could be so important?

"Lock? Are you awake?"

The voice was too soft to be Jett's. He cracked open an eye. The sunlight pressed against the window shades, trying to break up the darkness in his room. The storm must have passed.

Bodie stared down at him with wide eyes. His hair fell over his forehead. He wore a Backwater Sheriff's Department T-shirt that hung to his knees. The sleeves scraped his elbows.

Everything came flooding back. He had a kid in his house now. Gage had babysat for him. Maeve and he had made love last night, and now they might not be speaking.

"Hey, pal. Everything okay?" He scrubbed his face with his hand to set loose the fog in his brain. He needed some very strong coffee.

"I think we're late for our Pathfinders' meeting." Bodie showed him his phone.

Lock grabbed the phone and pulled it closer. He didn't have his contacts in, and his glasses weren't on the bedside table. He would need to find them.

"Is that today?"

"It's Saturday. Didn't you say we would start writing the script today with Miss Maeve?"

He had forgotten all about it. After Alessandra had called about the foster parent application, he hadn't thought about much else until he ended up at Maeve's. And there, he hadn't thought about anything at all except her naked underneath him.

"I need to get dressed, and so do you." He started to pull the covers back and stopped. Sleeping in the raw might have to end.

Bodie stared at him.

"Can you get yourself dressed?" He had so much to learn and not enough time to get up to speed.

"I'm ten, not five," Bodie said with more sass than Lock's niece ever did. "Why aren't you getting out of bed?"

"I'll explain later. Go throw on some clothes and brush your teeth. I'll be out in a minute, and we'll grab breakfast up at the main building."

"Why can't you explain now?"

"Because we're running late." And he didn't know if he should tell a kid he slept without any clothes. He might have to start making a list of questions to investigate.

"Will your mom be there?"

He hoped. Just so someone else could answer a question or two. "Maybe. Now, hurry. So we're not too late."

Bodie scurried out of the room. Lock got dressed. He didn't want to stir up trouble between him and Maeve, but he needed to know if he could still count on her for today's meeting. Today was about the kids, not them. He sent a text.

—Will you be at the meeting this morning?—

He waited for a quick second to see if Maeve responded, but she didn't. He shoved his phone into his back pocket and met Bodie at the door.

Bodie still wore the oversized T-shirt.

"Don't you want to change your shirt?" He grabbed his keys off the counter.

Bodie looked at the shirt, then back at him. "Do I have to?"

"It's kind of big. Won't it get in your way?"

"I like it. Mr. Gage gave it to me." Bodie's face lit up.

This kid was starved for affection. The urge to punch the daylights out of Steve, the foster parent, reared its head again. The urge to hurt that man might never go away completely.

"I get that. It's a pretty cool shirt. I don't even have one." He opened the door, and the cool morning air greeted them along with the bright sun and tree debris in the yard. He'd have to clean that up later and check on the rest of the ranch to make sure no damage had been done. He could bring Bodie along and let him get used to ranch life. If he was going to be a part of the Ryker family even in a small way, he would have to work just like they all did at his age.

"You don't have a sheriff's department shirt?" Bodie shoved his hair away from his round eyes.

"Nope." He ushered Bodie to the truck.

"Mr. Gage said he only gave this shirt to special people. Aren't you special too?" Bodie fastened his seat belt. His legs dangled over the front seat.

His brother to the rescue again. He would need Gage's help at every turn to take care of Bodie. Without

Gage, he was bound to screw this up. Maybe he should have stayed home last night instead of being with Maeve.

"I am his favorite brother, but I'm not as special as you. Do you think you could put a good word in for me? I'd like a shirt too." He backed out of the driveway.

"Sure thing." Bodie's smile touched his ears.

Lock's heart swelled until he couldn't breathe. He had never experienced that sensation before. He didn't understand parenting. How could he feel something for a person he hardly knew? Another question for the ever growing and daunting list.

"When we get to the main building, I'm going to have to take care of something first. Do you think you can start the meeting until Miss Maeve gets there?" He turned onto the main drive and headed for the front of the ranch. He had to take care of that application.

"You want me to start the meeting?"

"You're wearing the sheriff department's shirt. Gage must think you're pretty responsible. I do too." A few branches had fallen, and plenty of leaves and twigs were scattered around the property. He hadn't heard from Jett yet. That was a good sign. The damage might be nothing. Or the damage was hidden still, like what hid inside his heart. He needed to focus if he was going to get through the day.

"He did say I had to be on my best behavior in this shirt."

"See? You're practically a deputy. You can handle the beginning of a Downy meeting."

Bodie sat up straighter.

His phone buzzed, but he didn't want to look at it while driving even if he was the only vehicle on the road. He pulled into a parking space and checked the message.

He wasn't in the mood for this so early after the night he'd had. Mrs. Yearwood was already on her broom.

—*I hope that woman won't be at the meeting this morning.*—

He had no way of knowing what Maeve was up to and wouldn't blame her if she bailed entirely on this project now, but he couldn't keep Mia's mom waiting even if he wanted to.

—*She is still helping the group.*—

At least he hoped she could put their personal problems aside, and he would not send her away because of what had happened to her. She might have overreacted, but she had owned it. People made mistakes. Maeve was a good person who didn't deserve to be canceled because she had been human.

—*That's unfortunate. Mia will not be attending.*—

He fought the urge to write what he really wanted to say to this narrow-minded, overindulgent, overprotective mother who didn't see what a great kid she had.

—*I wish you wouldn't do that.*—

—*It's done.*—

"Can we go inside?" Bodie asked.

"Sorry about that. Let's hurry. We have about ten minutes before everyone gets here." He and Bodie went into the kitchen.

He could breathe a sigh of relief as his mother moved around the kitchen, taking care of breakfast. Autumn helped her. Ever since she and Jett became engaged, Autumn had taken on the role of cook for their meals.

"Good morning." Karen pulled a pan out of the oven. "Just in time for blueberry muffins. The blueberries are from the Jacksons' farm."

"Hey, Mom. Autumn. Why not from Zeke Barnes?"

"Didn't Zeke tell you? Of course not. You men don't really talk. Zeke didn't plant anything."

Zeke hadn't mentioned it, and whenever Lock did ask how business was—his mother was wrong about that talking point—Zeke always gave the same answer, saying things were fine. Lock would have to check into what this no planting was all about.

"I need to use the computer in the office. Can you get Bodie a muffin and something to drink? Our meeting starts soon."

"My pleasure." Karen scooped Bodie into a hug, and Bodie went willingly.

Lock closed the door to the office and took a deep breath. He pulled up the application that Alessandra emailed and filled it out. The process took longer than he thought, but he hit Send and conveyed a text to Alessandra, explaining the application was complete.

—*Great. Congratulations.*—

—*I haven't been approved yet.*—

—*Yes you have. I have that superpower.*—

He wasn't sure what she meant by *superpower*, but he didn't have time to decipher it. He went out into the kitchen. Some of the ruckus had died down. Only his mom was there, sitting at the table with a mug and a magazine. The quiet was a welcome change. He'd been running on overload for a while now.

"Do you want some coffee?" she asked without looking up.

"I don't have time." The kids were probably all on the patio by now. Maeve still hadn't texted him back. She might not be there, and he had to get them writing today with or without her.

"Pour a mug and take it with you. You have dark circles under your eyes. Did you sleep at all?" His mom looked up at him with concern etched on her face.

"Not much. The storm." He looked away before she could read into what he had said or more importantly, what he hadn't said.

"Something going on?"

Too late. "Plenty, but I can't talk about it now." He might not talk about all of it later either. Other than the foster parent part of his life, she didn't need to know about him and Maeve.

"I'm here if you need anything." She went back to reading, but those words were truth. She had been there for all of them, and in turn, they were there for each other.

"Can I ask you something?" He busied himself with pouring coffee into a Ryker Ranch travel mug so it would stay warm while he was with the Pathfinders.

"Anything, sweetie." Her smile brightened the kitchen. No one else had ever looked at him as if he could do no wrong. Each and every time he walked into a room, his mother beamed. He used to think she was over the top with her exaggerated smiles and constant hugging when he was a kid, but today he appreciated her more.

"How did you handle all of us by yourself?" Growing up, he never gave their situation much thought. They were the Rykers, and that was it. He had horses for playmates and an entire wilderness as his backyard. He had thought he was the luckiest kid around.

His big brothers had paved the way for him in school. And he always had Ajay tagging along after him. They had plenty to eat, clothes to wear, and warm beds to sleep in. She dished out love without so much as a price tag.

He'd never considered how strong his mother was until he took over running the ranch with Jett. In the beginning years as official owner, he'd thought the ranch would end him with its long days and endless demands, and he did not have five children to take care of as well. She never complained. Not once. The hard work she delivered she had demanded of them. Years of learning her work ethic had saved his sorry ass in the end.

Mom closed the magazine. "Well, the long answer, the one that might make you feel better about becoming a parent out of the blue, will have to wait because you have your fifth graders expecting you. But the short answer is that I took it one day at a time. No point in getting ahead of myself because I didn't have the energy for it."

"You did a great job." He never told her that enough.

"I did my best. I know that much. I made mistakes too." She dropped her gaze.

"You're talking about Ajay."

"Not just with Ajay, but I must've let that boy down somehow that he couldn't come to his momma for help." She lifted her glasses and wiped at her eye. "But in the end Ajay made his choice. I wish he had made a different one, is all."

"Me too." The hole Ajay had left never closed. Sometimes Lock could avoid it better, and other times he fell right in headfirst.

"You'll be a good foster parent, Lockwood. In fact, you'll be great. And we're all here for you. Izzy and Quinn can babysit. I'm sure even Royce would like to meet Bodie and have a playmate." Her smile remained sturdy and in place.

"Thanks, Mom."

He left her and checked his phone. Still no text from Maeve. With a heavy sigh, he went out to the patio.

Time to get to work.

****

The power had returned sometime during the night. Maeve didn't think sleep would ever come her way, but it finally snuck up on her, and she dozed a little. Her insides ached as if she had a virus. Maybe she did. Or maybe it was heartbreak on an already wounded heart.

She had decided not to go to the Pathfinders' meeting. She couldn't face Lock after last night. The children would understand eventually. Letting Bodie down buckled her knees, but Lock had texted, and she thought better of her decision. The kids shouldn't suffer for her mistakes.

Now she sat in her car in the parking lot. From her vantage point, she could watch the kids gathering at the picnic tables. They were missing one. Mia. The mother must have held true to her word and didn't want her daughter around Maeve. No one seemed to want to be around her at the moment.

Maeve had also reached out to her agent this morning, hoping to catch her before she had a chance to start her day. Kristen must have answered the phone without looking because when she had realized it was Maeve on the other end, she had stammered and stuttered her way through several excuses as to the lack of opportunities for a woman in her position.

The time had come to consider a new career. She didn't have the fight in her to crawl her way back from the rubble. Some people could wait it out. Fans had short-term memory, and eventually she would be able to slip back in without much notice.

But she wasn't getting any younger, and parts for women her age were harder to come by and went to the box-office guarantee. That wasn't her. She was a much more likely secondary character, but she had never been happy with that. She should have been. If she had been okay with second place, she wouldn't be in this trouble, but she hadn't wanted to settle for second. Foolish. Nothing wrong with the silver medal. Maybe if she had known where her lane was, she could have had it all.

Lock walked out onto the patio. Her breath caught. He wore a simple black T-shirt that accented his shoulders and hung loose at his waist. His faded jeans had some holes in them she would bet money he'd done himself getting caught on something or other while working around here.

His hair was a little disheveled, giving him a carefree look. Not that he needed any help in that department, but maybe he had rushed out this morning. He held a travel mug, probably filled with coffee and too much sugar because the heavy eyelids gave him away. At least to her. She had woken beside him enough times to recognize when he had a fitful night.

Her mind flooded with images of them last night, making love, his mouth on her skin, her legs tangled around his afterward. She could still sense the heat they had sent into the air against her skin now. He was only yards away, and she missed him deep in her bones.

Forcing herself to leave the safety of her car and walk over, she wobbled on her feet. She wasn't ready to face Lock. Bodie noticed her first. He jumped up from the table and ran. He knocked his thin frame into her and wrapped his arms around her. For a thin little boy, he held on to her with impressive might.

"Hey there." She hugged him but eased back. An unfamiliar warmth spread over her. Was this what it was like to be loved by a child? Would her own child race to her arms one day? She couldn't picture it.

"I didn't think you would come. Lock said you hadn't texted." Bodie stared up at her with wide eyes.

She brushed his hair away from his sweet face without thinking. She cared for this child and wasn't sure when or how that had happened. Actually, it didn't matter how her feelings grew. They had in an instant. "Sorry I'm late. My call ran longer than I thought." Not a complete lie, but the best she could come up with on the spot.

Bodie grabbed her hand and dragged her toward the others. "We can get started now. I have some ideas for our play."

"Morning," Lock said with a nod. "Thanks for coming." His face remained neutral. He could hide his emotions better than the truth behind a Hollywood scandal.

"Let's hear those ideas." She avoided Lock's gaze and hoped she had forced the right amount of excitement into her voice.

The meeting unfolded with ease as each child offered suggestions. Emma Sharpe took notes with her purple pen. They bounced ideas off each other like a good tennis match.

Maeve encouraged them to follow their inspirations and tried to rein in a few of the tangents that ran away from the main plot. The entire presentation would be only fifteen minutes. She would have preferred more time, but Lock insisted they would be timed and going over was worse than staying under.

She would argue the council was stifling creativity, but this wasn't her fight. She had enough battles on her plate. This time going along was easier. She did want everyone to have a speaking part even if it was only a sentence. They were all eager to please. She ate up their enthusiasm to learn and create like a salted caramel sundae. But the idea of all that cream and sugar turned her stomach.

Her phone pinged. She broke away to read the text from Zeke.

—*When are you coming to the house?*—

—*Do you need me?*—

—*There's someone here to see you, and she isn't leaving.*—

—*Who?*—

She couldn't imagine who would be at the house. All the well-wishers after her father passed had already come by, dropping off baking dishes wrapped in tinfoil. She highly doubted it would be someone from LA. A text or a call would be easier.

The typing bubble popped up on her screen.

—*Says her name is Dawn Yearwood.*—

She didn't know any Dawn Yearwood and replied as such.

—*Says she won't leave until you come here and talk to her. Seems determined.*—

—*Tell her I'm at the ranch.*—

She waited for a response. The typing bubble appeared again.

—*Says she doesn't want to talk in front of Lock. An old girlfriend? Doesn't look his type, though. Please come. Need her out of here.—*

—I'm coming.—

She put a hand on Lock's arm, interrupting his conversation with Nolan. "I'm sorry. Something has happened at the house. I have to go."

Chapter Seventeen

Maeve tore down the drive, kicking up dirt and rocks as she went. Zeke and this woman waited for her on the front porch. Maeve couldn't imagine what this was all about and why this woman didn't want Lock to know about the conversation. Zeke was probably right about the ex-girlfriend thing, but that would mean this person knew that she and Lock had slept together last night. Maybe she was a jealous employee who had seen Lock leave her house.

The woman standing beside Zeke was tall and thin. Her lanky hair hung in blonde streaks past her shoulders. She wore athletic clothes with a long wrap in a deep mauve. Recognition clanged in Maeve's head like a bell in a tower.

She unraveled herself from the car on a deep breath. "Are you okay?"

She kept her gaze on Zeke, trying to avoid a conversation that would not go well with this woman who was not Lock's ex-girlfriend. This was the mother of his Pathfinder. Maeve would have preferred an ex.

"I'm fine. This is Dawn Yearwood." Zeke waved a hand in Dawn's direction.

"Hello." Maeve stopped at the bottom of the porch steps.

Dawn marched down and stood inches from her. "Thank you for meeting me here. I didn't want Mr.

Ryker to get involved since he's meeting with the children."

Maeve took a step back. "What is it you want?"

"Are you two going to be okay? Or should I stay and chaperone?"

She wanted Zeke to stay because another confrontation might break her in two, but she didn't want to appear weak either. She had to prove to herself as much as to this woman with eyes of ice that she was more than her worst moment.

"Go inside, Zeke. If I need you, I'll yell."

Dawn's gaze bounced from her to Zeke. Maybe she was rethinking her decision to come here and corner Maeve, or maybe she was hoping Zeke would get out of there so she could blast Maeve without a witness.

With a final look over his shoulder, Zeke went into the house. The screen door slapped closed on his departure in its own protest of the entire scene.

"What is it I can help you with?" She might as well start as cordially as possible.

"Why are you still hanging around the Pathfinders?"

"I'm not hanging around. I'm helping them with one of their projects." She didn't want to have to explain herself, but she also didn't want to make trouble for Lock. He adored those kids, and he deserved to be the one to help them with their success.

"Your presence is harming my child." Dawn fisted her hands on her hips.

"I don't see how that can be. I've been in her presence a sum total of ten minutes." She would not buckle under the intimidation this mother assumed she wielded. Maeve would stand firm in her resolve to help the kids.

"I can't allow her to be in a group with a woman who clearly dislikes children. I'm coming to you as a mother to see if I can make you understand the importance of Mia's attendance in the Downy troop." She dropped her hands from her hips, but her stance remained rigid, and the glare in her eyes said things other than compassion for the situation.

Dawn Yearwood was most likely used to getting her way, and Maeve had enough of dealing with people who thought the world owed them everything.

"Mr. Ryker has asked for my assistance. In fact, the children have asked as well. You seem to be the only parent who is opposed."

She had no idea if any other parent was against her attendance, but Lock hadn't mentioned any complaints yet.

"I didn't want to do this. I truly didn't. I was hoping we could have a chat on your front porch like two civilized women. But you are forcing my hand." Dawn stepped closer, but Maeve remained planted.

"We haven't had much of any conversation. You asked me why I'm helping out, and you have determined that your child is somehow in harm's way. Which I disagree with. I'm not out to hurt anyone's son or daughter."

"Then why did you hurt that child you worked with?" A sneer curled Dawn's lip.

"I didn't hurt her." She had yelled because she had watched every ounce of her control wash away and be replaced with helplessness. Yelling had been a mistake, but her point had been correct. The child was spoiled beyond words.

"It's on the video."

"I never touched her. She threw herself on the floor." The video playing online, shared over and over, had been edited. Anyone with a keen eye would have seen that, but most people didn't notice or even watch the video that long. They just wanted to leave comments saying she was a horrible person and she should never be allowed back in Hollywood. They got what they wanted.

"It appears you pushed her."

"I assure you I did not." Anger started to boil low in her belly. She would not rise to the bait. That was one mistake she would not make twice.

"I've spoken with the Pathfinder Council. They will be issuing a letter." She checked her fancy digital watch. "Probably right at this moment. The letter removes Mr. Ryker as Flock Leader, which in turn will remove you."

The air left her lungs. Words failed her. Lock was being asked to leave? Because of her. She had hurt him again, and he would never forgive her for this.

"How could you do that to him? He's great with those kids, and they love him." They needed him. He had so much to offer, and they soaked up everything he said.

"He didn't see fit to get rid of you. So I did it for him. I told the council about you and what a detriment you are to those children and how he insists on keeping you around. After last year, when the group couldn't get promoted, they finally see his incompetence." Dawn rubbed her hands together as if to rid herself of something dirty.

"Don't allow how you feel about me to cloud your judgment. Lock is a good man with a big heart and a lot of love to give. He's an asset to those children. I'm asking you, nicely, to stop this from happening."

"You seem quite enamored of him. And if I think

about it, and he you. How well do you know each other?"

Maeve didn't have to stretch far to figure out what Dawn implied. She was most likely bluffing, having no way of actually knowing what was going on between her and Lock unless the woman had been standing at the window last night.

But Maeve could have easily given herself away. She had never truly mastered the skill of keeping her face neutral. For all she knew, each time she looked at Lock, anyone with working eyes would be able to see the expression on her face or the heat in her cheeks.

"I won't dignify that with an answer. I'll say you're making a big mistake by taking Lock away from those kids. I'll stop helping. Leave him out of this." She had given them plenty of feedback today. If Lock had any questions, he could text her. They would be fine from here on out. They didn't need her. She was the one who needed them.

"It's too late. They already have a replacement lined up."

She was afraid to ask. "Who is it?"

"Me. Of course. Please understand. Mia is my only concern here. And what's best for her is to get promoted to the next level so that when she's in high school, she'll reach her full potential and will be able to put having reached the highest level of Pathfinder on her college application."

"You are a vindictive person to take down Lock to benefit your daughter."

"I'm a mother who will do anything to see her child succeed. Nothing will stand in the way of Mia's success in this world."

"But Lock is not doing anything wrong. You can't

do this to him." She would never forgive herself for Lock losing his position because of her stupid behavior that had happened miles away. Her mind raced to find a solution, but nothing came up.

"He can't see clear when it comes to you. Anyone or anything that hinders Mia and the path she is on will have to deal with me. Any mother would be as protective of their child. I can only assume you don't have children. Otherwise, you would understand." Dawn pushed past her, not waiting for a response.

Women like Dawn Yearwood didn't need a response. She had the world at her fingertips. Something Maeve never really had, not even in Hollywood. Defeat hung in the air around her like the smell of stagnant water.

A truck sped down the drive and parked to the side with a flourish. Lock hopped out. Anger knitted his brows together. He swaggered over.

"Dawn, what are you doing here, harassing the Barneses?" He stopped with his hands on his hips.

"Hello, Mr. Ryker. I was just having a conversation with Maeve. But now I'm leaving."

"Spare me the formalities. There's no one here except us. I can't believe you had the council yank me as Flock Leader."

"You received the email." Dawn crossed her arms over her chest and hitched her hip to the side. The smirk on her lips screamed of the confidence she must feel for what she had to believe was a job well done.

Maeve wanted to be sick.

"Damn straight I received the email. What are you trying to prove?"

"That you aren't fit to lead these children into the

196

next level. You may do just fine running your ranch with your brother beside you, but guiding ten-year-olds should be left to those better equipped."

"I don't know how your daughter ended up such a sweet kid with a mother like you. I'm going to fight this." Fire burned in those dark eyes. A muscle in his jaw twitched.

"Fight it all you want. By the time the council meets to discuss whether or not to reinstate you, the badge ceremony will be over. Mia will advance, and you will no longer be the leader of that troop."

Maeve wanted to throttle this woman, who was using Lock as a way to get at her. "Dawn, be reasonable. If I weren't in the picture, you would not have stooped to these lengths. Call off your dogs and reinstate Lock. I'll go." She could even leave Backwater if necessary.

"Maeve, it's okay. I've got this." Lock put up a hand as if to hold her back.

"I brought this on, Lock. This is my fault." And she needed to make it right. For him. For herself.

"It's her fault." Lock pointed to Dawn.

"If you both will excuse me." Dawn slid into the car and slammed the door shut.

Maeve stood still as Dawn blew down the drive and out of sight. If she moved, she was afraid she might break.

"I'm so sorry." The words tasted like dust, not because she didn't mean them, but because they did little to make the situation better.

"Forget it. That woman has been looking for a way to kick me out for a year now." Lock paced in front of her. He clenched and opened his fists with each pounding step.

She wanted to take the pain away for him, but she was paralyzed to save him. Empty words were all she could offer. "You can't let her get away with this. The kids adore you. They need you."

She dropped onto the porch step. The weight of their time in bed together and the stress of the day wore her down. The fight had seeped out through her pores, leaving nothing but a stench behind.

Her eyes fought to stay open. The pregnancy made her tired, and she hadn't been getting enough sleep this last week. Maybe in an hour or two, she would feel up to solving this problem. She owed it to Lock to do that, even if he didn't want a chance to fix things between them any longer.

The air was still. Insects had gone into hiding, and the sun's heat pooled beads of sweat on her upper lip. Her stomach tried to reject the morning's cup of coffee and dry toast she had forced down. She had blamed her loss of appetite on Lock leaving in the middle of the night. Now she wondered.

Lock stopped his pacing and searched her face. "Are you okay? You look a little green."

"Gee, thanks." She rested her head against the porch banister and gave in to her heavy eyelids.

"Seriously, Maeve. Is something wrong? Do you feel okay?"

His concern lit a match under her. She opened her eyes and shielded them from the sunlight. She couldn't read what he was thinking, but his pinched brows said enough. "How bad do I look?"

"Like you haven't slept in days. Do you want to go inside and lie down? I can help you." He took a step closer.

"Not in that dust bowl. I'll drive back to the ranch and take a nap." She only needed to get some sleep. If she had a chance to rest, the nausea and the cramping in her belly would subside. If this were just her period, she would pop a few ibuprofens for the cramps, but she couldn't take anything like that. She had the baby to think about. The idea of going forward with this pregnancy wormed its way through the doubts and worry about how she would look having the baby of a thief and a liar.

When Dawn Yearwood nearly spat out that she wasn't a mother, Maeve had wanted to shout that she was. For the first time, she had wanted to defend the little person growing inside her. Did it really matter that Michael was the father? He would never know about the child.

She also had no idea how she would support herself or a baby, but she would figure it out. She could stay in Backwater and move back in with Zeke once the house was done. Maybe she could become an acting teacher...

"Let me drive you." Lock's words shook her from her daydreaming.

"That won't be necessary." But she was glad for the offer all the same. "What are you going to do about the Pathfinders?"

"I don't know. I want to be the one to tell the parents, but I might not get that option."

"What about Bodie? Does he know?" She grasped the railing and pulled herself to stand.

"I didn't say anything to him yet. I left him with my mom and came here."

"How did you know Dawn was here?" She hadn't thought about that until now. She had never said why she needed to return to the farm.

"I didn't. I read the email at the end of the meeting and came looking for you."

She didn't want to presume too much about his arrival. He might have just been mad and wanted someone to vent to. She was as good as anyone. Or he really wanted to talk to Zeke and didn't have the heart to tell her that. Still, the idea that he might have wanted to share his struggle with her sent a warm enough rush over her body she had to remove her cardigan. She used the sleeve to wipe the sweat off her upper lip.

"Why was Dawn here, talking with you?" he said.

"To gloat, I think. She may have gotten some pleasure from telling me you'd been kicked out."

"She's heartless."

"She's crazy." Her stomach clenched and stole her breath. The ground shifted underneath her. The sky swooped down in a bright blue arc and switched places with the hard earth.

She reached out for the railing to stop the spinning and caught herself before she fell.

"Are you sure you're okay?" Lock took a step closer.

"Just tired. I didn't get much sleep last night." She couldn't look him in the eye in case he could see right through her.

"Maeve, we should talk about—"

"I'm not up for that now. I'll call you later." She brushed past him and couldn't resist the urge to give his arm a squeeze. His skin was warm to her touch, but she wasn't ready to tackle what had happened between them.

He let her go.

She should be grateful. They weren't right for each

other anymore. Time had not been kind to them, and now both of their lives floated in the wind.

But she wasn't grateful.

Not at all.

Chapter Eighteen

A weariness hung on Lock like a wet horse blanket. He couldn't shake it off. He had to explain to Bodie what happened, and he didn't know where to start.

Just a week ago, coming home was one of his favorite things. His life behind that front door made sense to him. Now as he pushed it open, everything was jumbled.

His mother and Bodie sat at the kitchen table with their heads bent over a jigsaw puzzle. The ranch kept several up at the main building in the great room where the guests could hang out on bad weather days. He didn't keep any here, but if it was something Bodie liked to do, Lock would grab a couple or buy new ones.

"Hey." He kicked off his work boots.

"Hi, dear. Are you hungry? I fixed a little homemade mac and cheese. It's keeping warm in the oven. Bodie and I ate."

His mother had made his favorite meal as a kid. Lock was pretty sure that wasn't a coincidence. Bodie didn't look up from the puzzle with its thousand pieces all over the table. Lock took a detour past Bodie on the way to the oven. "Hey, buddy. That's a cool puzzle." He ruffled Bodie's hair.

Bodie brushed his hair back the way it was and shook his head.

His mother's eyes widened behind her glasses as she

met his gaze. He searched her face for an answer but couldn't find one. This was a hint at what parenting was all about. The parent walked in the door after a long day, hoping for a second to breathe, only to find the child upset about something that needed dealing with. He would forever be in awe of his mother.

"Did something happen?" He grabbed a plate from the cabinet to act as if everything was status quo. He would tell Bodie about the Pathfinders after he had a chance to eat something.

His mother came over to him. "He knows. The other kids told him. They were all texting." She kept her voice low. "I tried to talk to him about it over dinner, but he wasn't having it. I'm worried he thinks if you leave as the leader, you might leave as his foster parent too."

He pinched the bridge of his nose. "I'll take care of it."

"Boys, I'll be heading out now." Karen hugged Bodie, and he hugged her back but didn't say anything.

"Bodie, do you want to say goodbye?" he said.

"Bye, Karen. Thanks for the puzzle." Bodie kept his gaze fixed on what he was doing.

Lock opened his mouth to say something, but his mother shook her head and shot him a glare.

"You're welcome. See you soon." Karen patted Lock's arm as he held the door open for her. The cool night air swooped in as uninvited as he had been on Maeve's farm today.

"Good night, Mom." He joined Bodie at the table. Thoughts of Maeve would have to wait. "Do you want some help?"

"No, thank you." Bodie continued to fit pieces in their places without looking up.

"Could you look at me a second?" He didn't want that to sound too harsh, but Bodie's gaze snapped up anyway. "We need to talk about the Pathfinders."

"The other kids said you got fired." Bodie's bottom lip quivered. "I told them it wasn't true."

"It's sort of true. I've been asked to step down. But they can't actually fire me because I'm a volunteer."

"Why? What did you do wrong?"

In Bodie's world, it was probably that simple. Lock must have done something wrong if an adult punished him. Bodie didn't know how to consider that the people who were responsible for him had hurt him.

"I don't think I did anything wrong. One parent doesn't want Miss Maeve to help us out. Because I allowed her to, the parent was able to persuade the council I shouldn't be there. Does that make sense?"

"No. What's wrong with Miss Maeve? She's one of the nicest people I've met. What did she do wrong?"

"She hasn't done anything wrong with our group." He wasn't sure how much he should share. Telling Maeve's story wasn't for him to do. She had to decide what she wanted people to know. The video did her no favors, but anyone who really knew her would understand what had happened. He was certain Bodie would come to her defense.

"But she did something bad. Right?"

"Has anyone ever told you that it's okay to make mistakes?" He picked up a puzzle piece and looked for a spot. This conversation was about more than just his removal from the Pathfinders. Bodie needed better guidance than what he'd been receiving.

"Like in a math problem?" Bodie grabbed a piece too.

"Like in life." His mother used to do stuff like this with him when he was a kid and having a problem. She usually started baking something and let him help. He had shared plenty of stuff he thought he wouldn't have told any other way.

"I don't know." Bodie pushed his hair out of his face as his gaze moved toward the window.

"We make mistakes all the time. It's part of life. Mistakes aren't wrong." He grabbed a piece that matched the corner Bodie worked on.

"Okay. Why do kids get in trouble for making mistakes like talking in class or during church or when they don't make their bed?"

"What kind of trouble?" Maybe it was time to walk up to the discussion of what had happened to Bodie at the foster house. If he needed to talk about it, Lock would listen or get him to someone who knew how to listen well.

Bodie turned the puzzle piece in his fingers. He shrugged but kept his head down.

"Skipping bed making isn't a punishable offense in my house."

Bodie looked up, his face a smooth impasse.

"The people you lived with were not good people. You did not deserve what happened to you. Someone should have been looking out for you." This kid had been carrying some heavy load by himself. He would do whatever he could to make it right for as long as possible. At least until a family who could adopt him became possible. If it were possible. Older kids didn't often get adopted.

He would never understand the horrors people caused. No amount of anger would make him hurt a person or an animal. He'd been in fights to defend himself or his brothers, but he wasn't going to raise his hands to a child.

"But no one helped me. They let Steve hurt me."

"I know, and I'm sorry that happened, but it won't happen any longer. No one will hurt you while I'm around." That promise rooted itself in his heart. And if he thought—for the hundredth time—it would actually accomplish anything, he would track down the foster father and beat him to an inch of his life, but the justice system had him now, and hopefully, they did their job so Lock didn't have to.

"Can I ask you something?" Bodie returned to fitting pieces into the puzzle.

"Anything." He followed Bodie's cue.

"If you can get fired from the Pathfinders, can they fire you from being my foster dad?" A single tear ran down Bodie's round cheek and dripped onto the puzzle.

He cupped the side of Bodie's head. "Hey. Can you look at me?"

Bodie turned his gaze to his.

"Those two things are not the same. I'll figure out what to do about the Pathfinders. Once I get the official approval, nothing will stop me from being your foster father. Okay?"

Bodie nodded. The hint of a smile wobbled on his thin lips.

A knock came to the front door. It swung open, and Gage entered. He wore a light-blue collared shirt, dark jeans that didn't have a single crease in them, and black shoes. "Sorry to barge in, but I saw you two at the table through the window and figured you wouldn't mind."

"No problem." Lock stood and stretched his back.

His conversation with Bodie could continue another time.

"I was wondering if Bodie could come to the movies with us. We're going to see the new animated film playing in town."

"You and Izzy?" he said.

"Yes, and Calista, Quinn, and Royce too. It turned into a Ryker family night out. We thought Bodie might want to join us." Gage set his fatherly smile on Bodie.

Going to the movies was a great idea and probably what Bodie needed at the moment. Somehow Gage knew. His brother was so damn good at being a father. He could never live up to Gage in that area, or any other. The best he could hope for was to try. "The whole clan. Bodie, do you want to go?"

"Can I?" He came around the table with wonder in his eyes. This new movie must be a big thing.

But that excitement was not about a movie. Bodie was being included in a family event. He deserved to know his place was with the Rykers.

Lock squatted down to be at Bodie's level. "You can go anywhere with any member of this family. They're your family too. Okay?"

"I never had a big family before."

"Now you do." He pulled out cash from his front jeans pocket. No matter where life took them, he would keep an eye on Bodie. He would lend out his family too.

"I've got it, little brother." Gage put up a hand to stop him. "I told Kace and Jett the same thing. This uncle is treating. Bodie, grab your shoes."

Bodie hurried to his room.

Lock stuck out a hand to Gage. "Thanks, man."

Gage shook. "No thanks needed. You've taken Izzy

plenty of places when she was young and I needed help."

"You think I need help?"

"Lock, man, every parent needs help. There will be days you'll be exhausted, want to pull your hair out, just want five minutes to yourself. You don't have a partner. You can lean on all of us. Look how excited Mom is to go from just having Izzy to having a bunch of grandkids. Use her when you need her."

"This arrangement won't last forever." His mother always made room for others in her heart. Her big heart was probably why she had so many kids, and with Ajay gone, she always looked for ways to fill the void he left.

"Maybe not. Maybe it will. But until then, I'm here. We're all here." Gage patted him on the shoulder, ending the conversation. "We won't stay out late, but we might grab some pizza afterward."

"I'm not going anywhere tonight." He tried to ignore the relief rising up from his belly that he would have a few hours to himself. The long day had dragged on from the night before.

Gage was right, as usual, about that.

"I heard about the Pathfinders." Gage shoved his hands in his pockets.

"I'll work it out." He had no idea how he would begin fixing it, but maybe he could make a few calls. The people on the council weren't exactly his fans. Some didn't like that he didn't have a child in the troop. But that had kind of changed with Bodie. Others just didn't like him because some people in this town thought the Rykers had their hands in too many things, leaving fewer opportunities for others.

"If you need me to do anything, let me know."

"I will. Thanks. But this one I might be able to

handle myself."

Bodie tore back into the room. Joy radiated off this kid. "I'm ready." He held up his windbreaker.

"Have fun." Giving a kid love seemed like a pretty easy thing to do.

Bodie threw his arms around his waist and squeezed. "Thank you." He pushed away and ran out the door.

Gage gave him a nod and closed the door. The sudden silence curled up around him like white smoke. He wasn't sure if he liked the quiet. His life had been very quiet up until recently with Maeve's return and Bodie moving in. The noise added a layer he didn't know he was missing.

He left the puzzle on the table. They didn't need to eat at the table for a few days, and having it there would give him a way to talk to Bodie as more difficult subjects came up.

He returned to heating up the mac and cheese, but his phone rang, stopping him. He didn't recognize the number but swiped it anyway.

"Lock Ryker."

"Hello, Mr. Ryker. My name is Eloisa Humphrey. I'm the social worker assigned to your foster parent application. Do you have a minute?" Her voice crackled with age. Each word came out formal and exact, reminding him of a schoolteacher he once had.

Alessandra did work fast. He hadn't expected to hear from anyone so quickly.

"Sure. I can talk now." The conversation would break up the quiet he tried to adjust to. He plopped the mac and cheese into a bowl.

"Thank you. I've reviewed your application. Most of it seems in order. I only have one question."

"What's that?" One question wasn't bad. This should end up being quick, and he could get back to his dinner.

"Your application states you're single."

"That's right." An image of Maeve squeezing her eyes shut and laughing at one of his jokes poked through, but he forced it back down. He couldn't think about her now. He had because if he could be married to anyone, he'd want it to be Maeve.

"Why do you want to be a single foster father?"

"I didn't think my marital status mattered." Alessandra had told him his marital status would not be considered. The organization always needed people to become foster parents. They didn't have the luxury to turn away single parents. The question should have been raised as to why he wanted to be a foster parent, period, and until recently, he hadn't given that a single thought. He never expected to be a parent of any kind.

"Technically, it does not. You can't be excluded for that. I do want to understand how you'll care for…let me see…I have his name here—" The thwap of pages being flipped came through the phone. "—Bodie if you don't have anyone to share the responsibility with. Raising a child for any length of time is a large responsibility."

She didn't even know the name of the child she was supposed to look out for. If she didn't know who he was, how was she supposed to make sure Bodie didn't end up back in a house like the one he had left?

Lock pushed down the urge to point out her obvious inabilities. He could not make an enemy of her. Alessandra or not, the social worker could decide against him.

"To answer your question, Eloisa, was it?" He knew

it was Eloisa. He couldn't resist the smallest of digs.

"I prefer to remain formal during the process. Ms. Humphrey, please, Mr. Ryker."

He was glad they weren't in the same room or on video. His face would have said all he tried to keep under his tongue. "Ms. Humphrey, to answer your question, I have a large family ready to help out. You know, the whole it-takes-a-village thing."

Silence met him over the line. His joke had fallen flat. Ms. Humphrey was uptight and without humor. He needed to be more like Gage to win this woman over.

"Mr. Ryker, a support system is a wonderful thing for a foster parent to have, but the day-to-day activities will fall to you and you alone. Making sure homework is done. Grocery shopping, laundry, keeping the house clean, getting the child off to school. If Bodie participates in activities, you will have to ensure he has transportation. Some foster children suffer from mental health issues or learning disabilities, or both. You must be prepared to deal with those as well."

"I think I'm ready." He was concerned about how Bodie's experience with the last foster family affected him. Bodie could be moody and sullen. But Lock had checked with Alessandra, and Bodie did well in school most of the time. His grades had slipped some recently, but that was to be expected.

"I'll be the judge of that. I'd like to visit your home to see if you have adequate space for Bodie." Pages flipped again. She must take copious notes.

"I live on a ranch. He has acres around him. He won't run out of space." He punched the timer on the microwave to heat up his dinner.

"I meant the actual place where he will sleep and eat.

211

I need to make sure it's appropriate for a child." Her clipped words cut the emotion out of each one.

"Okay. Sure. No problem. When do you want to come by?" He looked around the cottage. It was small and basic. He kept it clean, mostly. But it wasn't as nice as the guest cottages with more up-to-date décor. He had never wanted any other space. This suited him just fine. Now he wished he at least lived in the main building with all the amenities or in the apartment upstairs where he'd lived growing up, but Jett now occupied it.

"Monday morning." Ms. Humphrey's voice pulled him away from his worry.

Monday mornings were busy on the ranch. He would need to tell Jett about his absence and make sure his work was handled. But it could be managed. It had to be. "How long will the meeting take?"

"As long as necessary. I've stayed as little as ten minutes and as long as two hours."

It was not the answer he wanted, but he didn't push. It was just one meeting. He was certain that after the meeting, the paperwork would go through. "Okay, I'll make arrangements with work."

"Aren't you part owner of Ryker Ranch?"

"I am." That truth should be a point in his favor. Money wasn't an issue. He wasn't rich or anything, but he was comfortable and could take care of Bodie's needs.

"Doesn't the boss get to make his own hours?" Her words accused more than questioned.

"Ms. Humphrey, this ranch is a twenty-four-hour-a-day job." As soon as he said it, he wished he could grab the words and shove them back in his mouth. "That doesn't mean—"

"I know what you mean, Mr. Ryker. I'd like to speak

with Bodie, if I may."

Did she know what he actually meant, or had she just made some note in a file, claiming he wouldn't be able to make the time for a child? Had he ruined everything before it barely started? "You want to speak with him on Monday?"

"No, right now, please. He doesn't need to be present on Monday since it's a school day."

"He isn't here right now." The microwave dinged.

"It appears your food is ready."

"You heard that?"

"I did, in fact. Do you normally make dinners in the microwave?"

"Does it matter?"

"Don't you want to provide a well-balanced diet for the child?"

His insides heated up. How much judgment was she sitting on? Did she have any real idea how to raise a child, or did she just scare people out of wanting to be a parent?

"Ms. Humphrey, if I may ask you something. Who questioned the last man who fostered Bodie? Because that guy wasn't worried one ounce about Bodie or his eating habits."

She huffed but did not answer his question.

"Ms. Humphrey, are you still there?"

"I was not the social worker assigned to Bodie previously. Where is he? Bodie? Why isn't he home now?" Her tone implied Lock had screwed up by letting Bodie go out. She must be adding up his demerits quickly now.

But he would show her how wrong she was about him. His support system was firmly in place, and the foster parenting had not been made official yet. "Bodie went with my brother to the movies."

"Your brother? A man. Alone. Which movie? When will he be back? Why didn't you go?" She fired questions at him, not giving him a chance to answer.

"My brother is a man. Maybe you know him. He's Backwater's sheriff." The sarcasm left his mouth before he could put a lid on it. He didn't like her implying that any of his brothers would somehow harm a child. She seemed to have a twisted mind.

"I'm afraid I'm not from Backwater. I don't know your sheriff. Being a sheriff doesn't guarantee he's an adequate babysitter. What is his name, please?"

"Gage Ryker."

More pages flipped. "I see. Which movie did you say?"

"I didn't say. Some animated movie for kids. He couldn't remember what or if Gage had mentioned the title. He wished he had asked better questions before they left. He would have to start doing that from now on. Maybe he did screw this up. He wanted to hit himself for that kind of thinking. Allowing Bodie to spend time with Gage was probably the best thing he could do for the boy.

"Just because the movie is animated doesn't mean it's appropriate for a ten-year-old boy. Can you get a movie stub for me?"

"Excuse me?"

"I'd like to see the movie stub, if there is one."

"I can't guarantee that. But I can guarantee that Gage is more than capable of watching Bodie. Gage has a daughter, and he's a single father who also lives on the ranch. He's a well-respected sheriff and solid person in our community. He took all the Ryker kids, including

Bodie, to the movies with his fiancée Calista."

"How old are the other children?" This woman's questions never ended.

He glanced at the clock on the microwave. He wanted this conversation over, and there would only be more of it in a couple of days.

"My niece Izzy is seventeen. I don't know Quinn's exact age, but she's in high school, and little Royce is five or six, maybe."

"You don't know the ages of your niece and nephew?"

"Technically, Quinn isn't my niece. She's my brother Jett's fiancée's daughter. And Royce is my other brother's girlfriend's son."

"Quite the pack."

"I don't understand your meaning."

"I believe the young people call it a modern family. Not my cup of tea, but that's neither here nor there. Thank you for your time, Mr. Ryker. I'll see you Monday morning at nine. Good day." She ended the call.

He stared at his phone for a minute, unsure of what had just happened. He shot a text off to Alessandra, but she didn't reply. He wanted her to tell him he hadn't made a mess of everything before they even began. He couldn't let Bodie down.

He was no longer hungry.

He wanted to forget about this day and grabbed a beer instead.

Chapter Nineteen

Maeve sat in the car outside Lock's house. The light in the living room was still on. It wasn't terribly late. She could assume he was still awake.

She had no idea what she was doing. After she left him earlier, she had managed a couple of hours of sleep. Her energy was restored, and the nausea stayed away.

Yet loneliness filled the space around her, gathering in every nook of the cottage until she couldn't breathe or sit in it. She didn't want to be alone. Everywhere she turned, she was by herself. Before she realized what she did, she found herself driving around. The streets of Backwater held little interest, and she returned to the ranch. But instead of going back to her cottage, she'd come here.

Each time the memories of her life ripped her apart, she wanted to go back and make a different choice. If she had only been paying better attention to Michael's signs. Had he let something slip about who he really was? Or had she been so desperate for affection that she had simply closed her eyes to it all? Either option burned her face with shame.

For years, she'd run from the girl whose father was a farmer, the girl who pretended to be someone else on stage to hide the pain of being the girl whose mother was dead. She had wanted to be the girl from the big city with class and culture and not the simple girl from Backwater,

Montana. Yet here she was, right back where she had started with nothing to show for it. Not even the man who had loved her once.

Lock's front door opened, and the interior light spilled across the small porch. He was in silhouette on the brighter backdrop, but she would know his height and the line of his shoulders anywhere.

She debated on driving away, but he had seen her. Caught. Gaping like a stalker. She offered a small wave and hoped the shadows covered the heat in her cheeks.

He placed an arm on the roof of the car and leaned down to the window. He smelled of flannel and warmth. "What are you doing out here?"

A day's beard growth dotted his jawline, and he had traded his contacts for his glasses. His T-shirt dipped away from his neckline. Her fingers twitched with muscle memory to touch the soft spot where his collarbones met.

"I went for a drive and somehow ended up here. I didn't mean to bother you." She pressed the button to start the car.

He reached in and took her hand off the steering wheel, locking their grips together. "Why are you here, Maeve?"

"I told you." She had so much more to say but swallowed the words like medicine.

"Do you want to come in? I've had a long day and was about to have a beer."

"I shouldn't drink."

"I'll make tea." He straightened and opened the car door.

She could either slide out and follow him inside, or she could close the car door and go back to her cottage to be by herself. Choices. Wasn't she just wishing to make different choices? She had nothing to lose by going with him. And everything to lose at the same time.

"Well?" he asked.

She stood before him. He turned without a word, as if he were confident she wouldn't jump back into the car. She would follow him anywhere, and he seemed to know that.

He closed the cottage door behind her, then went to the kitchen without a word. He opened a beer and moved around the small space, filling the kettle and setting a mug on the counter. She remained in her spot by the door.

"Are you coming all the way in, or are you going to stand by the door all night?"

"Where's Bodie?" Besides an abandoned jigsaw puzzle on the kitchen table, no sign of the boy existed.

"He went to the movies with Gage, Calista, and the other kids." He leaned against the counter and finished off the beer.

They had some time alone. Her stomach clenched again. She could not ever remember being nervous around Lock, but this time her heart was exposed more than any other. She didn't plan on anything happening between them, but being in the same space with him turned up the voltage on her nerves. If he felt it too, he hid it well.

"Are you going to tell me why you were sitting in your car outside my house?"

"I wanted to see if you were home." She squirmed under his scrutinizing stare.

"And if I was?"

"I don't know. I thought maybe I'd apologize again

for what happened. Is there anything I can do to help you get your position back?"

He regarded her. His gaze followed the length of her body. She couldn't read his face, but she needed to know what he was thinking.

"Marry me."

"What?" Her stomach flipped again.

"I don't need help with the Pathfinders. I'll figure that out. Dawn Yearwood will have a hard time getting rid of me. I need a wife to win over the social worker who's coming on Monday to see if I have a stable home for Bodie."

"Did you tell her you were married?" She needed to sit and moved to the couch.

"No. But she seems to prefer foster parents to be married. I stuck my foot in my mouth a couple of times on the phone with her tonight. Maybe if she thinks I'm about to get married, she'll let up a little."

The teakettle interrupted their conversation. Lock brought her the mug. She was grateful to have something to do with her hands. He sat on the other end of the couch. Too close and still too far.

"You shouldn't lie to the social worker." She didn't want to lie. Her life was already in a mess because of too many nontruths.

"It's not a total lie. We talked about getting married." He propped his feet up on the coffee table, casually, as if this conversation weren't the most bizarre one she'd had.

"That was over six years ago." And she had balked at his offer, saying they weren't ready, it was too soon.

"She doesn't need to know that."

"But we know it. And what about Bodie? Are you

going to lie to him?" She couldn't stand to lie to that boy after what he'd been through and knowing how harmful lies had been to her.

"He's a savvy kid. He'll understand the bind I'm in. He wants to live here. He isn't going to care if I tell him this once it's okay to fib a little."

"And what happens when we don't get married?" She couldn't believe she was having this crazy conversation. "How many beers have you had?"

"You think I'm drunk?" He dropped his feet and sat on the edge of the couch.

"I think you've lost your mind." She might be losing hers for even entertaining this conversation.

"I'm desperate to keep this kid."

"Don't make a mistake out of desperation." She knew better than most what making that kind of mistake could cost.

"No lectures, okay? Pretending to be engaged for the social worker isn't a mistake. She won't know the difference, and we can officially break up after I'm approved. No one else cares about me being a single dad except for that uptight woman."

"I'm not comfortable with that. We already have Dawn Yearwood staring down her nose at us. If she gets wind of this, you'll never see the Pathfinders again. She'll probably also tell your social worker what she thinks of you." She pushed off the couch and threw her hands in the air. This day had gone from bad to nuts.

"And let me point out, Lockwood, I'm not exactly the best mother figure at the moment. One internet search of me, and you'll be cooked. You must be drunk to believe this would work."

He came to her and brushed her hair behind her

shoulder. His intense gaze bored into hers. "I'm not crazy or drunk. But I do like it when you use my full name."

For years, his name had been on her lips, whispered in silent heartbeats.

Heat rolled off him and filled the space between them. She should step away and take a cleansing breath, but her feet remained planted. This man had a power over her he didn't know he possessed.

She tried to form words, but her dry throat broke them into pieces. She swallowed and tried again. "How long do you need me to pretend?"

"Just for a meeting or two. Maybe more. I don't know. When are you leaving town?" He stepped closer.

She had to look up to meet his gaze. Time for the truth. "I'm staying."

He jerked back. "You're not leaving?"

"I have nowhere to go." It hurt to admit, but she might as well get used to it. She had to start over, reinvent herself. People did it all the time. Why couldn't she?

"What about your career in Los Angeles?"

"I don't have that career anymore. I think that's evident." She'd had her fifteen minutes. A lifetime had been too much to ask for.

"That can change. People forget." He moved toward her again.

This dance they did only made her want him more. Which was a bit of a problem since he had said he didn't want her.

"I don't want to raise a child in LA alone. At least here I have Zeke." She didn't finish that with what she had hoped for. She had wanted Lock too. Selfish, really.

She had nothing to offer him.

"You decided to keep the baby."

She tilted up her chin again and forced her trembling lip to still. If she was going to do this mother thing, she had to be ready for whatever people thought of her. The father question would always come swinging, and she'd have to decide what to tell this little person growing inside her about his or her paternity. She would deal with whatever she had to, but she would be brave. Maybe for the first time.

"Do you think I'm making a mistake?" She held his gaze. He never gave a damn what anyone thought of him. He lived his life his way. She would have to become like that for her child.

"What I think isn't important. What's important is that you're making the best decision for you." He turned away from her, and she wanted to pull him back.

He grabbed his phone and tapped at the screen. Had he received a text he couldn't ignore? Did Bodie need him? Was he trying to find a way to get her to leave?

Nat King Cole filled the room.

"Music?" It was a dumb question. Of course, he had turned on music, but why?

He returned to her, took her hand in his, and pulled her close. "Speakers in the ceiling. I installed them years ago."

His other hand slid onto her waist. She leaned into him, and they swayed to the soft music. The why didn't matter when he held her this way.

"This is nice." Being so close to him also scared the hell out of her. Did she dare trust what might be happening? She didn't want to ask and shatter the little bubble forming around them tonight.

"You're going to be a good mother." He turned her with ease. For a man his size, he was light on his feet.

"How do you know?" She risked laying her head on his chest. His heartbeat kept time to hers.

"Because I know you. You're determined to be the best at whatever you do."

"I don't know if I'm that person anymore." Whoever she was, she wanted to stay in this moment for as long as possible. The rest of the world was on the other side of the walls, and she was in no rush to share him with that world.

"She's in there. Trust me." He placed a kiss on the top of her head.

Being with him hurt. Knowing he was in her arms but out of reach, not to be hers again, destroyed her as if a storm tore through her insides. She could not pretend to be his fiancée and then go back to a life that didn't include him. She would drown in that despair.

"I think I should go. I've taken up enough of your time tonight." She eased out of his embrace as the song switched to another ballad.

He gripped her arm. "Don't go."

"I can't stay. I have feelings for you, feelings that don't belong here anymore. Our lives are so different now." She moved away from him, and he let her go.

"I have feelings for you too. I don't know what to do about them." He pushed his glasses up his nose. Every time he did that, she saw the boy behind the man, and she loved him more.

"But you don't want to try and figure it out."

"I don't know, Maeve. I don't want to get hurt again, and you can't promise you won't."

"No one can ever make that promise." Michael had

promised to love her and take care of her, and look where that ended. Words were easy to deliver on a shiny platter. But they were hollow unless action could sturdy them.

"Maybe. But we have a history where that exact thing happened. I know you said you're staying, but what if you get another chance at making movies? You'd go, and I would let you, but that doesn't mean I won't get hurt. I don't want to lose you twice."

"Life doesn't give us guarantees. I wish it did. You should know that. You've had your share of hardships."

"So why do I want to add to my list?"

"Because you love me." Frustration or anger pushed those words out and into the room. She reached for them, but it was too late. He hadn't promised her anything, and she bared her soul to him.

She wanted to be worth the risk. She wanted him to take a chance on her. She didn't deserve it, she had hurt him badly, but she had been flapping in the wind for so long she needed him to reach out and anchor her before she blew away for good.

He stared at her. The song switched again. A painful piano melody drifted around them. Her heart ached, but she didn't move. He would have to be the one.

"You never answered my question. Will you pretend to be my fiancée?"

She straightened her shoulders and met his gaze with all the effort of moving a mountain. "I can't. I'm sorry. You don't need me. You'll do just fine in the interview. That social worker is going to take one look at you and know that you'll be an excellent father. You're a good man. Honest and true. You know how to live life to its fullest. You fight for what's right. You—"

His mouth swallowed up the rest of her words as he kissed her hard and fast.

Chapter Twenty

Lock held Maeve in his arms while she slept. Her body was hot against his, but their lovemaking had ended a little while ago. He was surprised how much heat she generated.

He grabbed his glasses and checked the time on the bedside clock. Gage would be back soon with Bodie. Lock would have to wake her. She wouldn't want to be caught in his bed when Bodie got home. But a few more minutes with their bodies tangled together wouldn't hurt.

Making love had happened in the most unexpected way. He hadn't realized he kissed her until her tongue found his.

He kissed her because he couldn't stand another second of not touching her or watching her leave. In moments, their clothes were on the floor, they were in his bed, and he was inside her. He meant to make it last, make sure she was taken care of before him, but their actions had become almost feral. She had straddled his lap, gripping his shoulders and calling out his name. He chuckled to himself. Hot and steamy were all right with him if that was how she wanted it.

"Mmm." She snuggled against him. "You're nice and warm."

"Are you cold?" He tugged the blankets up over them.

"Yes. I feel like I'm shivering." She burrowed

deeper.

"I can get you a sweatshirt." He eased out of the embrace, but she gripped his arm.

"Don't go."

"I'll be right back." He laughed.

She pushed up on her elbow. "Would it be too much trouble to get a cup of tea? My little bunny here is making me nauseous again."

"Are you okay?"

"I think so."

"I'll get you that tea." He shoved his legs into his jeans. He would find a shirt for her because he wanted her warm and safe. This child she carried might not know its biological father but could have a father who would love him…or her.

"Do you want anything else?"

"No, thank you. I don't feel like eating. I thought when you were pregnant you wanted to eat all the time." She tugged the shirt over her head.

It swallowed her up, and he grinned, liking her in his clothes. "Couldn't tell you. I'll leave the baby cooking to you."

She tossed a pillow at him. "Funny. I have to pee." And she slid out of bed.

He put up the water to boil and prepared a mug with a tea bag. His mind revisited the last hour. He could get used to having Maeve in his bed every day, but he did want to be careful. He was already falling for her again, risking his heart again.

He should slow down, put some space between them and let this thing grow at a slower pace. He had Bodie to think about now. If Maeve and he didn't work out, how would that affect Bodie? He finally understood why

Gage had barely dated when Izzy was little.

He could love her child as his own. They could be a family, the four of them, and maybe someday, Maeve would give him a child of his blood. He still wanted a chance at that, if possible.

"Lock." Maeve's voice shrieked out his name at a deafening decibel.

He tore down the hall. *What the hell happened?*

The bedroom was empty. He turned for the hall bath. She sat on the floor with her back pressed against the tub and her hands in her lap. She squeezed her eyes shut and panted.

"What happened?" He didn't see signs of something broken on her or in the bathroom. She had no head wounds, just tears streaking her pale face.

He dropped down to his knees, not sure if he should touch her and make things worse. "What is it? Tell me."

"Something's wrong. The baby." She moved her hands. Blood was on the shirt's hem. "I don't feel so good."

"I'll call an ambulance." His phone was in the bedroom.

"Don't go." Her nails dug into his skin.

"I just want to get my phone. I'll be right back." He pried her fingers from his skin with some regret and bolted for his phone.

He hesitated. An ambulance might take too long to get to the ranch and then make it to the hospital. He could drive her in half the time. He shoved his feet into shoes.

"I'll get you to the hospital." He put an arm behind her back and under her legs. Time wouldn't wait, and she needed a doctor. If whatever she had turned out to be nothing, she could fight with him about it afterward. But if it was something more… He didn't want to think about the worst.

"No hospital." She rested her head on his shoulder.

"You can hate me later." He scooped her up and strode to his truck. She weighed nothing in his arms, making him want to protect her even more.

He placed her in the truck and belted her in, then jumped in behind the wheel and tore down the road to the ranch's entrance.

He pushed the truck's engine to its limit as he flew past homes and buildings, not caring about traffic signs and rules. Every minute lasted forever and brought them no closer to the hospital.

She sat beside him, groaning and clutching her stomach. "I'm ruining your truck."

"That's what you're thinking about? Screw the truck, Maeve." He took her cold hand in his and gave it a squeeze.

She returned the gesture with enough force he could allow himself to take a full breath. He didn't know a whole lot about pregnancies or babies, but he did know bleeding was not usually a good sign.

He pulled into the emergency room parking lot and slammed on the brakes right outside the door. He raced around the front of the truck to get Maeve out of the seat.

"It's going to be okay." He kissed the top of her head and hurried through the automatic doors.

"Help us. We need a doctor." He turned in circles, looking for anyone who could help them. His heart pounded in his ears.

A short, round woman wearing blue scrubs ran out from behind the long desk. Her mouth moved, but he couldn't hear her.

Her name badge and the details of her face blurred. Maeve groaned in his arms.

The woman grabbed a gurney and rolled it over. "Lock, put her on the table."

Did he know this woman?

"Lock, can you hear me? It's Marjorie Simms, darling." She snapped her fingers in front of his face.

Marjorie Simms. His mother's longtime friend. The school nurse when he was a kid.

"Put her down now." She reached for Maeve.

He did as he was told, placing her down with care as fear ate through him.

Maeve clutched his arm. "Don't leave me."

"I'm right here." He gripped her hand and held her gaze.

"What's going on, sweetie?" Marjorie said to Maeve.

"I'm pregnant."

Something passed over Marjorie's face, but it was gone before he could figure out what it was. "We're going to take good care of you. Lock, fill out some forms." Marjorie wheeled Maeve away.

"Wait. I want to go with her." He still hadn't let go of her hand. He'd promised to stay with her.

"You can't come in with us. Fill out the forms, and I'll be back." Marjorie ran down the hall, shouting orders and whisking Maeve away.

Someone came up to him. He didn't want to answer questions he didn't know the answers to. He wanted to be with Maeve, holding her hand and telling her it would be okay.

"Are you the father?" the young male nurse said with his hand hovering above the form.

He could lie. They might allow him to be in with her that way. Would she want everyone in Backwater to find out he was the father? It wouldn't take long for the gossip to spread if the right person overheard. He had asked her to pretend to be engaged to him. Would that be enough?

"I'm her fiancé."

"Have a seat in the waiting room. Someone will be out shortly to speak with you."

****

Maeve wasn't sure how long she'd been out, but the sky beyond the hospital window was dark. The single light above her bed reflected in the glass. She was alone in the room. Completely alone.

She'd lost the baby. And just when she had begun to imagine an existence as a mother. Life did not spare its cruel jokes. Bad things could crash down like an angry ocean, pummeling the swimmer until every breath was stolen.

The doctor had told her she would be fine and could easily get pregnant again, if she wanted. The miscarriage wasn't her fault and happened in a small percentage of pregnancies. She had earned herself a bit of bad luck, was all.

Somehow this was her fault. Everything that had gone wrong in her life was her fault. Maybe wanting a chance with Lock after what she had done to him was too much to ask for, and the universe reminded her.

Would Lock want her now that she had failed in the worst possible way? She couldn't even take care of her baby. He would be within his rights to think she wasn't suitable to watch Bodie either.

She had said she loved him right before he kissed her. He hadn't said it back. There hadn't been time. Once he kissed her, words had disappeared and touching took its place. She had planned on mentioning her slip after they made love, but she had fallen asleep wrapped in his strong arms. Then the worst had happened. Now she was glad she hadn't said anything. Better if they both forgot it.

Images of her hands gripping her belly, of Lock carrying her into the hospital, of the doctor's grave face as he spoke played like a slasher film. She squeezed her eyes shut to make the images go away, but the tears burned trails down her cheeks anyway.

"Hey." The door swooshed closed on the whispered word.

Lock came toward her. He wore a scrubs shirt and a pained expression behind his glasses. His hair appeared to have been in a battle with his hands. He offered her a thin-lipped smile.

He was as solid as the mountains and as gentle as a breeze. He loved with all his heart when he opened it up to love at all. She had to let him go. She couldn't risk hurting him again.

"Hi." She pulled the covers up to her chin.

He cleared the room in two steps and reached for her hand. She hesitated but slid her fingers through his cold ones. He opened his mouth to speak, then closed it over what must be on his mind.

"Did they tell you?" She had to suspect someone had. He had rushed into the emergency room without a shirt on and holding her bleeding body in his arms.

"The doctors didn't want to, but I convinced them. I'm sorry. I wish there was something I could do for you to make this better." A single tear fell.

Her heart shattered for the second time. She had

never seen Lock cry.

In another world, this baby would have been his. Part of her was relieved it hadn't been Lock's. He didn't deserve to lose a child after losing his father at such a young age and later losing his younger brother. He'd experienced enough tragedy.

She could tell him to hold her because she thought she might shatter into a million unfixable pieces if something didn't keep her in place, and he would climb into this too-small bed for his large frame and keep her in his arms as long as she needed. But she didn't say that, because what she really needed was for him to leave before her bad luck poisoned him.

"You did plenty. Thank you for bringing me."

"Was it us? Did we…with our…" His eyes swelled with pain.

They had made love with a renewed fierceness. She couldn't get enough of him in that moment and had pressed hard against him so he would fill her up until she exploded. "It wasn't us. That's not how it happens."

His shoulders sagged. "I wouldn't have been able to live with myself—"

"Don't worry about it, Lock. You didn't cause this." She couldn't watch him carry any of the weight. He would easily take ahold of the burden and make it his own so she would suffer less. He took on Bodie with barely a second thought because that was the kind of man he was. Her man. No, not hers anymore.

"I am worried. What can I do for you?"

"Go home and get some rest. I'll be fine." She wasn't sure if she would ever be fine again.

"I'd rather stay with you. I can sleep later. I told Gage you were in the hospital so he would keep Bodie overnight, but I didn't say what happened. I don't have to go home."

"But I want you to." She sat up straight to appear strong even though on the inside she was dying.

"Why?" He pushed his glasses up his nose, her sweet man who would protect her, but she couldn't allow that.

She took a deep breath and held his gaze. "Because I told you I loved you and you didn't say it back." It was a cheap shot, but she had to take it.

"I kissed you. We had some pretty good sex afterward."

His teasing smile tugged at her heart. She told her heart to shut up. "Sex is easy. Love and commitment are hard, and you don't want that." She didn't blame him. Committing to her would be a detriment. She was bound to bring him more grief. What if they tried to have a baby and she miscarried again? She was damaged goods, and he deserved better.

"I never said that I didn't want a commitment."

"You said you didn't trust me."

"I said I needed time. There's a big difference."

"I don't have time. I'm too old to wait for you to decide if I'm worth it."

He reached for her hand, but she pulled away. Confusion twisted his features. "I want to be with you. After tonight, I know that better than ever. I can't lose you again."

She had been waiting a long time to hear those words. She wanted to jump into his arms and tell him she loved him all over again. But she stayed as still as possible, not trusting herself to behave. This had to be the best performance of her life. Her face had to remain void of emotion, the one thing critics said she could never do. She had to convince Lock she spoke the truth.

"I'm in no position to make promises, and neither are you. You're about to become a dad even if it's temporary. Bodie needs your undivided attention. Focus on him. It's too late for us."

"Don't talk like that. You've been through a terrible thing tonight. You know what? We shouldn't even be having this conversation right now. In a few days, we can talk about us."

"I won't change my mind."

"I'm not giving up, Maeve. We're right for each other. No one has ever made me feel the way that you do. Please give us a chance."

He made this difficult, giving in to her every wish. She needed him to leave before she pulled him against her and cried until she couldn't breathe, knowing she was safe with him. That was all she ever wanted. To be safe, knowing she was loved. And the only man who had ever loved her was Lock. She had not taken care of that truth, and now she was so desperately alone.

She rearranged her face into what she hoped looked like she had seen the light of day and would give them a try.

"There is something you could do for me. If you don't mind." Her throat burned with lies.

Joy burst his face open. Her stomach folded in on itself with what she was about to do to him. But she had no other choice. He had to go and get on with his life without her, and she had to move on too. She had no idea where, but the first thing she would do was get off the ranch. After that, she would find a way to rebuild her life without Lock Ryker. That would require her to leave

Backwater. Even if she couldn't make movies, maybe she could get lost in Los Angeles.

"I'll do anything for you."

His words pierced her. "Could you get me something to eat? Anything. Crackers. Pretzels. I haven't eaten since this afternoon, and now that… Well, would you mind?"

"I'll run down to the cafeteria and see if it's open. They might have cake. We could share a piece. Unless you want your own."

"That would be nice. One piece. Two forks. Thank you."

He hesitated but turned to go without a word. Did he want to kiss her goodbye? She wished he had.

She pushed off the bed. She had no clothes with her, but she had come to the hospital in nothing but Lock's shirt, and that was gone with everything else.

At least the hospital gown was long enough, and they had given her a pair of those slipper socks.

She just had to get out without being noticed.

It would be the other hardest role of the night.

Chapter Twenty-One

Lock stepped off the elevator onto Maeve's hospital floor with a piece of lemon cake and two forks. He had shoved a bottled water into the back pocket of his jeans.

The floor was quiet with the doors to the rooms closed for the night, though morning attempted to push its way into the darkness. The floor nurse was behind the tall desk, busy with work and not paying much attention to him, but in no time, the hospital would wake up.

He wanted a few more quiet minutes with Maeve before nurses and doctors interfered. He had to convince her he was ready to take the chance. He would tell her he loved her over the cake.

His mind raced ahead. They would need a bigger place to live. The three of them would be tight in the employee cottage he'd been living in for years. Jett and Gage were building homes on the property. Maybe he could too. He would like to build his house with his own hands.

He pushed open the door to her room. The bed was empty. She must be in the bathroom.

"Maeve, I'm back. I got lemon cake. They didn't have any chocolate, but this looked pretty good. I also got some water. Hope that was okay."

No answer from the bathroom. He went to the door and tried to hear if she was having any problems. He wanted to give her space, but if she had fallen…

He knocked. "Maeve, you okay?"

Nothing.

"Maeve?" He forced away the thoughts of her on the floor bleeding. "I'm opening the door."

He shoved the door open.

Empty.

He went back into the room as if she would appear. The bed was unmade, and all other signs of Maeve didn't exist. In the hall, he called out to the nurse.

"Did Maeve Barnes come out this way?" Had she gone for a walk while he was downstairs?

"I haven't seen her since I did rounds. Are you sure she isn't in there?"

He didn't dignify that with an answer and went back into the room. He dropped onto the edge of the bed and held his head in his hands.

Maeve had left. Alone.

Because she didn't want to be with him. She had lied to get him out of the room. He was a sucker. How many times was she going to hit him over the head with that?

He tossed the cake in the garbage and headed for home.

****

"You're making a mistake." Zeke leaned against the bedroom doorway with his arms crossed over his thin chest. "Lock is the best man I know."

She had snuck out of the hospital against doctor's orders, still wearing only the hospital gown. Taking the stairs down three flights and leaving by the back proved easier than she thought except for the cramping.

Grateful for the lucky break—if being in a hospital at all could be considered lucky—she called Zeke collect from a bank of payphones near a side exit by the emergency room. She couldn't believe payphones still existed, but this was Backwater. They were always a little behind the times. For once, she was grateful.

Zeke came for her with a change of clothes and too many questions. She tried to avoid them while dressing in his truck as he sped home, but her brother was as relentless as a garden sprinkler, and she was too tired to keep up the fight. She just wanted to close her eyes and not engage as he drove back to the ranch to get her belongings, but he wasn't having it. Lock was his best friend and deserved better than what she was giving him.

"This isn't a question of his character." It was a question of hers. Zeke was right about Lock deserving better treatment than she gave him. In the end, he'd see it was for the better. She was no good for him.

"He's going to come here, looking for you. What are you going to say when he does?"

They had made it back to the ranch so she could pack her things. Resting would have to happen later.

"I don't have to say anything else. Lock will let me go." He wouldn't come for her. She had walked out of the hospital while he was doing something nice for her. As soon as he realized she was not there, he would know she had done it to him on purpose.

She had broken his heart twice, and he would not stand for that. His integrity wouldn't allow it. Truth and honesty ran through his veins as thick as blood.

"Why don't you want to be with him?"

"Because I'm not good for anyone. I can't give him the kind of life he wants. He wants a family to hand his legacy down to." What if she couldn't give him that family? What if she didn't want to? Maybe she had lost the baby because she hadn't really wanted to be a mother and nature had done her a favor. She didn't want to think about the possibility of becoming the mother of Lock's children and not wanting that role. She didn't trust herself.

"You don't know him as well as you think." Zeke shifted from one foot to the other but didn't come any closer as if sensing she needed every inch of space to keep sane.

"I know him well enough." Lock would probably forgo a family for her. He would adopt, if necessary. But she couldn't ask him to do any of that because she was foolish and selfish.

She closed her suitcase and took one last look around. "Okay. I'm ready."

"Are you sure you want to come back to the house? It's still in the construction stage."

"I don't care anymore. I just can't stay here." She had to get off the ranch before she saw Bodie too. That sweet boy who needed so much love might break her in two if he tried to hug her as his hair fell over his eyes. No, she had to go before that. For the first time, she was glad Dawn Yearwood didn't want her around the Pathfinders. She might poison them too.

Zeke took her bag, and she followed him through the cottage. She had checked out online as soon as she returned from the hospital so she didn't have to face anyone at the desk and could disappear without questions.

She tried to avoid the space in front of the fireplace where she and Lock had first made love this time. Her gaze betrayed her and landed right on the spot where he'd held her close and run his fingers through her hair, whispering her name over and over.

Zeke pulled open the door. The bright sunlight momentarily blinded her. She blinked against the glare.

"Looks like you have a visitor. I'll meet you at the truck. Howdy, Karen."

"Zeke. Good to see you again. Maeve, may I have a word?" Karen closed the door and dimmed the light before Maeve could answer.

Karen pushed her black glasses up her nose, and Maeve fought the thoughts of Lock doing the same. She could not think about him with his mother in the room. Her face would give her heart away.

She willed Karen to turn on her heel and follow Zeke, but not even Moses could move Karen Ryker from her task once her mind was set. Maeve didn't have to wonder where Lock got that trait from. She was pretty sure all the Ryker men were the same.

"Zeke is waiting for me."

"He'll wait. Or you can send him ahead. I can drive you to the farm if you don't want him hanging around."

"No, thank you. I'm sure we won't be long." If she were feeling better, she might put up a bigger fight, even push past Karen and tell her to mind her own business, but Maeve's strength slipped through the holes of her constitution, leaving her weak.

"Why don't we sit? I've been on my feet all morning and could use a break." Karen claimed a spot on the sofa and patted the cushion beside her.

Maeve sat on the edge of the cushion as close to the arm as possible. The limited space gave a small amount of emotional protection from whatever Karen had come to talk about. Maeve assumed it didn't have to do with a guest survey.

"How are you feeling?"

"I'm fine." She dropped her gaze to her lap because she couldn't hide the truth.

"Oh, sweetie, I'm so sorry about the baby. I'd hug you, but you look like you might break if someone came near you."

Maeve's gaze snapped up. "You know about the baby?" Had Lock run to his mother as soon as he realized she had left the hospital? Well, it would serve her right for ditching him that way. If Karen were her mother, she would have been her first call too. The closeness this family shared never ceased to amaze her. She shouldn't be surprised that Lock called his mother.

"My dear friend Marjorie Simms was on duty when Lock brought you in. When she heard what happened, she reached out to me, thinking I might need comfort too."

"Why?"

"Because Lock told them you two were engaged. Marjorie assumed the baby was his."

"Why did he do that?" She hadn't agreed to his request, but she had jumped his bones rather effectively right after. Her actions might imply her concession, and if she knew Lock at all—she had made it clear to Zeke she did—Lock would have made that story up to save her reputation. Even in the present day, the residents of Backwater could be backward.

"Because the doctor wouldn't tell him what was going on and he wasn't going to stand there without information. He was alone, and you couldn't advocate for yourself. It was him or no one. So he fibbed a little."

"He's resourceful." And a whole lot of other wonderful things. Her fingers danced over the spot on her neck where his teeth had nibbled her skin while he came.

"He is that. I actually didn't come here to talk about Lock. I don't know what's going on between you two." Karen put up a hand. "Don't bother denying there's something."

"There really isn't anything going on."

Karen arched a brow over the top of her glasses. "I have had a very similar conversation with all the women in my sons' lives about their relationships. I know my boys. Lock is committed to the things he cares about. Until recently, that was only his family and this ranch. Now he's included Bodie and you."

"I don't know what to say. I mean, I can't speak for how Lock feels."

"You don't have to say anything. You'll figure it out. I wanted to see how you're doing since the baby. I know what it's like to lose a child. I thought I might be able to help."

"Oh, Karen. This isn't the same. You lost Ajay in the most horrible way. I hadn't even heard a heartbeat yet." And she hadn't even wanted the baby for weeks. She wouldn't dare compare her loss to Karen's.

"Loss is still loss. It's okay to grieve if you need to. Don't feel as if you have to put on a good face because you were only pregnant a few weeks."

"No one even knew. How would they understand my insides have been raked dry?"

"They don't need to understand. It's none of their business. Many people didn't understand how I could grieve over Ajay when he had caused all his own problems and the problems of others. Especially the pain he caused the Hartmans. What they didn't know was he wasn't just a confused, lost eighteen-year-old. To me, he was a chubby baby who threw his head back and laughed at anything his brother Kace did. He was the three-year-old I sent to preschool who turned to look back at me as he walked down the hall and said in a big voice 'Bye, Mom.' Or the eleven-year-old who cried at a scary movie Jett convinced him to watch. Or the fourteen-year-old who baked Christmas cookies with his brothers. They only saw that one horrible moment as the sum of his life. That wasn't Ajay Ryker. My son was so much more."

Maeve wiped away the tears on her face. "My baby was important to me for such a short time."

"Of course, she was." Karen gripped her hand.

She liked to think the baby might have been a little girl. "Thank you for coming here. Lock is lucky to have you."

"I'm sure it's been hard not to have your mother around, especially at a time like this. If you need a shoulder, you can call me anytime."

"I can't do that to Lock. He won't want to share you with me." And she couldn't do it to herself. When she walked out of this cottage, she would walk away from the Rykers once and for all. Any ties would only confuse things and stir up dirty water. A clean break was better for everyone.

"Well, lucky for us I get to decide who I spend my time with." Karen stood.

Maeve followed.

"I think we made Zeke wait long enough. Take care, Maeve. Don't be a stranger."

"I won't." But she suspected Karen knew that wasn't the truth. She longed to ask for a hug, but she stayed silent and watched as Karen opened the door.

"Oh. Hello, Lockwood. We were just talking about you."

Chapter Twenty-Two

Maeve wanted to scream. If she had only left five minutes sooner, she would have missed him completely. Now she stood before Lock, trapped like a skittish animal. She didn't know what to say or how to make him understand she wasn't any good for him or anyone at the moment.

He filled out the doorframe with his wide shoulders and long legs. He fisted his hands on his hips, taking up more space than he needed. The light filtered in behind him. She couldn't make out his expression, but she could guess what his face said.

"Why did you leave?"

His hollow voice crashed against her heart. He had changed out of that scrubs shirt for one of his own, but he hadn't bothered with his contacts. His glasses added to the vulnerability of him standing before her in the aftermath of her deception.

Of course, he would get right to the point, leaving her little choice except to deal with the situation headfirst. She wouldn't get a chance to figure out her story or if she even needed one at all. If she had just left when she planned, this encounter would not have happened, and in time, he would have gone on with his life. Just like he had the first time.

"I needed to get out of there." Many layers piled onto that truth and bent it.

"To get away from me." It wasn't a question.

She didn't have to confirm what he believed, but she wouldn't deny it either. "I couldn't stay in the hospital."

"I would've taken you home."

She knew that, and it was part of the reason she'd left that way. Lock would do anything for her. All she had to do was ask, but she would not allow him to give his life over that way. She could make no promises. Standing in this room, she wasn't entirely sure she could get through the next five minutes.

"I didn't want you to drive me."

"Why?"

"I can't be with you." She prayed her face stayed neutral and he would give up sooner rather than later because she might just cave, and that couldn't happen.

"Tell me something that makes sense, Maeve. I'm trying to wrap my head around what's been going on between us since your return, and I can only come back to we still care for each other."

"I'm not in a position to be in a relationship." Funny, how after so many years apart, all it took was for her to come face-to-face with him and the time vanished like rainwater in the bright hot sun. She had taken one look at him, and she had returned home. How simple would it be to get back on that road now, but she didn't want to take the chance that she would hurt him worse. He'd hate her for now, but not forever this way.

"That isn't true. You told me you loved me." He strode into the room and reached for her hands, but she pulled back. Shock flashed over his face, freezing his features.

"And you didn't say it back." That part of the argument didn't hold up well, but if she said it long enough, maybe he would believe it.

"I wasn't trying to avoid saying it. I…I got caught up in the moment." His lip twitched toward a smile, but the smile didn't quite take hold.

She fought the urge to smile back. If she did, that would break her, and the selfish part of her, the part she fought against, would take him for her own. "You don't have to make excuses."

"They aren't excuses. I didn't want the first time I said it again to be like this, in the middle of what feels like a war I don't understand, but I will say it."

"Don't."

"I love you, Maeve."

She closed her eyes against the rush of pain. All she had ever wanted was to hear him say he loved her again. Even in the hospital room, his love and strength were what she craved, but she couldn't give anything back. Holding back her feelings was the best way to keep him safe and prove to herself she wasn't selfish.

"I can't think about us right now. I lost my baby. Why can't you understand that?"

"I'm not asking you for anything other than to let me in. Let me be there for you and help you through this. We can do this together. You don't have to be alone."

Almost the exact words he had said to her when she left for Los Angeles. He never wanted to hold her back. He only wanted to be a part of it.

Zeke appeared in the doorway, and without knowing it, he saved her from responding. "You're taking a long time. Everything okay in here?"

"It's fine. I'm ready to go." She kept her gaze on Zeke because if she looked at Lock, she wouldn't be able to leave.

Zeke looked between her and Lock. "I'll be at the car. Take your time." He left them.

She hurried past Lock, hoping to give herself a large berth to avoid touching him, but he gripped her arm with his long reach.

"Please don't go."

She pulled her arm away. "Take care, Lock."

She walked out without looking back.

****

Lock kicked over the small coffee table in the guest cottage. It splintered into two pieces as his foot went through the top. He reached for the lamp and hoisted it above his head, but with control he didn't know he had, he put it down, gritted his teeth, and kicked the table again.

He wanted to destroy everything in his sight, put a fist through the wall, but he marched outside, slammed the door shut, and tried to gulp down fresh air. Zeke's truck was gone, and Lock didn't know what to do. Out of options wasn't his strong suit.

He had to let Maeve go. That was what he had to do. But he didn't like that choice and couldn't believe he had allowed himself to fall for her again and end up exactly where he was six years ago—only worse. He should have known better this time. He should have known that she wouldn't stick around, that when life got hard for her, she pushed him away.

When she had decided to go to LA and make that movie, staying in a relationship had been hard for her. She hadn't wanted to work at it. She had wanted to go, with no strings attached, and walk down every path life presented her. Staying with him, the ranch guy, would have only limited her choices.

Now she was doing the same thing. Staying with him was hard because she would have to face what she was going through. He didn't believe for one second the window had closed on how soon he had said he loved her. Hell, the way they had made love last night should have told her everything he hadn't said yet with words.

He needed to go for a hike or take out one of the horses for a long ride, but he had to get back to Bodie. He'd been away from the boy for too long. He took off his glasses and rubbed a hand over his face. Being a parent seemed impossible. He had to get his life in order, and like he had thought days ago, a relationship was not a priority. He had lost his way—that was all—but now he was back on track.

Lock sent Jett a text explaining about the table and his fight with Maeve. He didn't want the cleaning crew to find it and blame Maeve.

—You had to kick it?—

He could imagine Jett's annoyance surfacing as he typed those words. Jett had little patience when Lock lost control. That was because Jett was wound too tightly and expected everyone to keep a lid on at all times.

—I lost my temper.—

But he had stopped himself at the last second. Jett should be glad the whole place wasn't in shambles.

—You're buying a new one.—

That translated to the cost wouldn't come out of building expenses, but Lock's pay.

—I don't care. Bill me.—

—You're too impulsive.—

—No lectures. Not now.—

The writing dots popped up on the screen. Lock wasn't in the mood for Jett getting on him about the table. He should put his phone on Do Not Disturb so his brother couldn't get through, but the text popped up.

—Are you okay?—

Lock stared at the phone before typing.

—Who has Jett's phone?—

—Shut up. It's me.—

Lock pushed down the warm emotion clogging his throat. Just when Jett could be the biggest pain, he turned around and acted like a big brother.

—I will be.—

He had to be. What other choice was there? He had brought on this disaster all by himself. He had no one else to blame. Not even Maeve.

—Good. If you need something...—

Jett didn't have to finish the sentence.

—Thanks. I know.—

—You're still buying that table.—

In spite of the situation, Lock found himself choking on a good laugh.

Chapter Twenty-Three

Lock dumped his keys on the table. Bodie kicked off his shoes and flopped onto the couch. They had come back from Gage's, where Bodie hadn't wanted to leave. He had been in a deep game of Monopoly with Izzy. But the day was wearing down, and Lock was ready to call it quits.

"I'm hungry." Bodie grabbed the remote for the television. Some kids' channel came to life and invaded the living room in bright colors and loud crashes.

"Could you lower that, please?" Lock's head had pounded most of the day. He had barely slept because he'd spent the majority of the night in the hospital and most of the morning hunting down Maeve. He hadn't eaten all day or even taken a shower. Getting dumped twice by the same woman also had a way of turning the screws in his head.

He still wanted that long hike by himself to clear his head, not have to make a late lunch or entertain anyone. Maybe he wasn't cut out for this foster parent thing. He'd been too selfish his whole life to start changing now.

"I thought you ate at Gage's." Lock checked the fridge anyway. The empty shelves stared back, laughing at him. When was the last time he'd gone to the grocery store?

"I did, but that was hours ago."

He was pretty sure it was only a couple of hours ago.

His mother used to complain that the five of them ate her out of house and home. This must be what she was talking about.

"We'll have to go up to the main building to eat. But that has to wait." He needed to talk to Bodie, and he didn't want to see anyone at the moment.

"I can go myself." Bodie jumped up off the couch.

"Not now. The kitchen will be closed for the day. I have to show you what is marked out for the family and where it is."

"Just tell me." Bodie pushed his hair away from his face.

"I can't explain it without showing you. We have a strict policy to keep family living expenses separate from ranch expenses."

"Can someone else show me? Can I ask Gage?" Bodie pulled his phone out of his pocket.

"No, pal. Gage went to work. Jett is working. Kace is working. My mom is working. Everyone works here." He should be working too, except these past few days he allowed his personal life to explode in front of him.

Bodie's face fell, but he rearranged it into something less emotional. Only it wasn't quick, and Lock could almost read his mind. He had screwed up, and he hadn't even started talking about the big issue yet.

He needed to try again and sat on the couch. "Can you sit with me a minute?"

Bodie shook his head.

"Please sit. I want to talk to you about something important. Then we can get food. In fact, you and I will go to the store and stock up on stuff for the house. Okay?" He needed to have the cabinets full anyway. The social worker arrived tomorrow to inspect the place. She would probably ask for his weekly meal plan.

Bodie pushed himself into the corner of the sofa, facing Lock, and pulled his knees up to his chin. Bodie kept him at a distance. He reminded Lock of a spooked horse. The best way to handle him was to wait him out.

"The social worker on your case is coming here tomorrow to meet with me." Honesty always seemed to work best in other situations like this. Best to know what to deal with straight up than have to play guessing games.

"Did you do something wrong?" Bodie picked at a thread on his pants.

There that question was again. "Pal, not everything is about being wrong. Her visit is part of the process."

"That's why the social workers come, you know, to see if the parents are messing up. Did you mess up? Are they going to take me from you?"

"Nobody messed up. You don't have to worry. I wanted to tell you about the visit. Like I said, it's part of the application process." He leaned over to pat Bodie's leg, but Bodie pressed himself farther into the corner of the sofa.

He tried not to take the slight personally, but at the moment, it was hard. He was trying the best he could to make Bodie happy and feel safe, and yet for every step forward, there was a step back.

"Do you have any questions for me?" He willed Bodie to say something that would help Lock help him.

"Are you going to pass the test tomorrow?"

"Test? Oh. You mean the meeting. It's going to be fine. She just wants to see where we live."

Bodie looked around the room as if seeing it for the first time. "It's pretty nice here."

"I like it. It's a little small, but we'll manage." Unless this thing became more permanent. If Bodie stayed around a long time, he might have to make a change.

"Are you going to marry Miss Maeve?" Bodie stretched out his legs.

The question clocked him in the jaw. "What would make you ask that?"

"Because you two like each other."

"We're just friends." This kid didn't miss anything.

"Social workers like married couples. If you married Miss Maeve, the social worker wouldn't get mad at you for being a dad by yourself."

"How do you know that?"

"I heard one talking. You don't want to make the social workers mad. They don't help when they're mad."

"Here's something you should know. I don't usually care if someone gets mad because that has nothing to do with me. If our social worker gets mad because I don't have a wife, I'll deal with it. Besides, even if Miss Maeve wanted to marry me, which she doesn't, we couldn't get married by tomorrow."

"I think you should marry her."

"You like her, don't you?"

"Yup. You like her too. I see the way you look at her. Like in those movies my old foster mom used to watch." Bodie put a hand over his mouth and laughed.

Lock shook his head and laughed too. "Miss Maeve doesn't like me that way, pal." A reality he would have to learn to live with. Maeve wouldn't have left him again if she had wanted to build a life with him.

Bodie slid off the couch. "I'll be right back."

Lock leaned back on the couch and closed his eyes.

All he had wanted to do in the hospital was hold Maeve and tell her it would be okay. Together they would make it okay. But her stone-cold eyes had frozen him in place. She hadn't wanted his touch anymore. Maybe all she had wanted was a couple of go-rounds in bed for old times' sake. If he had realized that, he would not have slept with her the second time.

"Lock, are you asleep?"

"No, pal." He lifted his head and met Bodie's gaze. Until he could clear his head, sleep would be a long shot.

In Bodie's hand was a picture in a frame. Lock rarely thought about that picture. He had shoved it in a drawer in the guest room because looking at it only brought back bad memories. But he could never get rid of the last photo he'd taken with all his brothers.

"I found this in my room. Could I put it on the table by my bed?"

"You want to put out a picture of me and my brothers?"

Bodie glanced at the photo. His hair fell over his eye. "I don't have any brothers or sisters, and I don't have any aunts or uncles. This would be kind of like having uncles. I mean, if it's okay to ask them to be my uncles."

"Gage, Jett, and Kace would like to be your uncles."

Bodie's face lit up. "I never had a family like this before. I saw the same picture in Gage's house on his fireplace."

"Yeah, we all have that picture, even Karen." His insides ached with the memories of that day, and yet he was still one lucky bastard for having three brothers here and in his life.

"Are you mad?"

"Mad? Because you found the picture? No way. You can put it out if you want."

"You looked mad for a second."

He held Bodie's gaze. "I promise you, if I'm mad, I'll tell you. You won't have to guess and worry you're doing something wrong, okay?"

Bodie nodded.

"Good. I want you to do the same. If you're mad at me or someone at school, or anything at all, tell me. We'll work it out. You won't get in trouble for being mad. Everyone gets mad. The horses get mad sometimes. Jett gets mad a lot, but he doesn't do anything bad except yell at me. Even Gage gets mad."

"Jett yells at you?"

"Yeah, but he never means it, and two minutes later he apologizes. He won't yell at you. He never yells at any of the kids. In fact, I think he loves Izzy, Quinn, and Royce best. You can add yourself to that list."

"Really?"

"Yes, really. Do you want to go get something to eat?" He pushed off the couch. His sore muscles protested. Even with the aches and pains, he wasn't as angry as he had been earlier. Spending time with Bodie seemed to help in a way he hadn't imagined it could.

Bodie pointed to Ajay in the photo. "Does he live somewhere else?"

Lock reached for the photo. Memories of that day were as vivid as a sunrise over the mountain. Jett had been so mad they were goofing around and wasting time even though he was the one with the unsmiling face.

Lock and Ajay had fought that morning. Ajay had called him from a motel two counties away. He had woken up there with little memory of what had happened the night before and didn't have any money to get home. Someone had mugged him. He had begged Lock not to tell the others. He never did. Not even now. But when he found Ajay, he had bruises over his torso and a cut on the back of his head. His money was gone, and so were his shoes. Ajay wouldn't tell him what happened.

By the end of that photo shoot, Ajay had made Jett laugh and jumped into his arms, saying "You're my favorite big brother, Jetty." That had stung even if Ajay was only joking, because Lock had been the one to come to his rescue that morning.

He missed his brother with every fiber. The pain never went away. It hid until it was ready to pounce, like now.

"Ajay passed away a long time ago. We took this photo for Karen, and a few months later, Ajay was gone." He put the photo on the table.

"Oh. I'm sorry, Lock." Bodie catapulted into him and squeezed his waist, sending Lock back against the sofa.

He wrapped an arm around Bodie and held him close. He smelled like soap and innocence. Lock held on for a minute more.

"Let's get that food, okay?" Lock righted Bodie and blinked away the tears threatening to give him away.

Chapter Twenty-Four

"I'm coming back to Los Angeles." Maeve folded her clothes and placed them into her suitcase. She was in her childhood bedroom and on the phone with her agent Kristen. The sun sank into the treetops and splintered its rays through her window.

She had decided to return after all. LA had opportunities, and even though she had told Lock her career was over, she wasn't qualified to do anything else. She needed to give acting one more try, and that idea had her calling Kristen again.

"Maeve, that's great, really it is. We'll have to grab a latte, but I still don't have any work for you."

"It's been weeks. Haven't the comments died down yet? Something else must've happened to take my place." Hadn't a pop singer started dating an athlete yet? Or a celebrity divorce? Something must have hit the airways. She had paid less attention during her stay here.

Being in Backwater had its advantages. The small town was so removed from the rest of the world it was as if no one else existed.

"You aren't front-page news any longer, but the stink is still on your back. I've asked around several times. Not even Ron Hansen wants to work with you." Kristen's razor-sharp words cut deep.

The famous director was known for his sunny personality and easygoing manner. She really was screwed.

"What do I do?" Her voice faltered with agony. The question wasn't just about her career. She didn't know what to do with any of her life now and had no one she could lean on for advice.

"Stay where you are. Take a class. Teach a class. Paint. Anything. I'll keep looking for you, and when something comes up, I'll call you."

Stay where she was?

Maeve closed her eyes and breathed in the idea of hiding out longer. She couldn't do it here. Not after what happened between her and Lock.

"Nothing is going to come up, is it?"

Kristen hesitated long enough that Maeve checked her phone to see if the call was still connected.

"You'll probably have to take a very secondary role. Maybe a streaming reboot of an eighties cult classic if you're lucky. There won't be any leads for a while. Unless you write and produce yourself. That's an option."

She hadn't thought about creating something for herself. Could she write and produce her own piece? Producing cost money, which she didn't have. But the idea took root. Maybe she could nurture it.

"I'll think about it." She zipped her suitcase.

"Great. I have to run. Another call. Stay well, Maeve." Kristen ended the call before Maeve could even utter a goodbye.

She opened the window. A breeze had picked up, tossing the leaves around in the shadows of dusk.

A knock came behind her. She turned. Zeke stood in the doorway. His eyes were hooded, and he slouched as if he carried a heavy weight.

"Are you okay?" she said.

"I took on more than I can handle with this renovation. I'm in over my head."

She didn't point out that she had noticed that the minute she stepped into the house. "Maybe you need to hire someone to help out."

"I wanted to do it myself."

"There's no shame in asking for help." She moved past Zeke and went downstairs.

He followed. "I don't think I want to turn this place into a vacation rental anymore."

She stopped in the living room and looked at him. "So, don't. I didn't love that idea anyway."

"If I'm not farming and I don't make this some kind of inn, I don't know what else to do."

"You don't have to have all the answers right now. And if you decide to do something you haven't done before, you'll learn." She could learn to be something besides an actress. Part of her was ready to call it quits. The business was hard, and she was always worrying about getting work. Finding parts became a challenge because every year her age showed more and Hollywood favored younger actors. She had never preferred the fillers and surgeries to stay young.

"Learn what? I'm in my forties."

"You're hardly old. There must be something you enjoy doing." She went into the torn-up kitchen. They couldn't cook in here. She couldn't even make a cup of tea.

"How are you eating in here?" Checking out of the ranch might have been a mistake.

"The microwave works, and the refrigerator is on the back porch. Can I show you something?" Zeke said.

"Sure. As long as it's not another hole in the wall."

"I'll be right back." He took off for the basement.

She peeked down the dark steps but decided to wait for his return.

Zeke pounded up the stairs and stood before her, holding a notebook. He flipped through it and settled on a page about halfway. "Take a look."

She took the book that was heavy in her hand and gazed upon a beautiful sketch of the beach with rough waves and grassy dunes. A slat fence leaned to its side under a stormy sky as if bracing itself against the wind.

"Did you draw this?"

"I did. And the others."

She flipped through more pages. Each one was a nature scene that looked more like a photograph than something done by hand. She had no idea that Zeke had this talent. He'd never said or even hinted.

"These are incredible. I can't believe you've been hiding this." She never possessed this much talent, not even in her acting.

His cheeks colored pink. "I tried to show Dad once after you left. You chasing your dreams kind of inspired me, but he told me I was wasting my time."

"He was wrong. You're talented." How could her father have dashed Zeke's hopes? Though Dad might have been afraid to be left alone or worried that Zeke would fail.

"I paint too. The one with the fence—I want to sell it."

"Zeke, this is incredible. You should absolutely show your work. How long have you been doing this?"

"Since I was a kid."

"How did I miss that?"

"Because other than an occasional art class in high school, I never told anyone. Not even Lock. I didn't want him to think it was dumb. But when you got your lucky break and left town for good, I thought why not me too? I'd go down in the basement night after night. Dad never asked what I was doing."

"That was Dad. If it wasn't work, he wasn't completely interested."

"Exactly. I entered a contest under another name, and I won. I couldn't believe it. That was when I showed Dad, and he said art was for other people. We were farmers. Always had been. Always would be. Told me I was wasting my time with coloring. He actually said 'coloring' and left the room."

"I'm so sorry. I wish you had told me. I've had a one-track mind for so long. Can you ever forgive me?" Shame burned under her skin. How could she have been so self-centered her whole life? She had hurt too many people because of it.

"Nothing to forgive. You're my sister. I'm glad I can tell you now, but if I don't farm, I might have to sell the land."

"So sell it. You said it was in your name anyway."

"What about you? What will you do?"

"I think I have to reinvent myself, and I don't know where to begin. Leaving town seems like the best option, but I don't know where. Never mind me, you should go for this." She handed back the notebook. "Sell the land. Sell the house. Do whatever it takes. It's your turn now."

Zeke ran a hand over the cover, then lifted his gaze to hers. "Thanks for saying that. I think I tore the house apart after Dad died as a way to handle my frustration. Dad left a lot on my shoulders, and I don't want the burden any longer."

"You don't have to carry it. I'm sorry I never helped out more. Dad let me out of so much because I was a girl, and I took advantage." She would do better with Zeke going forward. Maybe she had a connection or two left who might show his work. She'd check first before promising anything.

"You didn't want to be a farmer. You had your own dreams."

"Now you have yours. Chase them." She kissed Zeke on the cheek.

"Where are you going?" He followed her down the hall to the door.

"For a ride. I'll be back later." She grabbed her purse with no destination in mind, but she didn't need one. She only wanted to clear her head.

"Are you going to see Lock?"

She bit the inside of her cheek to keep from crying. "Lock and I are through."

"Why do you keep fighting it?"

"Fighting what?" She pushed open the door, wanting the breeze to carry her away.

"Fighting your feelings for him? What are you afraid of? Lock will never hold you back. He would give you the wings to fly."

"That was very philosophical of you."

"I have my moments." He smirked.

"It's me. I'll only hurt him. He deserves to be happy." And she couldn't take the risk that she would ever be the reason for making him unhappy. No more hurting him.

"Do you ever ask him what he wants?"

"He doesn't know what he wants." Lock thought he

wanted her, and at one time, he had. But things had changed, and he was clinging to the past as she had been since her return home and their first night making love. She had gripped onto him, hoping to find her footing, but after losing the baby, she was torn from anything tangible and had only managed to hurt him in the process. She loved Lock too much to keep breaking his heart.

"This is Lock Ryker we're talking about, right? When have you ever known him to not know what he wants?"

She slid into the car with Zeke's questions on her mind. What was she afraid of? Making more mistakes and this time hurting the one person she loved. She wasn't right for anyone. Maybe someday, but by then Lock would have moved on. If he could give her wings to fly, she could do the same for him.

****

Maeve pulled onto the gravel parking lot. Rocks crunched under the rental's tires. She missed her own car and would have to go back to LA to get it. Kristen might think she should stay away, but she had loose ends to tie up. Once her affairs were in order, she would find another place to live. She had decided that much while she drove from Backwater to Antique Hollow. Antique Hollow was another small town much like Backwater, tucked away from the main highway and sometimes forgotten as cars and trucks sped past to more exotic destinations.

Just like every other small town, Antique Hollow hosted a town fair. Maeve had noticed the lights and decided she was ready to stretch her legs. Her body ached from all it had been through, and she should be resting with her feet up, but that idea didn't seem possible at the moment. Her insides buzzed with restless energy she had to move to burn off. The fair seemed like as good a place as any.

She parked near the back of the busy lot. Children's screams of laughter drifted down from the Ferris wheel. The air smelled of burnt popcorn and fried dough. Her stomach growled. She couldn't remember the last time she ate.

Booths with spinning wheels and games of chance lined up on one side. Her sneakers slapped the hard ground as she navigated the crowd, avoiding caramel apples and sticky cones of cotton candy.

The booth with the zeppole called out to her, and she found a place in line. Music played through metal speakers on wooden poles. The noise and the lights soothed her. She could blend in here. No one paid attention to her. No one cared.

"What can I get you?" The tall man behind the counter had powdered sugar on his cheek. His red T-shirt was also dusted with white powder, as were his muscular arms. His dark hair was brushed away from his face, and his dark eyes shone with mischief.

He reminded her of Lock, and she had to push that thought away. Would she ever stop thinking about him? "Fried dough, please."

He handed her a paper bag with a big grease stain already forming on the bottom. She swapped him for cash, grabbed some rough paper napkins, and walked away.

A long picnic table under a tree offered a spot to sit with a view of the people walking by. Someone had hung twinkle lights in the branches, giving the tree a fairy-tale glow. Children carried balloons while they skipped ahead of their parents. Mothers pushed babies in carriages. One father carried his toddler son on his shoulders.

The dough tasted like cardboard, and she pushed the unfinished part away. All these families spending time together, making memories, dried out her throat. She was supposed to be a mom taking her child to the fair, stacking up the memories in so many layers she wouldn't be able to carry them all in her arms.

But before the seedling of motherhood had taken root for her, she thought she had been a woman in love with a man who had loved her. For a short while she thought she had it all. The career of her dreams and someone to share it with.

Life didn't care about foolish thinking. It took what it wanted and left ruins in its wake. Coming to this fair might have been a bad idea, but she didn't have the energy to get up. Sadness held her in place with its weight.

"Excuse me?" A woman who looked to be in her thirties with fake eyelashes swirling up to her heavily painted eyebrows appeared at Maeve's side. The woman's long black hair was parted in the middle and hung straight around her brown-skinned face.

"Yes?"

"Are you Maeve Barnes?"

She could deny it. She could say the woman was mistaken and go back to her quiet, lonely existence at this table. But the expectant look on this woman's face tied up Maeve's tongue. "I am."

"Oh great. My boyfriend told me not to come over here and bother you, but I loved that last movie you did.

I had to tell you. I'm a big fan. Would you mind taking a selfie with me? It's totally okay if you want to say no." The woman's hands fluttered around her face as if accenting every word with a gesture.

"You want a selfie with me?" She was Hollywood's pariah. Fans had run away from her. This woman must have the wrong person. No one should want to take a picture with her unless they were going to use it against her. Taking a photo with the woman would be a bad idea, and Maeve had had too many bad ideas lately.

"Of course I do. You're so talented. You're honestly my favorite actress." She batted those eyelashes.

This eyelash woman in her pink dress reminded Maeve of cupcakes covered in sprinkles for some reason. The sweetness of her smile? Or Maeve's desperation?

"Okay. Sure." She pushed off the bench, hoping she hadn't allowed her loneliness to get her into trouble.

The woman positioned her phone but dropped her hand and held Maeve's gaze. "I hope you don't mind me saying, but what happened to you during filming, when that video of you yelling went viral…" The woman pressed her lips together as if she didn't want the words to come out but changed her mind.

"You were robbed. I've read stories about Ivy Julia Longfellow-Simon online. My aunt—she's dating a makeup artist in Hollywood—said her girlfriend told her that she had to do makeup for that television show Ivy Julia was on last year, and Ivy made up a story about the teacher on set and got the teacher fired. Ivy got busted because the teacher had accidentally videoed the conversation. Ivy's bodyguard backed up the teacher. Crazy stuff, right? I know it wasn't your fault what happened. I just wanted to say."

"Thank you for saying that. What is your name?"

"Oh. Can't believe I forgot to tell you. It's Carina."

"Thanks, Carina. You're the first person to take my side."

"Oh, that's not true. Have you been on social? You need to look because there's a hashtag trending that says *Maevewasdonewrong*. I think a bunch of Gen Xers started it. You know them." Carina rolled her eyes. "Here. I'll show you." She tapped away at her phone's screen and pulled up the social app. Carina searched the hashtag, and there it was. Thousands of posts where people supported her.

And yet she was still canceled. All that support wasn't enough for her agent to stand behind her. It wasn't enough for the studio to come out on her side. All it took was as many haters to end her career. A career she thought she had wanted more than anything. A career built on a house of cards because in the end, nothing mattered except for what a few powerful people thought. They wanted her out, and she was. She would never rise above that. Never be an equal.

Since coming home, she'd had another taste of the life she turned away. It might not be bright lights and a big city, but it was filled with real people who loved her and cared about her. It was a place that second chances could be built on.

"Honestly, I'm surprised. I had no idea I had supporters. Thanks for showing me." Having fans stand by her side warmed her heart some, but this business was fickle. She had overstayed her welcome.

"No prob. Let's take the picture, and I'll tag you. My friends are going to die when I tell them. Ready?" Carina positioned her phone.

She was ready—to get on with her life.

Chapter Twenty-Five

Lock debated on a tie. He hated ties and only owned two. He couldn't decide if Ms. Humphrey would expect one or frown at the sight of one because he was trying too hard. He decided he'd go without and closed his closet door. He would be himself, and that meant no tie.

The house was in decent shape. He'd been up before the sun and cleaned. Jett had taken over in the stables for him today so he didn't have to worry about work and could focus on this meeting that had his gut turning in on itself.

He went out into the living area. Bodie shoved his feet into his sneakers. They'd had a good morning, though Bodie hadn't said a lot. Lock chalked it up to not everyone wanted conversation with the birds.

Bodie would take the bus this morning. Lock had promised to pick him up after school and tell him how the meeting went. They were going to visit Kace's garage and get hamburgers at the diner.

"You all set? Did you pack your lunch?" He wiped his sweaty hands on his jeans. He didn't remember ever being this out of sorts.

"In my backpack." Bodie stood. His thin arms swayed at his side. His hair fell over his eye.

"It's time for the bus." He grabbed his keys.

"I don't want to go on the bus."

"You have to. Ms. Humphrey is coming this

morning. I won't be back in time if I drive you."

"Can Gage drive me?"

"No, pal. Gage is busy, remember? We talked about the bus. You have to take it in the morning." He wasn't ready for an argument, and they didn't have time to debate. He needed Bodie on that bus today.

"I don't want to go on the bus. I hate the bus." Bodie flopped back down onto the sofa.

"I know you don't like it, but today I need you to get on it. You can look at your phone during the ride." At this point, he'd bribe Bodie with whatever it took to get him to go to school. Probably not the best parenting technique, but he was desperate.

"My phone only uses Wi-Fi for data. I don't have cellular access. You haven't switched me over to your plan yet."

He had forgotten. "Okay. I'll do it today. I'll get you a new phone added to my plan."

"I want the same number." Bodie gave a defiant tilt of his chin.

"I'll see what I can do." He had no idea how that even worked. And trying to figure it out would suck up more of his day. How did parents get anything done?

"I want the same number."

"I heard you. I'll try. Now, let's get in the truck, and I'll drive you to the front of the ranch." He opened the front door, hoping this would get Bodie moving.

"Why can't you take me?"

"Bodie, you know why. Please, let's go. You're going to miss the bus."

Bodie didn't budge. Lock took a long breath. He needed to stay in control. This whole scene wasn't going well, and if he had to guess, Bodie was refusing to take the bus on purpose.

"I don't care if I miss the bus. The kids are mean on the bus."

He wasn't sure if this was true or not, and he didn't have time now to dig deeper. "Ignore the kids. Let's go."

"No."

He marched over to the sofa and stood over Bodie. "You have exactly five seconds to get in the truck, or I will take that phone from you."

"You can't take my phone from me. I'm allowed to keep it in case I have to call for help."

He remembered something about that in the folder Alessandra gave him. As long as he was in the system, they gave each kid a phone. "You've contradicted yourself."

"I don't know what that word means."

"It means you said two truths that you want to be the same but are opposite. You said you want to be on my phone plan, but your phone from the system can't be taken from you. You can't have it both ways."

"I don't care about that."

"Yeah? Well, I don't care about that phone rule. This is my house, and it's my rules." Even to him, the words rang with a harshness that hurt his ears.

"You're not my real dad. You can't make me do anything."

Rage shook him to his core. The whole morning depended on Bodie getting on that bus. He couldn't be here when Humphrey showed. Bodie couldn't miss a day of school, and he couldn't stay home alone because Lock had things to do after the meeting.

He had no idea how to handle this situation except for maybe flipping this kid over his shoulder and dumping him in the truck. That wouldn't work, but he still wanted to do it.

"If you don't want me to be any kind of dad for you, just say so. I'll call Ms. Humphrey and tell her to forget the meeting. After I call her, I'll take you to school and go to work, where the animals and the guests are a lot nicer to me."

"Knock. Knock. Anyone home?" Gage tapped the open doorway with his knuckles. He wore his crisp uniform, as usual.

"Hey. We're just about to go to the bus stop. Weren't we?" Lock looked at Bodie.

"You said Gage had to work." Bodie nearly spat at him.

Gage stepped inside. "I do. In fact, I was already at the station today. I had to come back and grab something. I thought I'd swing by and wish you both good luck today."

"Lock doesn't want to be my dad now."

"I never said that. I asked you if you want me to be your dad."

Gage looked between the two of them. "Looks like you two have a lot to discuss before the bus comes. I'll let you get to it. Good luck today."

"Can I talk to you a second?" He needed his brother's advice on how to handle the derailment of the situation.

"Sure. Bye, Bodie. Have a good day at school."

"Bye." Bodie kept his gaze planted on his phone.

Lock followed Gage outside and closed the door behind them. "I have about two minutes, but he won't get on the bus, and I don't know what to do. Can you help me?"

Gage scratched the back of his neck. "He's probably scared about today. He might be afraid if he goes to school, he won't get to come back here. The system hasn't proven to be very reliable to him. He might not know who to trust just yet."

"I wouldn't let anyone take him away from me."

"He's ten. He doesn't logically understand that. Just go inside and tell him you care about him and that you'll be there for him no matter what. That's all he wants to hear."

"How do you know?"

"I raised a daughter. Plus, that was what Mom told me when I first struggled with how to handle Izzy. She was about Bodie's age."

"I had no idea." Gage made everything look so easy.

"Now you do." Gage patted him on the shoulder. "You're doing great. Don't worry."

"Can you stay for the social worker meeting? I can't do this by myself. That woman hates me." At least with his big brother beside him, he'd be able to hold it together. Too much rode on today.

Gage choked out a laugh. "I doubt that woman hates you. You'll be fine. You don't need me."

"Gage, man, I do. I can't do this. I don't want to screw it up."

"Lock, trust me. You've got this. You're going to be a great dad, and she will see it the minute she looks at you."

"What if I'm not?" If he was going to be such a great father, why hadn't Maeve told him she was pregnant before they had made love? She continued to believe he wouldn't stand beside her and support her. She wanted to do everything herself without any help. Here he was, asking for help. Why didn't she see that asking wasn't always hard?

"The fact that you're worried says you'll be just fine. Go get your son to school."

"This whole thing is nuts. Me a dad. I never thought it possible." And not this way. He had wondered if the right woman would come into his life and they would build a family, but no woman ever stuck with him the way Maeve had. He chalked it up to not being able to find love twice.

Now he was about to embark on becoming a single dad. At least temporarily, but would it be? How could he bring Bodie into his life and then send him away to someone who wouldn't care about him the way Lock already did?

"Anything is possible. Anything at all." Gage slipped into the police car and drove away.

Lock slipped inside but stayed by the door. Bodie remained on the sofa. The top of his head stuck up from the back of the sofa like an alpaca's. Lock wanted to go over and ruffle his hair, but he didn't. He had one last try before they'd miss the bus and Bodie would miss the school day.

"It's time to go."

"I don't want to go."

"Are you scared about the meeting?" He came around the sofa so Bodie could see his face.

"No."

Maybe Gage was wrong. "You don't have to be afraid. No one is going to take you from me today. I won't let that happen."

"How can you stop it?"

"Because Ms. Gomez recommended me, and you

asked for me, and I want you to live with me. That's plenty." He knelt down in front of Bodie to be at eye level with him.

"You might be wrong. Or you might do something wrong. If I stay, I can help you in the meeting." Bodie fixed the collar on Lock's shirt.

"It's better if you're at school today. We want to show Ms. Humphrey that we can get you off to school without a hitch. There will be another meeting with you."

"I wish Miss Maeve were here." Bodie looked down at his feet.

So did he. Lock gripped Bodie's knee. "Listen, pal. It's going to be just you and me from here on out. We're a family. We can do this thing together."

"Can I see her?"

"I don't think she's staying in town. But she likes you very much. Don't worry."

"And your brothers will be my uncles?" Bodie's bottom lip quivered.

"Absolutely. You get three uncles, three aunts, three cousins, and a grandma all at once. They already love you. But every day, here in this cottage, it's just you and me. We make up our rules and do things our way. We have each other's backs. Okay?"

Bodie nodded and threw himself into Lock's arms. Lock had to brace himself from going down, but he held Bodie close. They would figure this family thing out, father and son. Gage was right after all.

"I love you, Dad," Bodie said into his shoulder.

He hesitated but only for a second. "I love you too."

Chapter Twenty-Six

Maeve checked the time on her phone. Lock's meeting would be starting. She had debated all night on whether to go to his house and tell him she'd pretend to be whatever he wanted so he could keep Bodie.

She had decided to leave well enough alone. She had caused enough trouble for the man, and he would be fine without her. Better. He and Bodie would build a good life together. She only wished she could have been a part of it.

Now she sat on the bed in her childhood bedroom with her back against the headboard and her knees pulled up to her chin. She had returned last night after her time at the Antique Hollow fair. She had nowhere else to go and truly didn't want to be anywhere else but back in the house where all her dreams had begun. She missed her father too, and at least at home he was nearby.

Except for her car, her life in LA could be packed up and sent to her without too much hassle anyway. She wouldn't set foot in the city for a while. Missing it wasn't an issue.

After that, she only had a few crumbs of an idea. Maybe she really could produce her own movie or television series. She had always enjoyed the behind-the-scenes workings of films. She could come behind the camera and create something truly hers with people she liked and respected, not spoiled children with vengeful parents. The whole idea of her as a producer seemed crazy, but nothing was gained without trying.

She checked the time again. How was Lock getting along? Was Bodie with him? She couldn't sit still any longer. Going to the ranch was out of the question, but she could go to the hardware store, pick up a few paint supplies, and start helping Zeke with the renovations. If she had something to keep her busy, her mind wouldn't drift back to Lock. She would have to figure out how to exist with him in the same town, but one step at a time. Running into him at the store wasn't going to be a problem this morning.

The doorbell interrupted her newfound goal, but she hesitated at the top of the steps, unsure of who that might be and whether she was ready to talk to them.

Zeke didn't appear to check on the visitor, and she didn't want to call for her brother in case she needed to remain unseen, but the person on the other side of the bell was determined to be heard. If she didn't get down the steps, they would need a new doorbell as well.

A trim figure stood in silhouette on the other side of the frosted glass. Judging by the shape, this person was not Lock. Maeve let out a breath and fought the pang of disappointment at the same time.

She opened the door to Dawn Yearwood instead. "Dawn? What are you doing here?"

Dawn was dressed for a yoga class in her high-end mint-colored leggings and fitted zip-up jacket of the same color but with strokes of white running through it. A white headband pushed her hair from her makeup-free face.

"Hello, Maeve. I was hoping to talk to you for a minute." Dawn clasped her hands in front of her waist.

"I was on my way out, but I have a little time." She had all the time in the world, but Dawn didn't need to know that. She would probably use it against her somehow. "Do you want to come in?"

"No, thank you. Would you mind stepping onto the porch? It's a lovely day. We might as well enjoy it. I hear another storm is coming in tomorrow."

Curiosity did have the best of Maeve. She stepped onto the porch. "What brings you by?"

Dawn squared her shoulders. "I came to apologize."

"For?" Maeve braced herself.

"For the way I treated you earlier. I didn't know the whole story. I jumped to conclusions, and I shouldn't have."

"I don't understand. You've decided I'm not unfit to be around children?"

"I watched that awful video a hundred times. I searched you on the internet after that. You have a lot of fans, and that child actor seems to have none. In fact, she's so unliked that her mother also has a reputation for being the worst possible kind of mother."

"Well, thanks, but even that unlikeable child has fans who believe her."

"That may be true, but it's not the point. Mia saw me watching a video of the mother in an interview and said to me 'That's you, Mom.' I had never been so horrified in my life. When I asked my husband what he thought, he did what he always does when confronted with something that makes him uncomfortable. He ducks his head and pretends to be reading on his phone."

Maeve wasn't sure what to say to any of this. "Are you here for yourself or for me? I'm not sure because you've been a thorn in Lock's side for weeks. You expect me to believe you're doing a one-eighty about me now? Why?"

"I'm not doing this right." She adjusted her headband. "I have behaved badly, and I want to make it right. Have you ever had a moment when a light switch turns on for you?"

"Sure." Since she had been back to town, she had a few of those moments.

"I had one of those moments when everything becomes clear. When Mia said what she did about me, I knew I had been the worst kind of mother and it had to stop. I even said something unpleasant about Bodie Finch, and I shouldn't have. What kind of an example had I been setting? I didn't want to be that mother any longer. Call it a midlife realization."

Maeve sat on the step. She still found herself weary after the hospital. Her recent desire to move around and run errands seemed as if it had happened to someone else. Or maybe Dawn's truths weighed her down because a midlife realization had smacked her in the head too. "That's very big of you to say, especially about Bodie. He's a sweet boy who's had a tough life."

"I should've been more sympathetic." Dawn sat beside her. "Then something else happened... I hope you don't mind my being direct, but I heard about your trip to the hospital. I'm so sorry for your loss."

Maeve inched away. "What are you talking about?"

"Oh, Maeve, you don't have to pretend with me. I promise I'm not running to the tabloids with it. But this is Backwater, and only the rapids coming down the river move faster than gossip. I was sorry to hear what happened with your baby. I know how it feels. I've had two miscarriages of my own."

Words failed her. She wanted to get up and run inside, but her legs didn't move.

"It will get easier. And if you decide to try again someday, a new baby will help heal the wound. I think that's why I'm so overinvolved in Mia's life. When I found out I was pregnant for a third time, I was determined not to do anything to lose that baby. Once she was born, I didn't know how to let that promise go."

"I'm sorry for your losses too. It must've been very difficult."

"It was. And it is for you too. You don't have to pretend with me. You'll probably put on a good face for everyone else. I did. But if you ever need to talk or just want to be able to let out the pain and anger, I'm here. I know we got off on the wrong foot, but I hope you'll give me a second chance."

She needed a friend since all of hers were gone now, and Dawn's apology seemed sincere. "I'd like that."

"Great. I also wanted you to know I'm having Lock reinstated as the Flock Leader. It doesn't make what I did to him right, but it's a start. I hope you'll still be able to help him with the play. The kids could use you. He's a good leader, but he can't make up a story to save his life." Dawn tilted her head back and laughed. "Don't tell him I said that."

"I won't be helping with the play any longer."

"Please don't let what I did stop you." Dawn gripped Maeve's hands in her own.

"It's not you. It's me. And him." The tears threatened again. She did not want to be an uncontrollable weeper, and yet here she was.

"I thought you two were an item." Dawn eased back.

"No. Not in many years."

"So the baby wasn't his?"

She wished. "Not his."

Dawn stood and wiped off the back of her pants. "Well, whatever is going on between you two, I hope you work it out for the kids' sake anyway. I have to run, but if you need anything at all—and I mean anything—just shout. I'll come running."

"Thanks, Dawn. Really."

"Thanks for taking a chance on me. You didn't have to. I hope to see you at the Pathfinder play." Dawn slid into the driver's seat of the car and made her way down the long drive.

She didn't know when the play was, but maybe by the opening curtain, she and Lock could at least exist in the same space. Until then, she had paint to buy.

Chapter Twenty-Seven

Lock handed Ms. Humphrey a cup of tea. She had wanted lemonade or water but with ice, of which he had none for some reason. He'd have to check the ice maker later. He also didn't have lemonade. He did have beer but refrained from offering her any.

She had settled for tea with a *tsk* and planted herself at the kitchen table, where the unfinished jigsaw puzzle sat.

"Where does Bodie do his homework if this puzzle is taking up the table? I didn't see a desk in his room."

He had given her the tour of the house, which took about two minutes. She hadn't said anything about the space until now. She hadn't even written a single note.

"He can sit at the couch and use the coffee table."

"Is that wise?"

"The table is pretty sturdy." It was sturdier than the one he kicked in the guest cottage.

"He would have to hunch over or sit on the floor. Perhaps you could squeeze a small desk into that tiny bedroom for him."

"I can do that." He took the seat opposite her.

"Mr. Ryker, is there any history of mental illness in your family?" She pulled out a leather-bound portfolio from her briefcase by her feet and opened to a yellow notepad.

"Not that I know of." He had never even thought

about that before now.

"Isn't it true that your brother was involved in a gang war and addicted to drugs?" Humphrey looked at him with her pen poised.

"Why are you asking me questions about my brother who passed away almost twenty years ago?" He needed to keep his temper under control, but his body ached from the stress and the relief of Bodie waving to him as the bus pulled away.

"I must have a family history. Was he involved in a gang war?"

He held his tongue, trying to figure out how to answer the question. "Ajay made some mistakes, but he was young."

She scribbled in her notepad. "I see. Weren't you involved in a shootout last year on this very ranch?"

"We were robbed. Some guns were fired, but not by my hand." He tried to see what she had written, but she kept the pad at an angle.

"Do you own guns?"

"I do. But they aren't kept here. I keep them locked away in the main building where we store all our firearms. We give shooting lessons to our guests." He also had a personal collection for when he went hunting with his brothers, but those guns were locked away in the main building too.

"So Bodie won't have access to them?"

"Not without an adult present, and by *adult* I mean myself, one of my brothers, or my mother. No one else has the combination to the lock." But if Bodie stayed with him permanently, he would teach him how to use the guns safely and properly. When the time was right.

"Do you plan on allowing a child to shoot a gun?"

"My brothers and I learned to shoot at twelve." Maybe he shouldn't have said that.

"Including the one who died from a gunshot wound?"

"Ms. Humphrey, with all due respect, you're walking very close to a situation you don't completely understand. What happened with my brother Ajay has nothing to do with me now."

"Fine, Mr. Ryker. We'll move along. Have you ever been arrested?" Her pen took up a frenzy on the page.

"Not officially." He shouldn't have said that, but he couldn't resist playing with her a little. This uptight woman needed to relax, and so did he.

"Excuse me?" Her gaze snapped up.

"My brother, the sheriff, thought it was funny to lock us up once, but it was a joke." What he wouldn't tell Ms. Humphrey was he, Jett, and Kace had left a fish in Gage's dresser drawer and Kace had accidentally broken Gage's toilet by jumping on it. Gage had gotten pretty annoyed with them and decided he would arrest his brothers. They'd all laughed about it after.

"Would you be playing that kind of a joke on Bodie?"

"Don't plan on it." He would never do to Bodie the things he and his brothers had done to each other. They were all young men with a lot of energy and wild streaks.

"Have you ever advocated for a child in the past?"

"I've been with my Pathfinder group for a few years now. I make sure they're okay. I've taken care of my niece Izzy. Does that count?" He wished he had thought to take this woman for a walk along the paved trail. If she saw the wilderness and felt its calming effect, maybe she would see her way straight to allow him to be with

Bodie.

"Not exactly, but nonetheless. Have you ever had a problem with drug abuse?"

"No."

"But you have a shelf in your refrigerator dedicated to beer." She pointed behind her.

"You saw that?"

"I see everything."

"Well, I'm not an alcoholic, but I do enjoy an occasional beer." He was starting to think he could use one now, but he remained seated.

She made more notes on her page. "How would you handle Bodie if he didn't want to go to church or eat dinner?"

"I don't go to church."

More scribbling. "Pick another place. Like school."

If this morning hadn't happened, he wouldn't know how to answer this or he would have said the wrong thing. "I would ask him how he's feeling and talk to him about what might be bothering him."

She pursed her lips and gave a tiny nod. "One more question. Do you ever plan on getting married and having a family of your own? If so, how would Bodie fit into your picture?"

"I don't know if I'll ever get married. I only worry about the here and now. Tomorrow isn't promised. For right now, Bodie and I are a family. If a woman comes into my life that I want to share it with, she has to take me and Bodie. We're a package deal. And if I have more children someday, Bodie can be a big brother."

"You won't send him back into the system?"

"You mean the very system I want him out of because of the last family you sent him to?"

"The system isn't perfect, Mr. Ryker."

"Your system sucks, Ms. Humphrey. Pardon my language. But to answer your question, I will never send him back into the system. As long as he wants to live with me, he will."

She put her pen down and closed her book. "Thank you for your time. I will have my report written up by the week's end."

He stood and tried to pull her chair out for her, but she waved him away.

"I can get out of the chair by myself."

"I was trying to be a gentleman."

"Try with someone your own age." The whisper of a something resembling a smile twitched over her lips.

"Can you give me a hint on how I did?" He walked her to the door. She couldn't be opposed to that, could she?

"A hint? Well, I will say this much. I don't like that you're single. You're still young and have a lot to offer a woman. I'm worried that you'll find yourself involved with a woman who doesn't want Bodie, and since he's technically not yours, you could give him back. It's happened before." She stopped at the door and turned her stern gaze on him.

"I'm not like those other people."

"That's what the other guy said too. Good day, Mr. Ryker. I wish you luck." She pulled open the door.

Jett and Gage stood on the other side. Jett faced away from the house. Gage, still wearing his crisp uniform, faced the doorway and flashed a grin as they stepped out onto the porch. Jett spun around at the scrape of the opening door. He grabbed the baseball cap he wore backward and put it right.

"Afternoon, ma'am," he said.

"Hello, Ms. Humphrey. I'm Sheriff Ryker. I wanted to welcome you to our family's ranch." Gage stuck out his hand.

She ignored Gage, which most people found difficult when he stood his full height in a sheriff's uniform and a gun strapped to his waist, but Humphrey had and looked between the three of them.

"You all have an uncanny resemblance to one another. Good day." She pushed past his brothers and worked her way into her small sedan.

They waited until she was out of sight before anyone spoke.

"Well, how did it go?" Gage said.

"She hated me." He slumped against the side of the house. Trying to be on his best behavior for the last hour stole what little energy he had left.

"You are a bit of a pain in the ass sometimes, but I doubt she hated you." Jett turned his hat back around, the way he preferred.

"What are you two doing here?" He had to admit he was glad to see his brothers.

"We came to see how it went," Gage said. "Kace was supposed to be here too, but he's late, as usual. We wanted to support you."

"Thanks, guys."

"We thought we'd take you out to lunch in case you needed some company. But a quick lunch because I have work to do," Jett said.

Gage shot Jett a sideways glance.

"What?" Jett asked. "He knows I'm only giving him a hard time. No one works harder than Lock. See? I can say it."

Lock wanted to hug Jett sometimes, but Jett never liked hugs or only liked them on rare occasions. Gage let Lock hug him anytime he wanted. He took the steps and stood beside his oldest brother.

Gage leaned into his shoulder, and he leaned back—a perfect hug.

"I really want this foster thing to go well." His mind raced over all the possible scenarios that could go wrong. "What if they deny me?"

"They won't. And if they do, we'll deal with it." Jett kicked the dirt. "We always do."

"Rykers stick together," Gage said.

A car's engine tore up the quiet. Kace's sports car came barreling around the bend, music blaring. The tires skidded to a stop.

"He's going to scare the guests. I will kick his ass," Jett said.

Kace jumped out of the car still wearing his mechanic's overalls. His hands were stained from whatever work he had done that day. "Did it start?"

"You missed it," Jett said.

"Is it over? I came as fast as I could. That's why I didn't change. Where is the social worker? I'll call her for you. Give me her number." Kace reached for Lock's waist.

He pushed Kace away. "What are you doing?"

"Looking for your phone."

"I said to be here after the meeting. Lock didn't need us during the meeting, but he might need us after. Do you ever listen?" Gage asked.

"He has too much grease in his ears." Jett shoved Kace.

Kace's smile exploded on his face as if grease in his

ears was exactly right. "Whatever you need, little brother. I'm here for you. Okay, who's hungry? I'm buying."

"Can't pass that up," Jett said.

Lock would never pass up time with his brothers. He didn't know where he would be without them. Growing up without a dad had been made easier by having three older brothers who always watched out for him. Without that, he didn't know what his life would have been like. Bodie deserved a chance to know what it was like to have men who would take care of him and not hurt him in his corner.

"I'll see you all at the diner." Kace hopped back in his car.

Jett and Gage did the same.

He hitched his leg into the truck. He wished he could call Maeve and tell her about the meeting with Humphrey, listen to her as she gave her opinion. Opening up that old wound would be hard to close again. In no time at all, he had become used to having her around, and now she was gone.

Another vehicle came around the turn. The fancy German car parked beside him. Dawn Yearwood slipped out from behind the wheel.

He fought the urge to groan.

"I'm on my way out, Mrs. Yearwood. Put whatever you have to say in an email." He closed the door and kicked the engine over.

She hurried around and knocked on the window. "You didn't check your emails. I need a minute."

He could pretend he couldn't hear her and pull away. Instead, he lowered the window. "One minute."

"Thank you. I'm assuming you didn't read your

emails this morning."

"I've been kind of busy. What do you want? I already received notice of my dismissal."

"You've been reinstated."

"What?"

"I'm so sorry, Mr. Ryker. I've been very difficult to deal with. For that, I apologize. I insisted the council reinstate you immediately."

"Why did you do that?"

"To make up for my behavior. I've seen the errors of my ways. If you're still interested in being the Flock Leader, the job is yours."

"How's the play coming?"

"Needs a little work." She smiled.

"Bodie and I will be there."

"Wonderful. If you need any help, let me know. I'm happy to put the costumes together."

"Costumes?"

"Of course, costumes, Mr. Ryker. This is a play. Our children must shine." She turned to go but turned back. "Oh, I thought you might like to also know I apologized to Maeve Barnes as well."

"You did?"

"She was wrongly accused by me and plenty of others."

"When was this?"

"Just this morning, at the Barnes's farm."

"She's still in town?"

"Well, she was at the farm. Have a good day, Mr. Ryker."

"Do you think you could finally start calling me Lock?"

"Lock." She nodded. "Thank you."

"See you at the meeting."

Chapter Twenty-Eight

"Do I have to wear this stupid costume, Dad?"

Bodie had been calling him Dad for two weeks now, but they only got word this morning that his foster parent application was approved. Ms. Humphrey had sent an email congratulating him and suggesting he wear a tie next time.

Him a dad. It still seemed surreal. He wished he could tell his dad, but instead he had called Gage when the news came through. He'd called Jett and Kace right after because he shared everything with his brothers. He had no family memories that didn't include them. This morning he'd stopped by the cemetery to tell Ajay too.

Now they were backstage in the multipurpose room of the elementary school. His Downys were about to perform their play to a small audience made up mostly of parents and siblings, including his own. His mother, nieces, and nephew were sitting in the audience too, ready to cheer Bodie on.

Gage came through the door that led from the hall into the back area. "You guys all ready?"

"Uncle Gage, I don't want to wear this." Bodie tugged at the giant pea coming out of the front of his costume.

Dawn had decided the kids would be vegetables for the show. Their play was about accepting each other for who they were, as they were. She figured making examples of green vegetables would get the point across. Lock hadn't minded. Bodie was peas and hated every minute of it.

"I think it looks adorable." The soft words drifted over to him, stealing his breath.

"Maeve." Bodie ran to her.

She dropped down and pulled him and his awkward costume into her arms. "You look great," she said to Bodie.

She hadn't looked at him yet. The hustle of backstage activity went on around him, but he shut it out. Maeve was here, and he didn't know what to do.

"Talk to her, Lock," Gage whispered in his ear. He said hello to Maeve and stepped back into the hall.

"Bodie, darling, can you come here for a quick cast picture?" Dawn, with her newfound smile, waved over Bodie. She had become a very different woman in the past two weeks.

Lock stared at Maeve. She was stunning in a blue flowing blouse with wide sleeves and black leggings. Her curly hair framed her face, making his fingers want to tangle with it. She kept her distance, and he let her have her space.

"Hi, Lock."

"What are you doing here, Maeve?" His treacherous heart pounded, stealing his breath. He wasn't over her, maybe never would be.

"I came to see the play and say hello to Bodie. I hope that was okay."

"He was glad to see you. He's asked about you." Lock was glad too.

"What did you tell him?" She dropped her gaze.

"That you were busy." He would never allow Bodie

to believe anything else.

"Thanks for letting me save face." She gnawed on her bottom lip but did not move.

If she had come for Bodie, her mission was accomplished, and he needed her to go. He had secretly hoped she wouldn't stay in town much longer, because he dreaded turning a corner to find her there. But with her standing before him, all he wanted to do was bury his face in her neck.

"Well, thanks for coming. I have to get back to the troop," he said.

"You have a million reasons why you should walk away from me right now. I've been horrible to you. But I was wondering if I could give you one reason to let me back in."

"You ended it, Maeve. Not me."

"I'm sorry for that. Sorrier than you'll ever know." She reached up a hand but dropped it.

"Now isn't the time for this conversation."

"I know, but I didn't know how to approach you. I was afraid. But some things are worth fighting for, and I have to try."

His pounding heart kicked into a gallop. He had to stop her. "Maeve—"

"I love you, Lock Ryker. My feelings for you have never changed. If yours have, I understand. But if you have any feelings left for me, please give me another chance to make it up to you. I'll spend my life making it up to you, and you will never have to wonder how I feel about you or if I'll ever leave. Because if you let me back in, I'm yours forever. Yours and Bodie's."

Dawn called for him somewhere backstage. The play was about to start. He wished he had more time to tell Maeve how he felt about how she treated him, to wonder if they would make a mistake they couldn't survive.

But of all the Ryker men, he had been the last one to overthink anything.

And he went to her.

Epilogue

December

Snow drifted down in large flakes over the Montana mountains. The Rykers were running out of daylight, but they would finish what they started if it killed them. And it might. Four strong men with their just-as-strong respective women had a lot of opinions.

Everyone was in attendance. Everyone except Karen. She had no idea what her children and grandchildren were up to on this Sunday evening.

The first time they gathered this way, it had been Ajay's idea. Gage had suggested tonight's meeting at Thanksgiving. With speed usually reserved for Kace, they pulled together a family photo shoot as a Christmas present for their mother.

For the fourth time, the photographer attempted to arrange the clan dressed in white shirts and blue jeans.

"Can I have the kids in the front this time?" the photographer said with a slight exasperation.

Izzy, Quinn, Royce, and Bodie sat cross-legged in a row on a wool blanket with its buffalo-plaid pattern that Lock had laid down on the cold ground at the last second.

"Okay, Sheriff, you and the missus stand behind Izzy, please." The photographer waved Gage and Calista into place.

They took their spot. Gage pulled Calista close. She

rested her head on his shoulder.

"Next Christmas we'll have Luna with us," Calista said. Gage and Calista had decided to follow in Lock's footsteps and foster an older child.

"We will." Gage placed a small kiss on Calista's lips.

"Okay, Jett and Autumn behind Quinn, please." The photographer waved Jett and Autumn into place. Jett crossed his arms over his chest. Autumn flipped his baseball cap forward. He flipped it back.

"Now, I need Kace and Tara, please, right behind Royce."

"Can I stand to the side this time? I want to make sure this next Ryker baby is in the photo too and so Karen can see my big belly," Tara rubbed her belly and laughed.

"Fine. Kace, next to Jett. A little closer. More. Great. Tara, lean into Kace. Yes. Like that." The photographer gave a thumbs-up.

"Stop pushing, Kace," Jett said.

"I'm not pushing. You're a grump."

"Gentlemen, please. My equipment is getting snowed on, and we're almost out of light."

"Sorry," Jett and Kace said in unison.

"Okay, finally, Lock and Maeve, please, behind Bodie."

Lock took his spot in line, the birth-order line, and Maeve stood beside him. He wrapped an arm around her waist and kissed the top of her head.

"Wait. Don't take it yet." Maeve hurried away to her purse sitting on the hood of Lock's truck. "We can't forget this." She moved back into position and held up a sonogram. "All the grandchildren need to be present and accounted for even if this Ryker won't be born until March."

"Karen will love that," Tara said.

"One more thing." Gage held up a hand.

"What now?" Jett rolled his eyes. "I'm freezing out here in a dress shirt."

"It was your dumb idea to take it outside again." Kace punched Jett in the shoulder.

Jett punched him back.

"Knock it off," Gage said. "We need to say something about Ajay."

"Should we have brought something of his?" Autumn asked.

"I've got that covered." Lock pulled an old watch that had once belonged to their father out of his pocket. Ajay had worn it until the brown leather was worn down, the glass face scratched, and the watch no longer kept time. Lock had taken it from him that last horrible night. He handed it to Bodie.

"Will you wear this for the picture? Make sure your arm can be seen."

"Thanks, Dad," Bodie said and strapped on the watch.

"To the best brother anyone could ever ask for. We miss you, Ajay," Lock said.

"Amen," from Kace.

"To Ajay," Gage said.

Jett looked from one brother to the other. "To Ajay. Now, take the damn picture."

A word about the author...

From an early age, best-selling and award-winning author Stacey Wilk told tales as a way to escape. At six, she wrote short stories in composition notebooks. At twelve, she wrote a novel on a typewriter, and in high school biology, she wrote rock star romances in her binder instead of paying attention.

But it wasn't until many years later, inspired by her children and a looming birthday, that she finally took her storytelling seriously. And published her first novel in 2013. Since then, she's gone on to publish twenty-nine more so women everywhere can indulge in books that hook them heart and soul.

She isn't done telling stories. Not by a long shot. If you want to read her emotional and honest books about family, romance, and second chances, visit her at www.staceywilk.com

To see what she writes next, follow her Facebook group for her amazing readers – Stacey's Novel Family https://bit.ly/2FK8Lae

Or join her newsletter - https://bit.ly/2A0jEFk